Praise for

MURDER AT THE
MOONSHINE INN

"Buckle up. Hazel Rose and her book group are not your granny's amateur sleuths. Southern, sassy, and a wee bit sexy!"

—**Mollie Cox Bryan**, author of the Agatha-Nominated
Cumberland Creek Mysteries

"Colorful characters, dark secrets, and heart make Maggie King's latest edgy cozy a standout. You'll be clamoring to join Hazel Rose's book group."

—**Dianne Emley**, L.A. Times bestselling author of
the Detective Nan Vining series

"With *Murder at the Moonshine Inn*, Maggie King has once again created a book group to die for. The investigative techniques and reading choices of Hazel Rose and her friends are equally amusing and suspenseful."

—**Judge Debra H. Goldstein**, award-winning author
of *Should Have Played Poker*

"In *Murder at the Moonshine Inn*, Maggie King distills book clubs, author deadlines, and undercover ops at a redneck bar into a cocktail of pure delight."

—**Diane Vallere**, National Bestselling author of
the Madison Night Mystery Series

"A brilliant, twisty mystery with fun and memorable characters. King is a writer to watch!"

—**LynDee Walker**, Agatha Award-Nominated author of *Lethal Lifestyles*

"When Hazel Rose is asked to look into a grisly murder, she realizes her long lost cousin is the prime suspect. With her book group, she runs into hidden lives, more distant relatives and more bodies."

—**Betsy Ashton**, Author of *Mad Max Unintended Consequences*, and
Uncharted Territory, A Mad Max Mystery Mystery

"It's as if Nancy Drew grew up and put together a crew of smart, funny, brownie-baking avengers."

—**Lyn Brittan**, author of the Mercenaries of Fortune Series

"A good mystery teamed with humor and characters you won't forget make this a read that goes down smooth as a mint julep—with a kick!"

—**Sunny Frazier**, author of the Christy Bristol Astrology Mysteries

"Hazel Rose and the women of the book group are at it again, investigating two murders while pretending they are doing nothing of the sort! With suspects and possible motives aplenty, they have to consider: Was it for love, for money, or for revenge?"

—**Maria Hudgins**, author of the Dotsy Lamb Travel Mysteries

"A must read for those who prefer homicide served up with a large dose of hilarity. From the opening scene, where Hazel Rose finds herself—against her better judgment—astride a barstool dressed in her most sensuous "ho" outfit, to the grand finale where Hazel again finds herself in an inappropriate place—this time against her will—King masterfully mixes humor with homicide. Five stars!"

—**Ellen Elizabeth Hunter**, author of Magnolia Mysteries

"Suspense, family secrets, and seduction make *Murder at the Moonshine Inn* a clever read."

—**Teresa Inge**, *Virginia is for Mysteries*

"*Murder at the Moonshine Inn* abounds with interesting characters, plot twists and turns and unexpected revelations sure to please mystery fans."

—**Sybil Johnson**, author of the Aurora Anderson Mysteries

"Terrific characters that really crackle and lovely, lively dialogue."

—**C.A. Larmer**, author of the Agatha Christie Book Club Mysteries

"I love complex, twisty plots: family and friends, love and money—and murder! This book has it all."

—**Vivian Lawry**, author of Chesapeake Bay Mysteries and
Different Drummer

"If Hazel Rose could say no, she wouldn't find herself knee deep in another murder case whose list of suspects includes some of her own relatives. In this rollicking fun read, Hazel and her fellow book group members investigate, exposing one astounding secret after another. The murder count goes up and Hazel discovers she's destined to be Victim Number Three. This second in the Hazel Rose Book Group mysteries series is clever and charming! I thoroughly enjoyed it!"

—**Marilyn Levinson**, author of the Golden Age of Mystery Book
   Club Mysteries

"Maggie King delivers a cracker-jack second episode in the Hazel Rose series. The book group is up to its collective nose in murders connected to Hazel's new-found relatives—and there are plenty of suspects to go around."

—**J. R. Lindermuth**, author of the Sticks Hetrick crime series

"*Murder at the Moonshine Inn* has everything you'd want in a cozy mystery: an intriguing puzzle, the demise of the despised, and a colorful cast of characters including a nosy book group. The insider knowledge of the mystery world, authors, and books makes it a delight for the addicted reader who wants it all in one clever package. Maggie King writes with grace and humor; you won't be disappointed."

—**Lise McClendon**, bestselling author of *Blackbird Fly*

"Hazel Rose's reluctant return to murder investigation will have you flipping pages as fast as you can to reach the solution of this engagingly puzzling mystery."

—**Karen McCullough**, author of *A Gift for Murder* and *Wired for Murder*

"I liked this book from the outset; there's a quality to the inner voice and a tongue-in-cheek humour that I found appealing. It's an excellently written story drenched in detail that carries the mounting tension along a treat."

—**Pat McDonald**, British crime author

"Move over, Jessica Fletcher! Make way for Hazel and her book group of sixty-something women who do more than read mysteries—they solve murders."

—**Mary Miley**, author of the Roaring Twenties mysteries

"Whodunit? Maggie King did! She's served up a fun, great read in the Murder at the Book Group mysteries. If you're a cozy reader, you better join her group!"

—**Tj O'Connor**, author of *Dying to Know*

"Hazel Rose and her book group are back on the case. From the opening scene where Hazel goes undercover, to the final scene where she comes face-to-face with the killer, this story will keep you turning pages. Fun, fast-paced, and well plotted, this is the perfect 'cozy' read."

—**Jayne Ormerod**, author of the Blonds at the Beach series

"With a likeable heroine, suspicious deaths, feuding relatives, love triangles, and a peppering of literary references, readers will be kept guessing until the final pages of this enjoyable and saucy whodunit."

—**Kathryn O'Sullivan**, author of *Foal Play, Murder on the Hoof* and *Neighing with Fire*

"Maggie King has achieved what mystery lovers crave: a surprise ending which makes perfect sense. The clues are there, but Maggie's sleight of hand weaves them skillfully into a story that has readers looking in every other direction. I highly recommend *Murder at the Moonshine Inn* to anyone who relishes a great mystery. Hazel Rose and her book group have done it again!"

—**Amy M. Reade**, bestselling author of *House of the Hanging Jade*

"Hazel Rose and her book club are back for more discussions and sleuthing in *Murder at the Moonshine Inn*, a good read and fun romp through Central Virginia. Hazel and her friends need to uncover the killer before he or she strikes again and again!"

—**Heather Weidner,** author of *Secret Lives and Private Eyes*

"In *Murder at the Moonshine Inn* author Maggie King's smooth style and subtle humor has created a well-crafted cozy mystery that is enriched with plot twists, realistic dialogue, home town references and a list of engaging characters that will keep readers turning its pages."

—**P. J. Woods**, author of the Harper Simone mystery novels

MURDER at the
BOOK GROUP

A Book Group Mystery

Someone's about to turn the last page.

MAGGIE KING

Also by Maggie King: *Murder at the Book Group*

"This promising series debut—edgier and sexier than many cozies—
should intrigue anyone who enjoys biblio crime."

—Booklist

"The characters in this story are fascinating,
and for the side of humor that the author delivers,
there is definitely a dark side to go along with it."

—Mary Lignor, Suspense Magazine

"Murder, books, and a book group . . . this is a perfect series for me!"

—Teresa Kander, Book Babble

Murder at the Moonshine Inn:
A Hazel Rose Book Group Mystery
by Maggie King

© Copyright 2016 Maggie King

ISBN 978-1-63393-281-4

Published by

210 60th Street
Virginia Beach, VA 23451
800-435-4811
www.koehlerbooks.com

MURDER AT THE
MOONSHINE INN

A Hazel Rose Book Group Mystery

MAGGIE KING

VIRGINIA BEACH
CAPE CHARLES

To Glen, with all my love

ONE

IF ONLY I could learn to say no, I wouldn't be perched on a barstool in a redneck bar, breathing secondhand smoke and pretending to flirt with men sporting baseball caps and Confederate bandanas, their eyes riveted on my Victoria's Secret-enhanced cleavage. I wouldn't be tricked out in a bizarre hairstyle, frosted blue eye shadow, painted-on jeans with strategically placed slashes, and a two-sizes-too-small Harley Davidson tank top.

I hit the rewind button on my life and stopped a few days earlier, at the point where Phyllis Ross threw a cup of coffee in Nina Brown's face. How that led to this undercover assignment—finding out who killed a middle-aged drunken woman in the parking lot of the Moonshine Inn—is quite a tale.

• • •

When I walked into one of the many Panera restaurants that dotted the Richmond, Virginia landscape I didn't spot any rednecks. Perhaps they were traveling incognito. The Panera denizens wore standard summer garb: shorts, capris, sandals,

T-shirts, with a baseball cap here and there. They sat hunched over laptops or swiping the screens of their smartphones. Some retro types chose to absorb the day's news on paper.

Trudy Zimmerman's long white mane made her easy to spot in a booth that overlooked Panera's patio and the parking lot beyond. When I took the seat next to her, she introduced the woman sitting across from us as Nina Brown.

Nina Brown. Where had I heard that name? Trudy pronounced Nina like the number nine followed by a short a—*Nine-ah.* Short and long vowels brought back memories of long-ago school days: were vowels still a part of the teaching curriculum?

Nina's appearance spoke volumes about her health. A heavy layer of makeup didn't hide the shadows under her dark eyes. Vertical lines bracketed her mouth like parentheses. I wondered if she suffered from depression, perhaps brought on by a serious health condition or recent trauma.

She extended her hand. "Nice to meet you, Hazel," she assured me in a surprisingly strong and melodious voice, one I associated with telephone sales or disc jockeys.

Trudy had called me the night before, saying she had a friend who needed a favor that apparently only I could grant.

"What sort of favor?"

"I can't say. She made me promise not to."

"Huh? What is this, some kind of spy operation?"

"I think you'll be intrigued by what she has to say. Please, Hazel. Do this for me."

"For you, huh? Who is this woman? How about a hint?"

"I *can't*. I'm sworn to secrecy. Just come and hear her story. You can always say no."

I'd laughed. "Yeah, just say no." One would think that at my age I would have learned to say no. But I suspected I'd be filing for Medicare without mastering that useful skill. Oh well, I had two years to work on it.

"Okay, I'll listen to what she has to say. I'll say 'yes' to that." We decided on Panera at Stony Point at eight the next morning.

Introductions made, Trudy looked at me and said, "Why don't you get something and then we'll chat." I noted her party hostess tone and gave her a look.

When I returned to the booth with coffee and croissant in

hand, Trudy stood to let me slide into the booth. "I might have to leave early. We have a staff meeting at nine-thirty."

"We" referred to the library where Trudy worked. *Great,* I thought. I hoped Nina got her tale told before Trudy deserted me.

Nina smiled and started with an icebreaker. "So Hazel, Trudy says you two are in the same book group."

"Yes, for, what is it, ten years now?" Trudy nodded.

Nina sipped her coffee, bleached by a heavy dose of creamer. "And you're a writer?"

"Yes, I write romance novels for baby boomers."

"How many books have you published?"

"Six, so far."

"A lot of people like your books."

I smiled. "So, what kind of work do you do?"

"Oh, nothing much right now. I help out at my . . . my sister's non-profit." She inhaled heavily and grabbed my arm, startling me. "I have something to ask . . . a favor."

"Why, Hazel Rose and Trudy Zimmerman. Fancy meeting you here."

"Hi, Phyllis." In one voice Trudy and I greeted Phyllis Ross, another member of our book group. Phyllis fixed her attention on Nina—not on us. Her do-I-know-you look was a little too probing, but Phyllis wasn't known for her subtlety.

Trudy put down her egg sandwich and wiped her mouth before making introductions. "Phyllis Ross, Nina Brown. Nina—"

"So it *is* you! I can't believe it." Phyllis pointed a shaky finger at Nina.

Nina looked alarmed. "Who *are* you?" she asked.

"Who am *I*? I'm Phyllis Lassiter Ross. Charlie Lassiter's sister."

"Oh! I didn't recognize you."

Phyllis glared. "Well, it's been twenty years."

I could understand why Nina didn't recognize her. I'd seen pictures of Phyllis from her younger days and the years hadn't been kind to her. Likely her love of the sun had accelerated the aging process.

Her face darkening with anger, Phyllis leaned over the table, hovering over Nina. Her brown-going-gray hair fanned out around her head and I covered my mug with my hand lest a stray hair invade my coffee.

"Charlie *loved* you, may he rest in peace," Phyllis railed. "But you dumped him like he was yesterday's garbage. After taking his money for that pyramid scheme."

"Charlie died?"

"Yes, two years ago."

Charlie Lassiter had suffered a massive heart attack. At his funeral I'd met his current wife, former wife, his children and grandchildren. I felt sure he was long over Nina. So, why was Phyllis pinning his demise on her?

"Phyllis, I'm sorry he died, but I had nothing to do with it. I hadn't seen him in years. As for the money, I paid him back."

"Not according to him you didn't. Two thousand dollars to invest in nutrition supplements." Phyllis gave Nina the once-over. "Obviously a poor investment."

Trudy and I looked at each other, not sure if we should intervene. But I felt like I had to do something. "Phyllis, please—" I started.

Phyllis ignored me. I hoped she wouldn't follow in her brother's footsteps and have a cardiac event. Could one of the device-addicted customers be a doctor? Eyes flashing, she continued to challenge Nina. "So tell me, how many children did you have?"

Nina opened her mouth as if to answer, then closed it.

"You told my brother you wanted children; you said your clock was ticking. Even though when you met him you claimed you didn't want them."

"I changed my mind."

"So how many little rug rats *did* you have? Or was it all a ruse to get rid of Charlie?"

"I didn't have children. I broke up with your dear brother because he was a jerk. God rest his soul, but he was a jerk!"

"He loved you and so hoped to get back together. God knows the whole family told him you weren't worth it."

"Yeah, I know. He stalked me for two years. And another thing—he was weird sexually."

Weird sexually? I privately hoped she'd expand on that item. As a romance writer I was always on the lookout for new material.

Up to then the two women had kept their voices modulated, but now Nina amped up her proclamation about Charlie's peccadillos, pulling people's attention from their newspapers and electronic devices. It also put Phyllis over the edge. In less time than it took to blink, she picked up Nina's mug and tossed the contents into her face, adding a few choice expletives.

Nina sat open-mouthed in shock, face and hair dripping with coffee.

I handed Nina my napkin and Trudy's. "Are you burned?" Trudy made a dash for the napkin dispenser on a nearby condiment station.

"No, just wet." Nina wiped her face. No doubt she could thank her over-creaming habit for cooling her coffee enough to save her from injury.

Then several things happened at once. A handsome young man whose name tag read "Todd Makin, Manager" appeared and asked if there was a problem. A member of the waitstaff trailed behind him with a wet cloth in hand.

"I'll say there's a problem," said a woman who had been sitting in the booth behind us. She stood and pulled off her up-to-then pristine white jacket, now splotched with coffee. Droplets of the brew clung to the woman's blonde curls.

By that time we were all standing and had the attention of the whole restaurant. Phyllis had vanished. Trudy handed Nina more napkins and escorted her to the restroom like she was a young child. As they walked away I noticed that Nina's clothes hung on her, almost requiring suspenders to hold up her capris. A recent weight loss was my guess.

The irate woman spoke up. "That woman, the one with the wild hair—" she pointed out the window. Phyllis was now headed for the parking lot, her hair and loose-fitting top flowing around her. "She threw a cup of coffee at that woman in the red shirt." She turned and pointed out Nina, now almost to the restroom.

"We'll get you all seated at clean booths." The manager smiled, his voice soothing. He'd make a great diplomat. Or playground referee. His assistant set to cleaning up both booths while Todd transferred our dishes.

That left me standing with the irate woman who wailed, "My beautiful jacket is just ruined!"

"Oh, the stain will come out," I assured her. "I have the same jacket and once spilled coffee on it. Cold water works like magic.

You'd better go to the restroom right away before the stain sets."

I'm not usually called upon for impromptu performances, but I did a fair job spinning this tale. The woman looked uncertain for a moment, like she suspected a trick. Then she sighed and went to join Trudy and Nina in the restroom.

I sat in the new booth and waited for Trudy and Nina to reappear. When they did, Nina was still a bit damp.

She explained, "They only have automatic hand dryers in the restroom. They don't dry the rest of the body too well."

Having never found myself dripping with coffee in a restaurant, I hadn't considered the limitations of hand dryers. Todd refreshed our beverages and offered any other services he could provide.

We assured him that we'd let him know. When he left, the three of us looked at each other and laughed. We had some "other services" in mind for the attractive Todd.

I said, "Nina, we're sorry about Phyllis."

Nina's shrug suggested that she tangled with enraged women on a regular basis. "It's okay. Charlie's whole family hated me. They thought he was so wonderful. But he wasn't."

I knew Phyllis had been close to her brother and had taken it hard when Charlie died. Perhaps she had a blind side for her brother. Of course, she hadn't known him in the same context as had Nina. Or so I hoped.

"You know," I said, "You could file assault charges. That's what Phyllis did, assault you."

"No, no, no, no, no." Nina waved both hands in front of her like they were windshield wipers. "Let's just forget about it."

I waited a beat for Nina to offer anything else about Charlie. When she didn't, I said brightly, "Well, let's start over. You said you needed a favor."

My earlier reluctance to come to this meeting so early on a Monday morning had yielded to an eager curiosity. A woman who caused other women to throw coffee in her face had to be interesting. And a woman with a sexually weird man in the past—well, I was all ears.

Nina bit her lip and set to twisting her napkin. "Um, yes. A favor." Nina looked around, like she feared someone might overhear her or sneak up behind her. Was she about to confess to a crime? If so, she didn't need me, she needed a lawyer.

Leaning in close, she lowered her voice. "I want you to find out who killed my sister."

TWO

BEFORE I COULD recover my power of speech, a melodious tune sounded from somewhere on Nina's person. She pulled her phone out of her pants pocket, checked her caller ID, punched the talk key and said "Hi."

I welcomed the interruption of the phone call. The last thing I wanted to do was find out who killed Nina's sister. Or anyone's sister. Hopefully the caller would distract her and she'd forget about me.

No such luck. She ended the call and gripped my arm a little too firmly as she said, "So how about it?"

"Uh . . . I think I need some information." Did she really expect me to agree to such a request on the spot?

She laughed. "Yes, of course you do."

I sighed. How could I turn her down without seeming cold? "Nina, I'm sorry about your sister. Truly sorry. But I'm a writer, not a detective."

"You found that other woman's killer. Trudy told me all about it."

When I turned to Trudy she held her hands up, miming "What

could I do?" I made a mental note to tell her not to recommend my services.

"That was years ago," I said to Nina. "And it was luck, not expertise." Nina referred to Carlene Arness. Eight years earlier, Carlene died after sipping cyanide-laced tea at a meeting of our book group. Somehow I'd managed to flush out the killer. I considered it a one-time thing and didn't relish a sequel. I said to Nina, "Isn't this a matter for the police?"

"They're stuck on Brad for my sister's murder . . . and aren't even looking at anyone else. And Brad's such a nice man, he'd never kill anyone."

Brad? My ears perked. It couldn't be *that* Brad. It just *couldn't* be.

But Nina's next words told me that it could be. "Brad Jones. My brother-in-law. I guess he's still my brother-in-law."

"Brad Jones, huh? If I have my facts straight, he was married to Roxanne Howard—and she would be your sister, right?"

"Right. You must have read about her in the paper."

"Well, yes, I did." Who hadn't read about Roxanne Howard? Besides her stabbing death in the parking lot of a disreputable bar three months earlier, there were the various newsworthy deeds and misdeeds over the years, especially the DUIs and public fights with her young employee-lover. And Nina wanted me to find out who killed her? I imagined more than one person had wanted to end that colorful woman's life: anyone that given to public displays was bound to have enemies.

Now I said, "Nina, this is quite a coincidence, and an awkward one—Brad Jones is my cousin."

• • •

Conflict of interest. That meant I was off the hook. I hoped my sigh of relief wasn't audible.

Nina's eyes widened. "Yes, Brad mentioned that. He said you and your sister contacted him out of the clear blue sky."

When my father was two years old his parents divorced and my grandfather disappeared from the lives of his child and former wife. In recent years, my sister Ruth took up genealogy and unearthed a slew of relatives previously unknown to us. I was now in touch with family members from around the country via e-mail and Facebook. A few of the relatives hailed from Richmond.

Now I told Nina the story of Ruth's family tree discovery. Trudy and the other members of the book group knew this tale. I explained that my deserter grandfather eventually remarried and had three more sons, each of whom had one child: Marcie Jones, Brad Jones, and Patty Jones Ratzenberger.

"So Marcie, Brad, and Patty are all first cousins and I'm their half-cousin. I wish I'd met Marcie before she died. When was that? Two years ago?"

"Almost," Nina said. "November of 2011."

"And she had breast cancer?"

"Pancreatic."

"My sister came down from New Jersey this past January and we met Patty. She and I hit it off and have lunch together most Thursdays."

Nina smiled. "Oh, I love Patty. She's so sweet." I allowed that she was indeed sweet.

"But Brad chose not to meet us. He told Patty that Ruth and I were probably after his money, and so why else would we get in touch after all these years?" I had even sent Brad a sympathy card when Rox died in March. Not surprisingly, he didn't acknowledge my gesture. But not sending it would have felt worse than dealing with his ignoring me.

Nina waved her hand in dismissal. "Yes, I know Brad has some issue with you. I'm sure it's just a misunderstanding. Anyway, I'll introduce you to him. He really is a nice man. Did you ever meet Rox?" Nina asked.

"No, I never did." I guessed that the woman was my half-cousin-in-law. Was there such a thing? Talk about unwieldy relationships.

"Well, I'm sure Patty told you all about her."

"She didn't, really. She said she didn't know her that well, but she was pretty upset about how she died. Patty seems very private with her feelings."

"Yes, she is private. I noticed that when Marcie was so ill." Nina excused herself to get more coffee. "Can I get you some?" Trudy and I assured her that we were fine.

I turned to Trudy. Keeping my voice low, I asked, "Why did

you suggest that she talk to me?"

"I didn't. It was all her idea."

"Later," I muttered as Nina returned with a fresh mug of pale coffee.

Nina said, "You know, don't you, that Rox took care of your cousin Marcie during her final days and months. She even served as her power of attorney, medical and financial."

I recalled the little that Patty had told me about Rox's role in Marcie's care. She had mentioned that Rox was Marcie's POA. When I'd asked why Rox and not a family member, Patty said that Rox had been POA for both her parents and so had a lot of experience.

When I posed the same question to Nina, she gave me much the same response, adding, "Marcie and Rox had been friends for a long time and Marcie felt closer to her than she did to Brad or Patty."

Nina leaned toward me, all earnestness. "So, Hazel, you have to clear Brad as a suspect. He's *family*. He needs your help."

How far does one go for one's family? There must be limits, boundaries. Brad had certainly set clear boundaries with me.

It would be interesting to meet Brad and see his reaction to me. I knew he was the chief suspect in Rox's murder. Maybe he'd welcome my discovering who killed his wife—unless he killed her. No question about it, I could be putting myself in danger.

Despite Nina's impassioned plea, I saw a perfect opportunity to exercise that elusive skill of saying "no" and leaped on it. "Nina, my answer is no. I can't investigate your sister's murder. You have my deepest sympathy, but you'll have to find someone else. A qualified PI."

A mixture of disappointment and anger flashed across Nina's face. During a moment of uneasy silence it suddenly came to me why her name rang a bell.

"You and Trudy are neighbors, right?"

"Why, yes . . . yes, we are."

At the time of Rox's murder, the book group had discussed the crime at length. Trudy and Eileen Thompson, another book group member and Trudy's co-worker at the library, told us that their neighbor—Nina Brown—was Rox's sister. Had Trudy withheld Nina's name during our conversation the night before, thinking that I'd guess that Nina wanted to talk to me about investigating and would refuse to meet with her at Panera? If so, she would have been right. Maybe. I knew I'd regret bringing up the subject of Brad and Rox again, but I found myself asking, "How long had Rox and Brad been married?"

I cringed at Nina's hopeful look. "Three months. They got married last Christmas."

"How did they meet?"

"I introduced them. He's been my dentist for years and he's on the board of the Alzheimer's Research Society of Central Virginia. I used to run into him at fundraisers. My father had Alzheimer's and so did Brad's mother, so it's a cause that means a lot to us." That reminded me that I needed to get a medical history for this new-found wing of my family.

Nina continued. "Brad recommended Rox for the Development Director position at the ARS—that's the acronym for the Alzheimer's Research Society—and when she left there he got her the job at the Hamlin Group. That's where she was working at the time of her death."

Brad sounded like a tolerant and solicitous person to this woman who, by all accounts, ran on the wayward side.

"And didn't she become the Executive Director of the ARS?"

"She did. She was there for a long time." I recalled that the most colorful stories about Rox coincided with her tenure at the ARS.

Nina's dark eyes took on that now-familiar pleading look. "Sure you won't change your mind, Hazel?"

"No." I put out my hand in a stop position. "Leave it to the police. And if you don't like what they're doing, hire a PI."

Nina sighed. "To be honest, I can't afford one and Brad won't foot the bill. Oh, I'll pay you, don't worry about that. But hopefully you won't charge as much as a PI. Not that I know how much that is."

"I don't either," I said. "Why won't Brad foot the bill?"

"He's against the PI idea. He wants to leave it to the police. They want it to be him, but apparently haven't found enough proof. They probably think he hired someone, and they're not looking for anyone else. At least that's the way it seems to me."

"Why's he content to leave it to the police?"

"Because he figures they know what they're doing and have the resources to solve the crime."

And if they think Brad did it but can't prove it, he's better off. Aloud, I said, "He's right."

Nina pressed on. "Hazel, you did this before. You found that other woman's killer. Carlene."

"I knew the people involved in Carlene's death, so it was natural to talk about her and ask questions, but I had to be subtle. In your case, I wouldn't know how to begin."

I instantly regretted my words. Nina knew how I could begin.

"Let's start with the Hamlin Group. I can set you up there and you can talk to people."

"What's the Hamlin Group?"

"It's an association management firm for non-profits. Rox was vice-president."

"What would be my cover?" I held up a hand. "Not saying that I'm going to."

"Research for your books. You have a lot of fans who'd love to talk to you. Especially middle-aged women. You could say you had interviewed Rox for a book." She gave me the same pleading look as my cats do when begging for food.

Nina had a point. I did have a lot of fans, especially in the non-profit world that teemed with women of a certain age— meaning middle-aged. My core group of readers. And I enjoyed mingling with them.

"Why would I have interviewed her?" I asked.

"I don't know. Make up something. You're a *writer*! I know," she snapped her fingers. "You can say you're writing a story set in a non-profit and want to soak up the atmosphere. Sex in the non-profit world."

Laughter broke the tension. Briefly. Trudy took our mugs to the coffee station for refills.

Nina went on. "And Brad is still on the board at the ARS. He can get you in there."

"I doubt that he'd do that."

"I'll talk him into it." I noted Nina's confident tone with interest. Did she have a lot of influence with my cousin? Did Brad know about this conversation? If I took this on, I wouldn't want him to know. But I wasn't taking it on, so the matter was a moot point.

Nina was growing more animated. Perhaps doing something to uncover the mystery of her sister's murder was cathartic. If I could help someone in need of healing—but wait. Should I be putting myself in danger just because nice-guy Brad won't come up with the funds for a PI? I'm sure a PI would manage a better healing process than I could with my amateurish ways.

"Look, Trudy thinks the world of you. And your husband could help."

Nina referred to Vince Castelli, a homicide detective-turned-true-crime-writer, who had amassed a file of information about Rox in preparation for his next project.

I sipped my coffee. "Nina, my answer is still no. But I'll ask Vince if he knows a good PI."

Nina gave me a long look before drawing a deep breath. "Okay."

Trudy looked at her watch and exclaimed in dismay. "Uh, oh. I'm going to be late for my meeting." She gathered up her purse and the detritus of her breakfast. "See you all later."

Even though Trudy had contributed little to the conversation, I'd found her presence comforting. Fearing more arm twisting on Nina's part, I lost no time in changing to a mundane subject. I asked about her reading interests.

"I haven't read much of anything lately. I've been taking a playwriting class. The last class meets tomorrow."

"That must be the same one Mary Anne's taking." Mary Anne Branch was a member of the book group who was taking a break in order to devote herself to the playwriting class. When I started to describe her as an attractive woman in her forties, Nina nodded. "I know who you mean. There are only five of us in the class."

"What got you interested in plays?"

"Oh, I love plays. The, um, *immediacy.*"

We spent a few minutes discussing plays, naming the ones we'd seen or wanted to see. Nina touted anything at the Firehouse Theater, a local venue that staged cutting-edge productions. I chimed in with a vote for *Hay Fever*, a Noel Coward play Vince and I had seen the previous Valentine's Day.

Then Nina's phone sounded the same melodious tune as before. She assured the caller that she'd be there in less than an hour. "Gotta go," she said to me. "Someone at the Hamlin Group went home sick and they're asking me to fill in."

On our way out, Todd held the door open for us. "Have a nice day, ladies. Nice to see you again."

Outside, Nina gave me her card with her e-mail address, street address and phone numbers. I didn't think it a good idea to provide so much information—I only gave my e-mail and website on my cards. But I kept my words of caution to myself and tucked the card in a side pocket of my purse.

In the car I whooped and cheered. "I said *no*! At last, I've learned to say no."

What I hadn't learned was how easily a *no* could become a *yes*.

THREE

ON THE WAY home, I pondered Nina's request that I investigate her sister's murder. She had mentioned paying me. How much should that be? Or was bartering the way to go? Did Nina service cars? Clean houses? Do laundry? Color hair? Considering the condition of her own hair, I didn't think I'd have her touch mine.

But it didn't matter because investigating her sister's murder was an emphatic *no*.

At home Olive, our Norwegian Forest cat, rolled over in the driveway for a tummy rub. Olive was camouflaged, sometimes black, sometimes charcoal, and sometimes brown, depending on the play of light. Her green eyes often darkened and became opaque, blending into her fur. Indoors, Morris, an orange and white Manx cat and Olive's companion, greeted me, abbreviated tail bobbing.

Vince came down the stairs. "How did everything go?" He asked after kissing me.

I laughed. "That's a short question that requires a long answer. Do you have time now?"

"Sure."

My husband, Vince Castelli, stood at six foot one with broad shoulders. His shock of white hair, blazing blue eyes, mustache, goatee, and Brooklyn accent all added up to sexy as all get-out. He'd retired as a Richmond homicide detective to pursue a career writing true crime accounts. Like me, he's enjoyed publishing success. Vince was currently writing an account of how the housekeeper of a wealthy family in Richmond's West End used her employer's hunting rifle to shoot him and his family. Another case for gun control, in my opinion. Sometimes Vince joined the book group to tell us about law enforcement and police procedure.

I met Vince shortly after I moved to Richmond from Los Angeles in 2000. For five years we went through a series of breakups and make-ups, due mostly to the commitment phobia I suffered after four failed marriages. Finally, I took a leap of faith and found myself proposing. We married on a white sandy beach in Costa Rica almost eight years ago. Despite the chaos that marked our premarital relationship, we enjoyed marital bliss—for the most part.

I'd just sent my latest manuscript to my editor. It told the story of three friends whose spouses die and they wind up spending their golden years with their high school sweethearts. My baby boomer-aged characters enjoyed active and loving sex lives. The best thing was that I got to do my research with Vince and he was a willing partner. The research was more fun for my books than for his.

I started off by describing Phyllis's tirade at Panera. Vince laughed and shook his head. "Woman's a piece of work. Nina's lucky the coffee wasn't hot. So is Phyllis, for that matter."

"Let me tell you why Nina wanted to meet me."

No sooner had I mentioned the name Roxanne Howard than Vince cut me off. "Wait a minute—Nina Brown—is she Jeannina Brown?"

"I don't know—"

"Yes, I'm sure she is. Jeannina Brown. She's a suspect in her sister's murder and so is your cousin Brad. The police just don't have a solid case yet."

Vince knew all about the case. The Richmond Police Department was handling it and he kept in touch with his former colleagues. And he planned to publish an account of Rox's murder for his next true crime project.

"Why did she want to meet with you?"

"That's what I'm trying to tell you . . . She wants me to investigate her sister's murder."

"Why? Murder's a matter for the police."

"I know, I know." I didn't want to get him all riled up. "And I'm sure they're handling things."

"I don't like you looking for killers. I still shudder when I think of that time with Carlene."

"Yeah, tell me about it." I held up my hand in the stop position. "On second thought, don't. And I did say no."

"And remember, Brad's first wife died under suspicious circumstances. According to reports, police don't think foul play was involved. But I'm not so sure."

"Oh, that's right." How had I managed to overlook that small detail? Vince referred to Brad's first wife, who drowned in the James River about four years before. Maybe it was just as well that Brad wouldn't have anything to do with me—the fact that he had not one, but two dead wives loomed. "Brad's sure an in-demand suspect."

"Exactly."

Vince gave me an emphatic look. "What does Nina think you could do?"

"Talk to people at the places where Rox worked, like the Hamlin Group and the ARS." I explained that ARS was short for the unwieldy Alzheimer's Research Society of Central Virginia. "She says I have a lot of fans there."

"Hmm."

For a few moments the only sound came from Morris, snuggled in Vince's lap and purring.

"You need to tell Trudy that you're not a detective."

"Yes, I plan to do just that. Although she said she didn't tell Nina that I was."

"Of course, Nina may have remembered reading about you back in 2005, reading that you solved a real murder. That might have led her to ask Trudy about you."

"It's possible," I allowed. "I'll ask Trudy how this all came about." Thankfully, not many people clamored after my services.

I guessed there wasn't a big market for amateur detectives, aside from the fictional kind. "I told Nina I'd ask you for a name of a good PI. Do you know of one?"

Vince thought. "Yes, I know a few. I'll e-mail them to you."

"You have a folder of articles about Rox, don't you?"

"I do, but it's not complete. I'll show you what I have." Vince shot me a warning look. "As long as you promise—"

"Don't worry. I'm not investigating. I just want to refresh my memory on Rox." I returned to the unfortunate, and messy, reunion of Phyllis and Nina. "If I was Nina I'd file assault charges. Even with cool coffee. Plus, Phyllis was verbally abusive and in a public place to boot. The woman's often a trial at book group, but at least she limits her attacks to authors who aren't there."

"Does she post negative reviews on Amazon or Goodreads?"

"Hmm. I don't know. If she does, I'm sure she gives no higher than a two-star rating." A merry tune on my phone alerted me that I had a call. "Trudy."

Vince nudged Morris off his lap and got up. "I'll get you those articles."

Trudy asked, "Did you hear anything from Phyllis?"

"No. Do you think we will?"

"It would be nice if she apologized, but I wouldn't count on it. So, what did you think about Nina?"

"Oh, I don't know what to think. I feel bad for her, but I don't know why you recommended my services. And she's a *suspect*."

"But I told you earlier that I *didn't* recommend your services. Not exactly. First of all, I've only known Nina for about five years, and I still don't know her that well. We chat from time to time when I'm out walking Millie." Millie was Trudy's Golden Retriever mix. "One day last week she came over and asked me if I knew you. Figured I knew a lot of authors, being a librarian. I said yes and that we were in the same book group. She wanted to meet you, see if you'd help her find out who killed her sister. She remembered reading about you back in 2005. I told her I doubted that you would, but she persisted. I figured you could just say no. Which you did."

"And I'm sticking to it." Or so I hoped. "Trudy, this seems important to you. But you say you don't know Nina that well."

"Yes, I know it seems weird. It does to me too. But, well, I don't think she did it. I'm not so sure about Brad, but I don't think Nina did it."

"So Nina could be in danger from Brad?"

"Exactly."

"What makes you think Nina didn't do it?"

"A feeling."

A *feeling*! Feelings mattered. But like anything in the human realm, they were prone to error.

"And I want to see justice done," Trudy added.

"I can understand that. So why don't you investigate?"

Trudy laughed. "I have a better idea. We could get the book group involved in this—how does that sound?"

"You mean a group investigation?" Morris jumped up on my lap and I stroked his back. "Well . . . I don't know. I suppose we could discuss it at tonight's meeting." Uh oh, I could already feel my resolve crumbling.

Thanks, I mouthed as Vince handed me a manila folder secured with an elastic band. He gave me a suspicious look. No doubt he'd caught the part about the group investigation.

"What about Eileen?" I asked. "She's a neighbor as well. Did Nina talk to her about coercing me into doing this?"

"No, I'm sure she didn't. I don't know if she likes Eileen that much. You know how Eileen can be."

I did. Much as I liked our fellow book group member, she could be brusque and impatient. "Yes, I can picture Eileen telling Nina in no uncertain terms to hire an investigator and not try to involve hapless writers just to save money."

Trudy laughed. "I mean, they're neighborly enough. And Eileen went to Rox's funeral with me."

"I remember that you went to the funeral. Tell me again how it was." Vince and I had been out of town for another funeral and missed out on Rox's.

"Okay, as funerals go. But we were short-staffed at the library, so Eileen and I left right after the service. We didn't meet any of the family, but there wasn't much of one. Brad, of course. Aside from him, who was there? Brad's son. Some friends."

"I know my cousin Patty Ratzenberger and her husband Paul were there."

"Yes, I'm sure," Trudy said. "But I didn't meet them. Did I

tell you that Nina and Brad used to be an item?"

"Oh, yes, you did. I forgot about that."

"Well, now they seem to be back together. He's there a lot late at night. I see his car when I'm walking Millie."

"Interesting. And it lends credence to the two of them being viable suspects."

"Yes, unfortunately it does. Oh, and before I forget—at one point Nina told me she was estranged from Rox, but that was a year, maybe two years ago. I'm not sure if they still were at the time of the murder."

"Things don't look good for Nina."

Seconds after I ended my call with Trudy, Phyllis phoned. Without preamble, she started. "Is that bitch coming to book group?"

Morris, startled at Phyllis's harsh voice emanating from the vicinity of my ear, jumped off my lap. I didn't blame him.

"I take it you mean Nina. I don't know if she wants to come to book group. She didn't mention it."

"Well, if she does, I'm out of the group. I'm not putting up with her."

"Like I said, I don't know her plans."

"Nina was a real piece of work. So was that sister of hers."

Nina's sister? Did she mean Rox? Had Nina mentioned other sisters? "Did you know Nina's sister?"

"Yes, Roxanne. I met her once or twice. Brassy as all get-out. Why do you ask?"

"She was killed a few months ago. We talked about it at book group. She was stabbed in the parking lot of the Moonshine Inn."

"Yeah, I remember. She was quite a lush." Had Phyllis said anything about Rox at the time we discussed it? It was a hot topic and took up an entire group meeting.

"Well, let me know if she shows up tonight. But just in case she does, I won't be there."

I gave Phyllis a noncommittal "We'll be in touch." She didn't apologize for her outrageous behavior at Panera, but I decided to stay on her good side in case she had some useful information to share about Rox.

I'd first met Phyllis Ross long ago at another fiction group. Phyllis was given to overwrought harangues about the book selections. Poor writing, books too long, too short, and continuity errors in time and place were just a sampling of her pokes and jabs. She generally dominated the discussion.

Years later, Phyllis showed up at our mystery book group. Since this group didn't read the same books, she could choose her own according to a theme. That cut down on her complaints—for a while. I put her critical nature to good use by having her read my drafts. Sure enough, Phyllis nailed every flaw. I guessed I'd have to find another proofreader as I didn't see myself carrying on any kind of relationship with the volatile woman. It was one thing to be a book group malcontent; being abusive was quite another. I'd never again be able to be in Phyllis's presence without thinking of her behavior at Panera.

It was time to tackle the articles. First I went to the kitchen and grabbed a couple of envelopes and a pen. My recycle practice included using the backs of envelopes for note-taking. I curled up on the sofa with Morris, opened the folder, and started reading.

My sister had told me a little about Brad's wife's tragic end, but I'd never read an account. The body of Veronica Paye Jones, missing since February 19, 2009, had been found about seven miles from downtown Lynchburg, Virginia. Her body was lodged in a tree, approximately five feet above the James River.

The article was dated March 26, 2009. The woman had been missing for more than a month? I shook my head in dismay. That must have been a hellacious ordeal for the family. Waiting always was. Even though finding her body was sad, at least they could then grieve and have closure.

Lynchburg was at least a hundred and fifty miles from Richmond. I'd been there a couple of times for book signings. I envisioned a map of Virginia, placing the city more or less in the center of the state.

Veronica's obituary listed her husband and son, Bradley R. Jones and Alexander M. Jones respectively, as survivors, along with a slew of kinfolk in Kentucky. The deceased earned her Ph.D. from Bryn Mawr College in Pennsylvania. Her academic expertise included 19th-century British and European literature.

Were Brad and Rox a couple during this time period? According to Nina, they'd met years before. Were they friends for years before ratcheting up their relationship?

The police didn't think foul play was involved, but my husband was skeptical about that view. Had Veronica committed suicide? If so, was it instigated by a possible relationship between Brad and Rox? Or Brad and Nina? I thought it unlikely that she'd had a sudden urge for a swim in February. Many questions, few answers.

On to the next printout. Oh yes, the movie theater incident, probably the most famous, or infamous, of Rox's many incidents:

> *On April 10, 2007 Roxanne Howard, 49, confronted Foster Hayden, 23, and his companion, Pamela Barry, during the screening of a film at the UA West Tower Cinema in Richmond. Howard spoke at high volume, using abusive and sexually explicit language. A patron summoned the manager who tried to escort Howard out of the theater, but she resisted and continued her profanity-laced tirade. She finally left of her own accord.*
>
> *But Howard waited outside in the parking lot where she keyed Hayden's car and smashed his windshield with a tire iron. When Hayden and Barry left the theater and approached the car, Howard threatened them with the tire iron. A police response was initiated by Barry, and Howard was arrested for assault and property damage. Later Hayden dropped the charges.*

I shook my head at Rox's bizarre behavior that made Phyllis's actions at Panera pale by comparison. A photo of Rox showed a woman who would look right at home at the Moonshine Inn, the redneck bar where she'd been last seen alive. The bloated face and disheveled hair suggested a hard-living life. Twenty-six years separated Rox and Foster—Rox was quite the cougar. So far, my female baby-boomer characters hadn't strayed outside of their age groups and set their sights on younger men—but I wasn't opposed to the idea, and I had a lot of stories to tell.

Why had Foster dropped the charges? I jotted that question on my envelope.

Another newspaper article detailed Rox and Foster having an altercation in the hall outside of his apartment which prompted neighbors to call the police. Neither party filed charges. I went on to read about her two DUIs, about her murder, and her obituary.

But the media celebrated Rox's accomplishments as well, including her reign as Executive Director at the ARS and later as Vice President at the Hamlin Group. A smiling Rox posed with prominent public figures, including politicians from both parties.

Was the murderer someone in these photographs or named in these news stories? Was it a hired killer? If so, who hired the killer? And didn't hired killers use guns?

No doubt about it—I was succumbing to the lure of this investigation.

Vince sat next to me on the sofa and scratched Morris's ears. "So, what's this about your book group investigating?"

"Trudy thinks they might be interested in taking this on."

Vince considered. "Well, a group project would be safer."

"And these women are well-connected in the Richmond community."

"True. Sarah Rubottom's the ultimate volunteer."

"And one of her organizations is the Alzheimer's Research Society. So that works out well. Eileen and Trudy know a lot of people from the library."

"And your cousin Lucy has all those contacts in the business community." Lucy Hooper was yet another cousin, but from my mother's side. She managed a job placement agency in downtown Richmond.

I told Vince what Trudy said about Nina and Brad being an item, past and present. I added that Nina and Rox had been estranged at one point.

"So that gives Brad and Nina possible motives to kill Rox." Vince sighed. "Well, I hope you decide against doing this. But, if you do go ahead with it, I'll find out the current status of the case. I haven't kept up with it."

Vince stayed in touch with his former colleagues at the police department. They were valuable resources for his writing. "I do know that they interviewed a number of people who all had alibis."

"Really? Like who?"

"As I recall, Brad, Nina, Andy, Foster Hayden, all the folks at the Hamlin Group and the ARS. And Foster's girlfriend, what's her name?" Vince touched his forehead with his fingers, a classic gesture used to summon elusive information.

"Pamela Barry," I supplied. "I just read about that theater incident and saw her name."

"Yeah. She's living in Boston now. She was with her church group that night. A number of people vouched for her. Oh, and your cousins, Patty and Paul Ratzenberger—they were questioned as well."

"That's funny. Patty never mentioned being questioned. Why would they be?"

"As far as I know, they questioned everyone in the family. I think money was involved, but I have to refresh myself on the details. As for Foster Hayden, they had to hunt him down in Atlanta. He was visiting his mother in the hospital at the time of the murder. His alibi holds up."

"And then there's Andy—he got a DUI in Owensboro, Kentucky that night."

A nice alibi, as alibis go, I thought.

"I never heard of Owensboro. Where in Kentucky is it?"

"In the western part of the state." Vince waved his hand in a westerly direction. "A ways from here."

Vince continued. "The police questioned Rox's neighbors, past and present. They questioned her employers from way back. No one knew anything helpful. No one at the Moonshine Inn saw anything." I expected that bar denizens might harbor hostile feelings towards the police and close ranks. "But someone at the bar heard Rox arguing on the phone. Her cell records showed a call from Brad, placed about thirty minutes before her death. Her last call was to Nina." Vince gave me a look of concern, but said nothing.

I rushed to reassure him. "If we decide to do this as a group, we'll just be talking to people, seeing if there're any possibilities aside from Brad. If not, we're back to square one with Brad being the main suspect, with no proof."

"Talking is one of the most dangerous things you can do." Vince sighed. "Does Brad know that Nina talked to you?"

"Um, I'm not sure."

"I'd just as soon he didn't know about this."

"I'll tell her not to let him know."

"When are you going to discuss this with the group?"

"Tonight. We're meeting here."

"Again?" He groaned. "Weren't they just here?"

"Not for a while. We're on a rotation."

"Pretty quick rotation, it seems. You meet every two weeks and you don't have a huge group."

"It motivates us to keep our houses clean. At least the downstairs. Silver lining."

Vince smiled. "Keep an eye out for those silver linings."

"Yes." I predicted that I'd need a silver lining. Or two.

FOUR

THE HEAVENS OPENED over Richmond just as the book group members arrived, some carrying dripping umbrellas, others soaked, unprepared for the downpour. I placed a wastebasket by the front door to collect the umbrellas and sent the wet folks off to bathrooms where they could help themselves to towels and hair dryers.

While Morris sniffed at the umbrellas, I went to the back door to let Olive in the house. But the rain came down in sheets and I figured she'd taken refuge under a car. For as long as the storm raged, the neighborhood rodents were safe.

Once everyone dried off, they gathered in the kitchen. I waved a hand towards the table. "There's iced tea and water. Help yourselves anytime."

Sarah Rubottom asked, "What are you baking? It smells wonderful in here."

"Brownies." Thankfully, they masked the smell of the broccoli from dinner. As if on cue, the timer dinged. After testing the brownies with a knife that came out clean, I took the pan out of the oven and let it cool on the range top.

"That sure was a quick storm," Lucy Hooper said. In fact, the tempest had now subsided to little more than a drizzle.

"Lucy, your hair looks great," I admired my cousin's short brown layers. All agreed that Lucy looked stunning with her new do.

Once we settled into chairs in the family room, I started, "Trudy and I had an interesting experience today at Panera—".

Eileen Thompson cut me off. "Where's Phyllis? Is she coming?"

Trudy and I looked at each other. I gave a short laugh and said, "Listen to what Trudy has to say about Phyllis."

Everyone listened agog while Trudy described the brouhaha between Phyllis and Nina.

Lucy was the first to respond. "I can't believe Phyllis would act like that."

"I can." Sarah crossed her arms.

Lucy looked incredulous. "The woman can be cranky about books, but overall she's fine. I've always liked her. But to assault someone like that—"

Sarah shook her head. "Totally outrageous," Her gray braid twisted behind her neck. The humidity created wisps of hair that surrounded her face like an electrocuted halo.

"Well, you haven't heard anything yet. Let me tell you what happened after Phyllis left." This time I took the floor and detailed the meeting with Nina and her request that I look into her sister's murder. The group had already discussed Rox's murder at length three months before so I didn't need to elaborate. Aside from an occasional clarifying question, no one spoke until I finished.

"What did you tell Nina?" Lucy asked.

"I told her no."

"Good. You don't want to get involved in another investigation—do you?"

"No, I don't. But Trudy and I thought maybe you"—I spread both arms in an encompassing motion—"might want to do this as a group."

"Yes," Trudy said. "Hazel doesn't want to take this on alone. We all remember Carlene."

"Yeah, we do." We exchanged sober looks.

"Hey, this could be fun," Lucy said.

Eileen looked doubtful. "I don't know if I'd use the word 'fun'."

"Well, not fun, but, well . . . "

"Fun!" We proclaimed in unison.

"What I mean is, it could be interesting," Lucy clarified.

"The thing that gets me is that Nina is a suspect," I said. "So is Brad."

"And they were an item at one time and are again," Trudy put in.

Lucy shook her head. "Well, that's not good. But, Hazel, since Brad is your cousin, I do understand feeling a family obligation to clear him." She grinned and pointed at me. "Don't look so sour."

"Well, the man won't even acknowledge me. But still."

"You feel that pull of family."

I shrugged. "I guess. And I want to see justice done."

"Ah, justice," Sarah intoned. "Isn't that why we read mysteries? To satisfy our need to see justice prevail?"

"Yes, but that's vicarious justice," I said.

"But what about your writing schedule? You don't want an investigation to impact that."

"It's okay, Lucy. I was thinking about taking a short break. I sent off my latest manuscript last week."

"But," Lucy pronounced, "Family or not, this absolutely has to be done as a group. By the way, what's the current status of the case?"

"Vince checked on that today. Nothing new. The case is open but stalled. They don't have anyone and can't get any proof. They still suspect Brad, with Nina running a close second."

"So Rox is your what?" Sarah asked. "Cousin-in-law?"

I nodded. "So she's family, too. Kind of."

"You probably explained this before, but refresh my memory: Lucy and Brad aren't cousins?"

"Correct. Brad's on my father's side and Lucy's my cousin from my mother's side. Her mother and mine were sisters."

"And they're spending eternity playing bridge together," Lucy added.

"Yes, they didn't get along here on earth so we figure they're inseparable now."

We segued into stories about our dearly departed relatives and our notions of how they spent their time in the great beyond. These speculations reflected our personal beliefs, or lack thereof.

Eileen corralled us back to earth and the present moment. "I have to tell you that Nina also told me she wanted Hazel to investigate her sister's death. I told her to get a PI and stop pussyfooting around." Trudy and I looked at each other. Eileen's report pretty much squared with what we thought she'd say. "I mean, I'm sorry about her sister, but I have my own problems." That was true. Eileen's mother resided in an assisted living facility and raised havoc at every opportunity with her rants about the inadequacies of the place where she clearly didn't want to be. She kept Eileen hopping.

Eileen wiped her gold-framed glasses with a cloth from her purse. "But I can see a group investigation. I don't have a problem with that. I just don't want you to get involved on your own, Hazel. Not after Carlene."

"So I can count on all of you?"

"Absolutely." Four heads nodded.

"Oh, I almost forgot," I said. "Phyllis called me after I got home." I described that conversation.

"So Phyllis knew Rox," Sarah mused. "Interesting."

"She said she met her once or twice. Probably when Nina and Charlie were together."

"They also might have known each other through VAFRE. Since they both worked in development."

"You're right, Sarah." Sarah and I started to explain about VAFRE, the Virginia Association of Fund Raising Executives. But this group already knew about the regional networking organization. They agreed that Phyllis and Rox likely both belonged to it.

"Vince has a folder of articles on Rox that he's gathered for his next project. I'll scan them and e-mail them to you." I summarized the contents.

"Brad's first wife drowned?" I saw the concern in Lucy's pewter eyes. "Oh, Hazel, maybe this is too dangerous even for a group project. This guy could be bad news."

Sarah chimed in, "I'll say. Maybe it's a good thing he does refuse to acknowledge you as a relative."

"My thoughts, exactly." I added, "I'll tell Nina in no uncertain terms not to let Brad know that we're doing this."

"But Hazel, we have to watch out for Nina as well," Eileen reminded me.

"Right, so let's not be alone with either of them. Or with anyone we talk to, for that matter. Either meet in public places or travel in pairs."

"Like Noah's Ark?" Lucy said with a laugh.

"Like Noah's Ark," we chorused.

"Sarah, do you see Brad at the ARS?" I asked.

"What's the ARS?" Eileen asked before immediately answering her own question. "Oh, right, the Alzheimer's Research Society."

"I don't see him often," Sarah said. "Every now and then he stops in for something. Signing letters. And, of course, board meetings. But they're on Wednesdays and Tuesday is my day there."

"Do you ever talk to him?"

"Not really. Hello, goodbye, that sort of thing. I've never had a conversation with him."

"I know Foster Hayden," Lucy said. "We have lunch occasionally. He's mentioned that incident at the movie theatre. I'll call him and set up a lunch date, see what I can get out of him."

"In a public place," Sarah sternly warned.

"Yes, of course. But I'm in no danger from Foster."

"How do you know him?" Trudy asked.

Lucy explained how she had helped Foster's older brother, who'd had a substance abuse problem, get a job when he got out of jail. Foster and his family felt indebted and would do anything for Lucy. "Plus the law firm he works for is a good client," she added.

Trudy said, "Refresh my memory about the movie theater." Lucy and I together recounted Rox's storming into a movie theater during a showing and continuing her rampage outside.

"Wow. That's a story for the ages," Eileen said. "How did she find them in a dark theatre?"

"Well, your eyes adjust to the darkness," Lucy said. "And she might have seen them go in. Likely she was following them."

"Likely the audience remembers the scene Rox made better

than the one on the screen," I said.

Trudy put in, "I remember reading about her going to Foster's apartment and they were rolling around in the hallway." We laughed, but these stories were as tragic as they were funny.

"Lucy, how will you broach the subject of Rox with Foster?" Eileen asked.

"Oh, I'll think of something. Last I heard he was writing a mystery. I could say 'I have a mystery idea for you. You could adapt it for your young adult readers.' Don't worry, he's quite forthcoming. Likes drama."

"Good match for Rox," Eileen noted.

"And Sarah—" I started.

"Yes, I can talk to Maisie Atwater at the ARS. She was the office manager when Rox was Executive Director. When Rox left, she became the ED. Now she consults, but she's in England right now so I won't see her until next Tuesday. Sorry to have to wait on this."

"It's okay. I haven't even told Nina we'd do it." Despite my words I felt a sense of urgency to get going on this project. But the rest of the world wasn't on our schedule. And it's not like I couldn't find ways to occupy myself. Like writing.

"Sarah, didn't Maisie talk about Rox when she was killed?" I asked. "If she knew her, it seems like she would."

"Probably, but I don't remember. I don't always see Maisie. Sometimes I have to switch days and I'm not there on Tuesdays when she's there. So I may have missed it."

Lucy looked at me and Trudy. "But back to Phyllis: do you think she'll apologize? Or something?"

"I don't know. She gave no indication that she would when she called. She just said she'd leave the group if Nina joined."

"Well, la di dah. Let her leave." Lucy tossed her layers and they fell back in place. Perfectly.

"I'd like to stay on her good side for the time being. I'm thinking that if we take this on, she might be a good resource because she knew Rox. And Nina."

"Doesn't sound like she knew them too well. Or recently."

"Maybe Nina *will* wind up joining us," Eileen said, eyes dancing. "Or we could tell Phyllis that she did."

Trudy gave Eileen a look. Eileen, unperturbed, asked, "Didn't

Vince write about a woman who killed her brother-in-law after they both killed her sister?"

Eileen referred to the case involving Rosita Yates, a Virginia Beach woman who was murdered in 2007. I summarized as much as I could recall about the case. Rosita's husband, John Yates, was the primary suspect in his wife's murder but the police couldn't pin anything on him. They got a break when Rosita's sister, Yvonne Tripper, gunned down John, who happened to be her lover. Ms. Tripper immediately confessed to killing both Rosita and John. According to her, John, luring Yvonne with promises of marriage and access to Rosita's vast estate, convinced her to kill her sister.

"Right," I said. "But John reneged on his promises and laughed in Yvonne's face when she flew into a rage at his betrayal. She retrieved her gun and put a hole through John's chest."

"That was his big mistake—laughing at her. That put her over the edge."

"Don't you think she was already over the edge, Sarah?" Lucy asked, her tone dry. "Imagine, killing over a *man*."

"Maybe the situation with Nina and Brad is a replay of that story," Eileen said. "If it is, Brad had better watch his step."

"Maybe Nina's the one who needs to watch out," I said. "She doesn't look too strong. A gentle breeze would knock her over."

"True," Trudy agreed. "And it seems like wielding a knife with enough force to kill a person would take quite a bit of strength. Although she wasn't quite as frail back in March when Rox was stabbed."

No one had anything to add to the Nina-as-stabber speculation. After a pause, Lucy asked, "What about Mary Anne? Should we ask her to join us?"

"I'll send her an e-mail now." Trudy dashed off her message in seconds. I envied her speed. With my knack for hitting the wrong keys it took me forever to compose on my smartphone. For me, the auto-complete feature was a godsend. And I still didn't know half the apps.

"I wonder if Mary Anne will come back here when she finishes her playwriting class," Trudy mused.

"I tend to think she won't," I said. "I didn't think she was that hot on mysteries. Nina's taking that same class. It ends tomorrow night."

"Is playwriting the 'in' thing now?" Eileen laughed. "Suddenly we're awash with playwrights."

"So, Hazel, will you call Nina?" Lucy asked.

"Yes, tomorrow. I have doctors' appointments in the morning. I'll call her after that. I need more information, so I want to meet with her again before I commit us to this."

Trudy asked, "How often are we going to meet about the investigation?"

That's when it hit me that I was in charge of this operation. "Let's make tentative plans to get together on Wednesday to see where we are with things. I will have talked to Nina by then."

"Can we meet at a coffee place? Like Taza's? Or Crossroads?" Sarah named a couple of independent coffee houses on Richmond's Southside.

"I love Crossroads," Lucy said. "But it's noisy and we don't want to be shouting. And Taza closes early, I'm not sure what time."

We reviewed the local coffee options, preferring a locally-owned and nearby place and needing for it to be open in the evening. But such places with evening hours were in short supply.

"That leaves us with Starbucks and Panera," Lucy said.

"You know, I love you guys, but I just can't spare another night to meet. How about Skype?"

"Great idea, Eileen," Trudy said. "I can't really set aside the extra night either. Skype will be quicker and easier. Except that sometimes I have trouble with the video part, especially if there're more than two of us."

"Then let's keep it simple and just do audio," I said. "We see each other all the time."

"I don't do Skype." Sarah was our technological holdout, e-mail and a flip-phone being her concessions to the ever-changing world of communication.

"You can come over to my house," Lucy offered. She and Sarah lived near each other.

"Okay," Sarah sounded unenthused but offered no further objections.

"Then Skype it is." Trudy looked around the room. "Is seven on Wednesday okay with everyone?"

A chorus of yeses indicated agreement. "And you'll send us

those articles, Hazel?" Eileen asked.

"I will. And let's make sure we all have each other's Skype handles."

A sound like wind chimes alerted Trudy that she had a new e-mail. "It's Mary Anne. She's passing on the group investigation. She's sorry about Nina's sister, but says investigating her death is way too scary."

"Smart woman, that Mary Anne."

No one disagreed with me.

FIVE

"SHALL WE DISCUSS our books?" I looked around at the group. "I guess we'll have to be quick about it."

Trudy kicked off the discussion with a spirited account of a tale set in ancient Mesopotamia that she'd read on her Kindle. A detective modeled on the likes of Dashiell Hammet's Sam Spade or Mickey Spillane's Mike Hammer is hired to find Abel, the brother done in by his brother Cain, recounted in the Book of Genesis.

"Of course, back in those days the detective had to use a stylus and clay tablet to take notes." Trudy passed around a picture of those items that she'd printed from the Internet.

As a librarian, Trudy had a love of books and knew how to draw listeners in and make them want to read whatever she described. We all took note of *Genesis One: Abel is Missing* by Martin Lorin.

"It's self-published, so you'll need to buy it online." When Trudy saw Sarah's sour expression she rushed to add, "They might have print copies." Sarah held a dim view of reading devices.

Lucy asked, "So why *did* Cain kill Abel?"

Eileen explained. "Envy. Cain took some of his harvest to the Lord. Abel offered his fattest lamb. The Lord preferred the lamb. Cain took great offense and killed his brother. Classic story." Apparently, some of us were more up on our Old Testament than others.

"Who could blame the Lord? I'd prefer a nice plump lamb any day over *wheat*." Sarah fairly spat the word *wheat*.

"Not me, I'm a vegetarian." Eileen proclaimed.

"There must be more to it than envy," I said. "Something that Adam and Eve did. They probably weren't good parents."

"I bet the eviction from the Garden of Eden took their focus off their children." Trudy fiddled with the silver barrette that held back her long white hair and exposed the rose tattoo that decorated her neck. I knew that she kept the tattoo hidden from her anti-tat library director.

"Some will do anything for parental approval." Lucy fanned herself with her book.

I heard an edge in Eileen's voice when she said, "If you read the OT you'll see that it's like I said: Cain didn't like the Lord preferring Abel's offering to his."

We went back and forth on the Cain and Abel story, the archetype of sibling rivalry, digressing into other takes on brothers killing brothers. John Steinbeck retold the Cain and Abel story in his enduring epic, *East of Eden*, naming his characters Caleb and Aaron.

"But the Caleb character didn't kill the Aaron character," I said.

"But Caleb's jealousy caused Aaron's death, indirectly," Eileen explained. "The two had so many conflicts that Aaron up and joined the military and got killed."

"*East of Eden* . . . that's pretty long, isn't it?"

In one voice, the rest of us assured Lucy that *East of Eden* may be long but it was a page turner. "Steinbeck knew how to hold the reader's interest," I said, adding, "The movie's interesting as well, especially if you're a James Dean fan. But it doesn't come close to the book."

Sarah asked, "How about what we were talking about before—sisters killing sisters?"

"I've come this close to killing mine." Trudy said, holding

her thumb and index finger a quarter inch apart. We laughed in rueful understanding of the ambivalent feelings some of us shared about our female siblings.

"My sister won't eat anything I cook," Sarah said, sounding nettled. "She's never even tried my cooking."

I bit my lip to keep from smiling. A glance at the others told me they were doing the same thing, thinking that Sarah's sister was lucky. Sarah wasn't known for her cooking, but that didn't keep her out of the kitchen. When book group met at her house, we had to rev up our diplomatic skills.

Trudy tapped the screen of her iPhone. "There was that movie, *Chicago*."

"Oh, yes," I said. "That woman who was serving time for murdering both her husband and her sister when she found them in bed together."

"Doing the 'spread eagle'," Trudy read from her phone display. We all hooted at that one. "And don't forget *What Ever Happened to Baby Jane?*"

"I don't think anybody was killed in the Baby Jane one," Sarah said.

"But they tried," Eileen said. "Those sisters tried to kill each other."

Carlene Arness and I had started the Murder on Tour group ten years before. It differed from other groups in that we each read a book of our choosing based on a travel theme, and then discussed our book along with each other's choices.

Carlene's death in 2005 and the ensuing investigation dampened our enthusiasm for murder mysteries and actually drove some members away. We reformed as a film group, first with Sarah, Trudy, Lucy, and myself. Eileen and Phyllis soon followed. We kept the travel theme. But it didn't work out: different opinions on what to watch, interruptions, talking, whispering, eating, distractions, short attention spans, cell phones.

So we returned to reading mysteries, settling on time periods prior to the twentieth century. Maybe we thought they were less violent. They weren't, but they were at a remove from contemporary stories. Trudy and Eileen had unearthed a treasure trove of online databases for readers that covered the ancient world and traveled through the centuries to the present day. We would pick a theme for the month and then meet biweekly, which didn't give us much time to read an entire book, but we didn't have a problem with that. We never gave away the endings, so we could discuss our book in progress. Plus, we liked to socialize, so more frequent meetings suited us.

Eileen brought us back to our primary purpose. "Okay, this is a book group. Let's hear what the rest of us read. Hazel?"

This month's theme was the ancient world and I raved about *Silver Pigs* by Lindsay Davis, the first of Ms. Davis's historical series set in Rome and Britannia in AD 70. I planned to continue reading the series on my own.

"I'm so glad you read the first book of a series this time," Sarah said. I was known for starting a series at any point, a practice that infuriated the other members.

"It doesn't mean I'm changing my ways."

I heard the floor creaking overhead. Vince chose to hole up in his den during book group but Morris periodically showed up to make his rounds. Morris was shy but curious, so he kept track of any goings on in his territory. Hands reached out to be sniffed and the cat obliged, getting a pat here and there.

"I read *The Germanicus Mosaic* by Rosemary Rowe." Lucy went on to summarize the plot and setting of the story set in Roman Britain. "I enjoyed it. And"—Lucy winked at me—"it's the first in this series."

"Did you post your review on Goodreads yet?" Trudy asked. We enjoyed Lucy's reviews on the social cataloguing site for readers.

"Not yet, but I will."

Sarah and Eileen hadn't finished their stories, both set in ancient Greece. While they offered general descriptions, I excused myself to get the refreshments together.

I cut the brownies into small portions. Thankfully, everyone in this group could eat walnuts. With allergies so rampant, finding brownies with nuts in bakeries and grocery stories posed such a challenge that I'd taken to baking my favorite dessert. As a plus, Eileen's brand of vegetarianism allowed for milk and eggs so I didn't have to alter the recipe to satisfy her requirements.

As I opened the refrigerator and took out a plate of fruit, the others wandered in from the family room, talking in high spirits.

I caught something about Matthew McConaughey, but in what context—acting, looks, six-pack abs?

When Eileen saw me lifting the lever of an old-fashioned metal ice tray to release the cubes she exclaimed, "I love it! So retro." Eileen had pulled her long brown curls back into a ponytail secured by a rubber band. Her slenderness made her appear younger than her fifty-three years.

I said, "I bought a couple of these trays on eBay. They go with my vintage Formica tops." I refreshed the water and iced tea with the ice cubes.

"Oh, are you a holdout on granite tops? Me, too."

"They look great but I won't be bullied in having them. I guess *House Hunters* won't put my kitchen on their show—unless they want to redo my counters." I referred to the popular HGTV show that seemed to require the homes they showcased to have granite tops in the kitchen; bathrooms, too.

• • •

The group stayed for another half hour, enjoying the refreshments.

When everyone had left, I gave Vince the all-clear. He came downstairs with Morris in tow. We brought Olive inside, checking first to be sure she was dry and not bearing a rodent gift. The cat passed muster and we let her in the house.

Vince asked, "How did the group go?"

"Oh, we talked about fratricide and sororicide." We both laughed. "Want some brownies?"

At his "Sure" I took the depleted plate down to the family room.

"So tell me more about book group. And I hope you ditched the idea of investigating." Vince bit into his brownie. "These are pretty good."

I smiled. "Thanks. And, to answer your question, we didn't ditch the idea. They were most intrigued."

Vince harrumphed. "Why doesn't that surprise me?"

I told him about the group's tentative assignments and our plan to meet by Skype on Wednesday for updates. I went on to the Cain and Abel discussion and the parallels we'd noted with Vince's true crime account involving sisters.

"Well, there's definitely a sisterly aspect to Rox's murder."

"How could someone kill their blood relative? I mean, I could see a spouse—"

At Vince's look, I laughed. "Oh, not you. You're one of the good guys. And you don't have enough money to make killing you worthwhile."

"Thank God for small favors. So, anything else you care to tell me about your discussion?"

I thought. "No, I pretty much covered it. Unless you want to hear about stories set in the ancient world."

"I'll pass." Vince waved his hand. "Want to split that last brownie?"

"Sure."

• • •

"Okay, Ms. Rose, you can get dressed. We'll be in touch once the radiologist reads your pictures."

I hoped my breasts forgave me for allowing a relentlessly cheerful stranger to flatten and compress them. I'd heard talk of a new and improved mammogram procedure, but it remained a distant dream.

I walked down the hall to my second appointment, an annual physical. The previous week I'd had blood drawn, and my doctor reviewed the report. I came away with a clean bill of health that put the odious mammogram out of my mind. Deciding that I deserved to treat myself I headed for Brio's Tuscan Grille at Stony Point Fashion Park and enjoyed a grilled salmon salad.

At home I found Vince sitting on the screened-in porch, bookended by Olive and Morris. They hoped for a sample of his potato salad and didn't take their eyes off the mayonnaise-laden mound of spuds. I kissed Vince, pet both felines, and ran down my medically-oriented morning. After getting a modicum of sympathy over the mammogram ordeal I said, "Well, I'm going to call Nina now and ask her to meet me at Joe's tomorrow." Vince rolled his eyes but said nothing.

After leaving a message on Nina's cell phone, I turned to the task of scanning the folder of Rox-related articles. Midway through the process, I got a call from Nina.

Without preamble, she asked, "So, are you going to do it?"

"Um, I'm not ready to commit just yet. I have some questions. Let's meet tomorrow for breakfast." Nina sighed but agreed. Not wanting a replay of the Panera episode, I suggested Joe's Inn in Bon Air at eight o'clock.

I finished my scanning project and sent the documents to the book group, including a note that Nina and I planned to meet at Joe's the next day. Then I composed an e-mail to my sister Ruth, asking about the medical history of the newly discovered relatives. She almost immediately responded that she didn't have any information. I spent the rest of the day outlining my next story about a group of women who form a secret Facebook dating group. They arrange a cruise of the Greek Islands and have romantic adventures.

Sometimes I got very jealous of my characters.

SIX

THE NEXT MORNING I set off on foot for my meeting with Nina. Richmond's summers could be insufferably hot and steamy, but the weather was usually bearable early in the day. Oak trees canopied my neighborhood, providing welcome shade. Along the way I met many dogs. I found it amusing that I could greet many of the dogs by name but I seldom managed to learn, or remember, their owners' names.

Vince and I lived in Bon Air, a 19th century resort area frequented by the wealthy that had been annexed by Richmond. Bon Air meant "good air" and carried more panache than the mundane Richmond. The air quality has certainly deteriorated since the 19th century but was still a hundred times better than in Los Angeles, where I'd lived for many years.

A part of Bon Air is designated a National Historic District, boasting a number of Victorian homes. But the house styles of our neighborhood reflected the 1960s building boom—split levels, ranch styles, Cape Cods, and the occasional Colonial Revival.

In twenty minutes I arrived at Joe's Inn, on the dot of eight o'clock. My mother would have been proud—she'd instilled in me the virtue of punctuality. Joe's was known for serving up unpretentious food at reasonable prices. As my father would have said, "Good plain food and plenty of it!"

Vince stood by the door but we made no signs of recognition. According to plan, he'd follow me into the restaurant and keep an eye on our booth from a discreet distance. I really thought I'd be fine at Joe's Inn but, as Vince pointed out, Nina was a suspect, so we couldn't be too careful.

The host took me to Nina, sitting in a wooden booth against the wall. She looked lost in thought as she stirred her coffee. She'd pulled her hair back and secured it with a white plastic barrette. Her colorful madras plaid shirt drained her makeup-free face of color, accentuating the shadows under her eyes.

"Thanks for coming, Hazel." A tepid smile appeared briefly. I gave my coffee order to the server. "Let's order now, so we can talk."

When I heard a voice with a Brooklyn accent say, "Yes, coffee, please," I knew Vince was sitting a few booths behind me.

I'd worked up an appetite from the walk, so I chose the Greek omelet and wheat toast. Nina opted for white toast. Once the server left, I waited a couple of beats before saying, "And now, if you're up to it, tell me what happened the night your sister was killed."

Nina sighed and began her tale. Apparently, the Moonshine Inn near the Westover Hills section of Richmond had been Rox's favorite watering hole. Brad had called his wife and they'd gotten into an argument over her drinking. As often happened when the newlyweds argued, Rox called her sister to come and pick her up.

"When I got to Moonshine's parking lot, Rox was nowhere in sight. I was annoyed but figured she didn't know which end was up. I only hoped she hadn't forgotten about me and tried to drive herself home. She already had two DUIs.

"The parking lot was crowded so I had to park towards the back of the lot. I got out of the car, not knowing if I should go into the bar or look for Rox's SUV. I sure didn't want to go inside. Have you ever been in the Moonshine Inn?"

I shook my head. I didn't frequent bars and I'm sure I wouldn't pick the Moonshine, even if I did: the clientele ran to the rough side. "Why would Rox have gone to a place like that, and so often?

It's not a place I'd expect to find a professional woman."

"I don't know. Maybe she didn't want to be recognized. It was quite an issue with her and Brad. Maybe she wanted a place where she could just drink and not worry about running into someone she knew, especially someone from the Hamlin Group." If that was her intention, she'd made a good choice with the Moonshine.

Nina went on. "I took my pocket flashlight and started to look around the lot as I walked towards the bar. That's when I saw Brad. He'd just been in the bar and Rox wasn't there. We looked for her SUV together."

Now her voice caught. "And we found it—parked alongside a chain link fence by a dumpster. Rox was lying on the ground by the driver's door. Blood everywhere." Nina's voice caught again and tears began streaming down her face. "No pulse."

I rooted through my purse for tissues and pulled out a couple that I passed to Nina. I grabbed her hand and said, "Take a rest, Nina. There's no rush."

Nina wiped her face and said, "No. I need to get moving on this. So I went to Florida for a while after the funeral and stayed with a friend. When I came back I got involved in the playwriting class. All that time I kept hoping the police would solve the case. But they haven't accomplished a thing. Not a frigging thing. Something has to be done."

She blew her nose and resumed. "Back then, that night, Brad called 911. It had only been thirty-five minutes, forty-five tops, since Rox had called me."

"I'm sorry. Did you see anyone else in the parking lot?"

"No. No one."

The waitperson set our plates before us. As we buttered our toast I said, "You said the lot was crowded?"

"Yes, with cars, but everyone was either inside the Moonshine or in one of the other places nearby. There's another bar and a restaurant." Nina sipped her coffee and nibbled her toast.

"Oh, wait, I'm forgetting about that guy with the baseball cap." Nina suddenly sounded coy. "I saw him when I got out of my car and turned on my flashlight. He walked towards me and we made brief eye contact. He had glasses and dark hair, longish. Baseball cap. Something happened, like his knee maybe buckled. He got into the car next to mine. I didn't notice the driver—remember, I was focused on Rox. Then I saw Brad. I forgot about the guy until later.

"Anyway, there was something about the guy that seemed familiar, but then I realized that I didn't know him after all. Oh, and I think I saw a glint of something, like metal."

"Metal. Like in a knife?" I asked.

"Maybe. But it could have been a gun . . . after all, Moonshine *is* a redneck bar. But I don't know. Belt buckle?"

Under the circumstances, I couldn't dismiss the knife idea, though the knife that had killed Rox was left at the crime scene—a kitchen knife, with no prints. "So this metal thing was on his person?"

"Yes. Around his waist area. I'm surprised I remember as much about him as I do . . . I keep thinking someone's out to kill me. Someone who thinks I saw him. Or her. Maybe this guy. Or the driver. I don't know." She waved her hand across her face like she was swatting at a bug. "Sorry. I still get so upset."

"Understandable," I assured her. "Three months isn't that long. And if you think someone's trying to kill you, it makes things worse."

"That's another reason I went to Florida. But I have to face things."

The omelet was good but I found myself mindlessly eating. Something about this account of the baseball-capped and possibly armed guy struck a false note—a red herring. The term "red herring" referred to anything that misled or distracted, a practice often employed by mystery writers to lead readers astray. But I'd have to ponder my doubts later. "Do you remember anything else about this guy?"

Nina thought for a moment before shaking her head. Figuring it was time to line up the suspects, I asked, "So, do you have any idea who could have done it?"

"Well, I don't like to point fingers." I waited for the finger-pointing to start. I didn't have to wait long. "There's Andy Jones. Brad's son. Your second cousin."

Actually, Andy was my first cousin once removed, but it wasn't the time and place for illuminating Nina on the mind-boggling distinctions that made up a family tree. "Why do you suspect Andy?"

"Andy loathed Rox and Brad. He blamed Rox for his parents' breaking up and he blamed both of them for his mother's death."

Ah, the mysterious drowning. Back when I investigated Carlene Arness's death, I often asked questions even when I knew the answers. More than once it had proved useful to see if the answers matched up to my knowledge. Plus, the person I questioned often provided new information. So even though I knew that Veronica Jones had drowned, I asked, "How did Andy's mother die?"

"Veronica drowned in the James River, near Lynchburg. It was ruled a suicide, but Andy is *sure* his father and Rox murdered her. Either that or they drove her to suicide."

"Really? That's quite an accusation."

"Yes, well, it is. And totally unfounded."

"How did Veronica come to be in Lynchburg?"

Nina shrugged. "No one ever knew how or why she came to be there."

Nina went on. "When your cousin Marcie died, Andy showed up drunk at her funeral. He started in on Brad and Rox and wouldn't shut up. He was really loud and abusive. Finally, Paul took him outside and got him calmed down."

"Paul? You mean Paul Ratzenberger, Patty's husband?"

"Right. Paul and Andy were always chummy. I remember when we all visited Marcie how the two of them would leave to go outside or go to the kitchen and make coffee. Male bonding. So Paul was a godsend that day at the funeral. At Rox's funeral Andy was sober and nice as could be. Go figure."

"Well, I don't think it's unusual for an alcoholic to act one way drunk and another way sober. Assuming he is an alcoholic. But I am surprised that he showed up for Rox's funeral if he loathed her so much."

"I know. Maybe he was just happy to see her dead." She twisted her mouth and added, "Or congratulating himself for a job well done."

I continued with my pretense of not knowing certain facts. "Was Andy ever questioned?"

"He has an alibi—he conveniently managed to get a DUI in Owensboro, Kentucky the very night Rox was killed."

Without prompting, Nina explained the Kentucky aspect.

"Andy lives in Kentucky, at least some of the time. That's where his mother came from and he has lots of relatives there. He also has a girlfriend there with their young son. When he fights with the girlfriend he hightails it back here. When he fights with Brad, he goes back to the girlfriend. The cycle repeats over and over."

"And where is Andy now?" I asked.

Nina shrugged. "In Kentucky, I guess. I haven't seen him since Rox's funeral, but I haven't been around. Brad hasn't seen him either . . . hasn't even heard from him."

Andy's silence must mean that peace reigned on the Owensboro home front. Had Brad tried to contact his son—or was their relationship a one-way street?

"The only other suspect I have is Foster Hayden. But that was years ago, 2007 or so. Why kill Rox now?"

Ah, yes, Foster, the most memorable of all the players in Rox's soap operatic life. I said, "That name sounds familiar. Tell me about him."

"They worked at the Alzheimer's Research Society. Rox was executive director and Foster interned for the communications director. She picked Foster as her special pet and showed him preferential treatment. She was just crazy about him."

Yes, it sounds like she was crazy about him, I thought. *Crazy* being the operative word.

I asked, "Wasn't there something about a theater incident?"

"Oh yeah, the movie incident." Nina sighed. "That was unfortunate. Rox was so distraught when they broke up and Foster went to work someplace else. When she saw him at the movies with that other woman, her grief just overwhelmed her."

And caused her to go on a rampage, barely escaping charges of assault and property damage.

"So Rox was seeing Brad and Foster at the same time?" I tried for a matter-of-fact, judgment-free tone.

Nina thought for a moment. "I don't think so. Rox and Brad were kind of on and off over the years."

"Were you ever involved with Brad?"

Nina looked startled, then wary. "I have been. At times." Had her involvement alternated, or coincided, with Rox's? A middle-aged threesome?

"Are you now?"

The server appeared and refilled our mugs. We stirred creamer into our coffee and didn't say anything for a full minute.

I broke the silence. "Look, I've heard that you are involved with Brad."

Nina took a deep breath. "Brad and I are just friends. We decided a long time ago that we weren't well-suited romantically." Nina looked right into my eyes as she said this and didn't look away. I figured she either told the truth or had passed Lying 101 with flying colors.

I noticed that she didn't question how I acquired my information. Maybe she assumed I was a crackerjack detective and wasn't surprised by any information I could unearth.

"Maybe Foster's girlfriend did it," I offered. "You know, the one with him at the theater."

"Maybe." Nina didn't sound convinced.

"Anyone else?"

Nina thought for a moment before saying, "No." She stretched out that no to a length that suggested doubt. "It *could* be someone at the Hamlin Group. Or the ARS. It's unlikely but they are possibilities. Oh—there's Rox's ex-husband. But that's pretty remote. They split up years ago and he lives in Australia with his wife and family."

"So he's a possibility, but an unlikely one. Did Rox have any children?"

"Yes, she and the Aussie had a daughter. She lives in Seattle. She flew in for the funeral and went back immediately. I haven't heard from her since."

"What about someone at the bar?"

"I don't know. They were all questioned, or at least the police took their names. Maybe you could go there and question people."

I didn't even respond. The mere idea horrified me.

I thought of Phyllis's unflattering remarks about Rox, and in particular her drinking habits. "Did Phyllis know Rox?"

Nina scowled at the mention of Phyllis. "I'm not sure. Maybe. They might have met back when I was keeping company with Phyllis's brother. Why do you ask?"

"Just wondered. So tell me about your family."

"No one really, just some distant cousins. And I have an ex, but he's not a relative."

After a pause, Nina said, "So you'll do it?"

I took a deep breath before agreeing. "But the book group will investigate with me. It's a joint operation."

"Does that mean they all have to go everywhere with you?"

"Not necessarily. But we will travel in pairs."

"Okay. I'll set something up at the Hamlin Group and Brad can get you in at the ARS—"

I held up my hand. "Don't tell Brad anything."

"Why? Maybe this is a way to get you two together."

"Don't tell Brad *anything*," I repeated. "Sarah from the book group volunteers at the ARS and she can nose around. Don't worry, she's good at it."

"Okay. You're the boss."

When Nina didn't look me in the eye, I asked, "Does Brad know you're talking to me?"

Her "Um, no" sounded tentative. "Not exactly. I mean, he doesn't know we're talking today."

"Nina, does he know or doesn't he?"

"Well, I brought up your name when Brad and I first talked about this. I told him about that other murder you investigated. That's when he said you were his cousin."

I sighed. If Brad even guessed what I was up to I had to watch my step. "If the subject comes up again, tell Brad I'm not investigating." I looked Nina straight in the eye and she nodded.

"Nina, I have a question for you, and you don't have to answer. But you need to keep it in mind: what if it's Brad?" To myself I added, *What if it's you?*

"It *isn't*," she said.

I relented. "Okay, fine."

"Let's start with the Hamlin Group—when can you go?"

"Friday. Nine o'clock?"

"Fine."

"What about my cover story?"

"Hmm." Nina smiled for the first time, like a burst of sunshine after days of rain. "The other day one of us suggested you say you're researching sex in the workplace. How's that?"

I laughed. "It's as good a cover as any. Maybe even a real story idea for me."

Nina paid the check, and we walked past Vince sipping his coffee and feigning absorption in his paper.

"Nina, Vince e-mailed me a list of PIs. I'm going to forward them to you. I still think you should consider hiring a professional."

"I'll consider it," Nina assured me, but with little conviction.

As she got into her Mitsubishi she said, "I'll let the Hamlin folks know you'll be there, so be ready with your research questions."

SEVEN

THAT EVENING, THE book group members assembled for our first Skype session. It took a few minutes of fumbling, cursing, and adjusting audio settings, but at last we each declared ourselves connected, voices coming through crystal clear.

I kicked off the discussion by sharing my morning conversation with Nina at Joe's Inn, including Nina's top suspects—Foster and Andy—who both conveniently had alibis. When I got to the guy in the parking lot, Sarah blurted, "Oh, what a load of crap! That's a red herring if ever I heard one."

"It could very well be a red herring, Sarah," I said. "In fact, I had that very thought when Nina told me about this guy. But at this point we have to be open to all possibilities."

"Whatever. I just *know* that Brad did it. Probably Nina does, as well."

"Well, I'm going to the Hamlin Group on Friday morning. Are any of you free to go with me?"

Eileen rushed to volunteer her services. "I'm off on Friday, so I can go. I'll be your research assistant. Is that okay with everyone?"

When no one objected, Lucy said, "That's a great idea, Eileen—being a research assistant."

"Actually, it is," I agreed. "But I feel kind of high and mighty having a research assistant. I'm not a big-name author."

"Act as if you're a big name and you will become one."

"I don't know if I want to be a big name, Sarah. But that's beside the point. Eileen, I'm happy to have you as my assistant. And protector. Just to give you a heads-up, my cover story is that I'm researching sex in the workplace."

They shrieked in delight. After a good long laugh, the kind that involved clutching our sides, I said, still gasping for breath, "Okay, Eileen, I'll pick you up at eight-thirty on Friday." I thought about traffic going into downtown Richmond at that time of day and amended the time: "Make that eight-fifteen."

"I'm having lunch with Foster next Wednesday," Lucy said.

"Not 'til then?" I sounded whiny to my ears.

"He's in Atlanta, visiting his mother. He'll be back on Tuesday."

Sarah said, "And I think I told you the other night that I won't see Maisie Atwater 'til Tuesday."

I felt impatient, but resigned myself to having to wait. "Vince and I are going to the Moonshine Inn on Friday night."

"You're kidding!" Trudy exclaimed. "I wouldn't go near the Moonshine Inn."

"Yes, it's a weird place. Be careful," Eileen advised.

"Bet you could pick up some good writing material there," Sarah said.

"Yes," Lucy said. "Baby boomer rednecks having hot and steamy sex."

We shared another laugh, a replay of the earlier round. "Hey, that could work," I managed between gasps.

"But you and Vince are so, well, *conventional* looking. No offense."

"None taken, Trudy. But I'm going to a couple of thrift stores tomorrow. Don't worry, I'll come up with something rednecky. We'll be fine."

"You need big hair," Lucy said. "And blue eye shadow, sparkly red nail polish, and let's see . . ."

"Can't I use green eye shadow? My eyes are green."

"No. Blue is more redneck." Eileen was firm on that point.

"Show some cleavage," Sarah put in.

"Okay, okay, I get the picture."

"I have some cowboy boots," Eileen offered. "Hand-tooled. They're a little beat up."

"Beat up is good."

"What's your size?"

"Seven and a half."

"I wear an eight. They'll probably be okay as long as you don't go hiking in them. I'll bring them on Friday when we go to the Hamlin Group."

"Hazel, when are you seeing your cousin Patty next?" Trudy asked.

"Tomorrow. We're having lunch. I may be able to extract something helpful from her, but that's iffy. She's not forthcoming and insists on saying only nice things about people."

"That's too bad," Sarah commiserated. "Investigating requires nasty people, not Pollyannas."

"Are you going to tell Patty you're investigating?" Eileen asked.

"Absolutely not! And don't you tell anyone either, other than spouses and significant others. The fewer people who know about this, the better."

"I'm zipping my lips as we speak," Eileen assured us.

"We operate like the CIA, on a need-to-know basis," Trudy put in.

"Exactly." I went on to summarize our assignments. "Okay, Lucy's having lunch with Foster, and Sarah will set something up with Maisie. Friday's the Hamlin Group and the Moonshine Inn. When should we Skype again? Next week at this time?" My suggestion met with everyone's approval.

"Wait, what about me?" Trudy asked. "I don't have anything to do."

"Oh, there'll be plenty later," I assured her. "I have high hopes that we'll unearth all kinds of dirt on Rox in the next week. Maybe on Nina and Brad as well."

Lucy suggested that we let her or Sarah know if we find out anything useful before they talked with Maisie and Foster. "And be very careful," she cautioned. "I know we said this the other night, but it bears repeating: don't be alone when you're questioning people. Everyone remembers Carlene's death. It was a long time ago, but not long enough." Murmurs of "absolutely" and "you're right" followed.

"And let's have our phones with us—turned on and unmuted," Eileen added.

"Just so you know," I said, "I sent Nina a list of PIs. So maybe she'll decide to go that route."

"Well, that would be better . . . but not as interesting."

"I wouldn't worry about it, Sarah," Eileen said. "I'm sure Nina won't hire a PI."

"I do have a question and maybe Trudy and Eileen can answer it," I said. "How truthful do you think Nina is?"

"I think there's truth in what she says—just not the whole truth. She does leave out stuff."

"I agree with Trudy," Eileen said. "But I think she does want to find out who killed her sister. Or for someone to be found to take the fall. Then she and Brad are off the hook."

"And can live happily ever after," Sarah quipped.

EIGHT

LAWN MOWERS, LEAF blowers, and weed whackers created a din at Patty and Paul Ratzenberger's apartment complex on Forest Hill Avenue. Thankfully, it was quieter where they lived in the back. The community accepted families with children—toys in primary colors strewn about attested to that. At the moment no one, adult or child, was out and about.

Patty opened the door, wearing an aqua cotton robe. "I'll be just a minute. Make yourself at home." She gave me a quick hug before turning back to her bedroom. Pleasant aromas came from the countertop convection oven in the kitchen.

I noticed a slight limp as Patty walked away and I asked if she'd hurt herself.

"A touch of arthritis in my knee. It comes and goes. Paul has it, too."

"I have some on-again-off-again stiffness myself. Especially in the humid weather."

The apartment was small and crammed full of overstuffed furniture in a charcoal gray that suggested hulking, prehistoric creatures. I doubted that the décor accorded with *feng shui* principles; not that I knew much about the Chinese philosophy of harmonizing with the surrounding environment, but surely these eyesores wouldn't harmonize with anything. But Paul and Patty planned to buy a house once they found one in an area of Richmond they liked. Patty had grown up in the city, so it seemed like she'd know the areas. And they'd been here a few years. What was the delay?

I perused the books in an overflowing bookcase. Volumes that couldn't fit on the shelves were stacked on the floor, flanking the bookcase. Patty once explained that she had acquired our cousin Marcie's collection of classics following her death from pancreatic cancer.

"I was so delighted when Brad arrived on our doorstep with these cartons," she had said. "*Such* a surprise." Since Marcie had died close to two years before, I guessed the stacking arrangement had become part of the décor—no doubt another *feng shui* no-no.

Marcie and Patty had both been high school English teachers. While Patty taught until her retirement, Marcie surprised family and friends by switching careers at age thirty to become a stockbroker, and a successful one to boot.

Who had inherited Marcie's money? She had no children or spouse. Obviously not Patty—I'd expect her to upgrade her living space, or at least her furnishings, if she'd received a windfall. But people didn't tend to leave their estates to cousins. As Brad was also Marcie's cousin, that idea also ruled out him as the beneficiary. But if Marcie left everything to Rox in gratitude for tending to her in her last days, that meant that Brad now had Marcie's estate in his bank account; it also gave him a powerful motive to kill his wife.

Had Marcie even left a will? Patty once told me that Marcie was diligent with financial matters for her clients, but fell short when it came to her own. "By her own admission, Marcie wasn't at all organized," Patty had said, her tone suggesting that her cousin's foibles were delightful. The disorganized part left room for doubt about Marcie leaving a will.

"There was that check." Patty had chuckled as she told me about finding an uncashed check for a thousand dollars made out to Marcie. "I found it in one of the classics. It was dated sometime in 2005."

When I asked Patty if Marcie had left a will, she shrugged, laughed, and said, "Who knows? If she did I guess she left everything to Rox. Rox was so good to her."

A small photo on the bookcase showed Patty and Paul with Marcie, Nina, and a man Patty had once told me was our cousin and Brad's son, Andy Jones. Andy sported longish dark hair, a vibrant mustache, and glasses with lenses shaped like mini TV screens. Marcie sat propped up in bed with a turban over her likely bald head, courtesy of her chemo treatments. Patty once told me the photo was taken a couple of weeks before Marcie died. The group was smiling. Life converging with death.

The shelved books were organized by type: fiction, nonfiction, art books, and classics. The plays of Tennessee Williams, William Inge and other preeminent playwrights of the past century made me think of Nina and her class. From time to time I toyed with the idea of acting in a play, fantasizing about transforming myself into Blanche DuBois in Tennessee Williams's *Streetcar Named Desire*. But maybe I should start out small—I could ask Nina to cast me in her play.

Patty emerged from the bedroom dressed in jeans and a linen blouse. Patty was a statuesque woman with a sleek cap of nut-brown hair. People always said we looked alike. She stepped into the kitchen and checked the progress of our lunch. "The quiche should be done in a few minutes. Iced tea?"

"Yes, thanks."

Carrying our drinks, we took seats in the tiny living room, sinking into the depths of the dinosaurs, my private nicknames for their unfortunate choice of furniture.

"How's Paul's mother doing?" I asked. She had broken her hip a few weeks before.

"She's in rehab and doing well. Paul and his brother are trying to get her to go to assisted living but she won't even consider it. She insists on returning to her house. We may have to go back up there and live with her."

"Up there" meant Pittsburgh. Patty and Paul had retired a few years earlier and relocated to Virginia from the Steel City, as Pittsburgh was dubbed. I couldn't for the life of me remember what Paul did for a living. I didn't want to let on that I didn't remember, especially after so many months had passed. It never came up anyway.

"Oh, I'm sorry to hear that, just when we were getting to know each other. I guess it's a good thing you didn't find a permanent place."

"Yes. Well, we'll keep in touch," Patty assured me with a smile. "Come and visit. Ever been to Fallingwater? It's not too far from Pittsburgh."

"I haven't." Fallingwater was a Frank Lloyd Wright-designed house, part of which was built over a waterfall. I'd toured a number of the architect's creations and admired them, but I found that he valued design over comfort so I never coveted one of his homes, even if one became available. Someday I hoped to make it to Fallingwater.

"So, what will you do with your furniture? Put it in your storage unit?" I knew they had a storage unit that supplemented their inadequate living space.

"Oh no, all the furniture in the apartment is rented." So these monstrosities were destined for someone else's living space! Despite the ugliness, they appeared to be indestructible, and so would saddle transient families for years to come.

"Well, that saves you from having to move it all back to Pittsburgh." I sipped my tea and broached the subject of Rox. "I hope you don't mind me bringing this up, but I met Nina Brown the other day."

Patty looked surprised. "Nina? How did you meet her?"

"She was at Panera with my friend Trudy. They're neighbors." I omitted any mention of the Joe's Inn breakfast.

"Paul ran into Nina one day in Walgreen's. She told him she went to Florida for a while after Rox Howard's funeral."

"Yes, she said that. She told me and Trudy about Rox, and said she wants to hire a PI to find out who killed her."

"Really? I would have thought the police were handling things."

"She doesn't think they're doing a good job. Or not doing it fast enough. And she thinks they're focused on Brad."

"That's probably true. I just hate it that he's a suspect." Patty shook her head, looking rueful. "I'd love to see Nina again. I liked her. She was so kind to us when Marcie was ill. And then when Rox was killed . . . well, I can't begin to imagine what it's like to lose a sister, especially like that. "

Patty went on. "But we never expected Nina to break up with Brad. We thought they'd get married. Instead, Brad married Rox."

"Really? Brad and Nina were a couple at one time?" I kept to myself the belief that they were probably reunited.

"Oh, yes. In fact I think they were a couple a few times around," Patty chuckled. "Obviously an attraction there."

"What did you think of Rox?" I asked. "Did you like her?"

"We barely knew the woman." I could tell Patty chose her words with care. "We didn't have much interaction with her at the hospital. We usually visited Marcie in the morning when Rox was working."

Obviously Patty's mother had taught her that if she couldn't say something nice about someone don't say anything. Or keep things neutral. Good advice, but not useful in a murder inquiry. I needed people who would dish. Patty seemed restrained about Rox, so I intuited that she hadn't found Rox quite so nice. Nevertheless I pressed on, hoping to get more tidbits that I could decode from the niceness.

"Were Rox and Nina estranged because of their tangled relationship with Brad?"

"Not to my knowledge." Patty got up and started bustling around in the kitchen. "Take a seat, we're just about ready to eat." I sat at a round laminated table and Patty appeared with two plates of broccoli quiche and side salads. We spent a few minutes enjoying the delicious food. Patty was a good cook with a kitchen stocked with everything a cook would need. I thought of her possible move back to Pittsburgh. The rest of the apartment suggested transiency but it would take Patty a while to pack up her kitchen contents.

"So you say Nina wants to hire a PI?" Patty shook her head in wonderment. "Is she going to do it?"

"I don't know. I got the feeling she was just considering it." I said. "Oh, and she's taking a playwriting class."

"Really?" Patty said. "Well, good for her. That should get her mind off her troubles."

"Maybe," I allowed. "By the way, Patty, this quiche is delicious."

She beamed her pleasure before asking, "Hazel, what's new

with your book group? What are you reading now?"

I told Patty about our current "tour" through the ancient world. "Feel free to join us whenever you want. I'll be happy to pick you up."

"Are there any of those, what do you call them—cozies—set in the ancient world?"

"Oh, sure. I can get you some titles." Patty was skittish about reading mysteries, saying she didn't want to read anything violent or gory. I had told her about the "cozy" style, mysteries where the murder takes place "off page," with little or no sex or profanity. "I'll bring them along the next time I see you. Or I can mail them."

"You can bring them. There's no rush."

With most people, I would send the list by e-mail. But Patty and Paul were self-proclaimed technophobes who didn't use cell phones or computers. Patty didn't own a car, but did drive until she started developing signs of traffic phobia and was afraid to get behind a steering wheel. She claimed that she liked being "contained." Considering their close living space, contained must be tantamount to confinement in a straitjacket.

Andy came up next on my mental agenda. "Nina mentioned our mutual cousin, Andy. Said she hadn't seen him in a while. Have you? Has he been around?"

"No, we haven't seen him. Not since Rox's funeral. I don't *think*." Patty seemed to be scanning her memory for an Andy sighting.

"Did he and Rox get along?"

Predictably, she said, "Oh, I think so. I don't recall hearing anything different." Apparently Patty not only spoke no evil, but heard and saw no evil as well.

We chatted for a while longer but I gained no more useful information about Rox, Nina, Andy, or anyone else. It would help if I was more adept at interviewing techniques.

As I was leaving, I turned to Patty. "Do you have any family medical history? I'd like to share it with my sisters. After all, we share a grandfather."

Patty thought. "Well, Brad's mother had Alzheimer's—but she's not your blood relative. My dad had cardiac problems. I'll have to think about it."

"By the way, how's Paul doing—other than the situation with his mother?"

"He's doing fine. Thanks for asking. He's out with the boys."

While Patty and I lunched together most Thursdays, Patty's husband did the same with a group of men—male bonding. I tended to think that entailed talking about cars. I thanked Patty for her tasty lunch and we made plans to get together the following Thursday.

• • •

Vince and I needed a few items for our visit to the Moonshine Inn, so on the way home from Patty's I went on a shopping spree. It only took three thrift stores and a stop at CVS and we were all set for our undercover operation.

Then I drove over to the Moonshine Inn for a preliminary check of the parking lot. I hoped the bar denizens would contribute some juicy tidbits of information. But I had to be prepared for them closing ranks.

The Moonshine Inn operated out of a weatherbeaten, white-shingled, main building with random add-ons, like a child's game of building blocks. A restaurant and another bar shared the parking lot.

I had no trouble locating the chain link fence and dumpster where Nina and Brad had found Rox's body. I got out of the car and examined the ground around the massive waste container. What did I expect to see after three months—blood spatters? The asphalt looked much like any other asphalt: dusty, muddy, oil-stained. Still, I might intuit something useful from visiting the scene of the crime.

But my intuition came up empty.

NINE

ON FRIDAY MORNING cotton-candy clouds paraded across the sky. A day that started out so lovely had to be a good one. The forecast called for eighty degrees with low humidity—a rarity in Virginia after Memorial Day.

I drove two streets over to Eileen's house, a white bungalow style with blue trim. She emerged carrying a tote bag screenprinted with an image of George Eliot.

"Here are the boots." She pulled a pair of tan hand-tooled cowgirl boots from the tote. "I tried to polish them up a bit, so they don't look too bad now."

"Thanks. They look fine. And these pointy toes could double as weapons." I laughed as I tossed the boots behind my seat. "I hope I won't need to resort to such measures."

I drove down Forest Hill Avenue through Westover Hills and crossed the James River via the Robert E. Lee Bridge. To my right, the office buildings of downtown Richmond offered a view of the skyline often seen on postcards. To my left, the Hollywood Cemetery perched on a bluff overlooking the river. Hollywood Cemetery held a place of honor as one of the most historic and beautiful cemeteries in the country. It served as the final resting place for a number of notable Americans, including two presidents and thousands of Confederate generals and soldiers.

I turned onto Franklin Street and passed the historic Jefferson Hotel, the Kent-Valentine House, and the main branch of the Richmond Public Library. After navigating a series of one-way streets I arrived at my destination, a narrow two-story building dwarfed by the taller buildings surrounding it. I drove into a shoebox-sized parking lot, turning my wheel completely several times before I crammed myself into a space. I recognized Nina's Mitsubishi three cars from mine.

I grumbled to Eileen, "If we have to come downtown again, let's take the bus and not have to worry about parking."

When Nina had called confirming the meeting for Friday morning at nine, she had given me the address, along with instructions for parking and getting in the building. So far, nothing daunted me—accessing the building involved pressing a button by the door and waiting for someone to respond. Nina greeted me with a modicum of enthusiasm, more than she had the other two times we'd met. She displayed no enthusiasm for Eileen, just murmuring "Hi, Eileen."

"Eileen's my research assistant," I said brightly.

Nina raised her brows. "Oh. Okay." She tried to smile, but her effort fell short. Trudy had suggested that Nina didn't care for Eileen—apparently she was right.

Nina led us into the office proper. "Dilbert"-style gray partitions divided the office space into sections. Along with the cubicles allotted to the worker bees, a section accommodated a refrigerator, brewing station, microwave, and toaster oven. A conference table and chairs were wedged into another space. The welcoming aroma of freshly brewed coffee filled the air. The closed doors I spotted at the end of a hallway suggested private offices for management.

Nina pulled me aside. "Look, I have to 'fess up about something: Brad saw your name and number on a note by my phone. He blew up, got really mad. He didn't believe me when I said you were coming here to do research for your book. He's sure you're investigating and that you're after money. He said, 'She'll find a way to get money. She won't get any out of me, that's for sure. She tried once before.' I told him that I did ask you to investigate and that you had refused. He still didn't believe me."

I felt furious with Nina for leaving my name and number in plain sight but said calmly, "Well, what's done is done. Continue to claim that I'm not investigating. What's Brad's problem, anyway? He sounds completely irrational. And paranoid."

Nina shrugged as she picked up the coffee carafe.

"And you said Brad was just a friend. So was he visiting as a friend? Or something more?"

"Okay, okay, we're together. Sort of. It's no big deal."

"If you want me to help you, be straight with me."

"It's really none of your business," she hissed before pasting a bright smile on her face. "Who wants coffee?" she asked. I noticed the stack of foam cups beside the coffeemaker. I tried to avoid foam cups and toyed with the idea of fetching my travel mug from the car but decided it was too much trouble.

As she poured coffee into the cups, Nina introduced me and Eileen to the abbreviated office staff. As June was a slow time for the Hamlin Group, it was a popular time for staff to schedule vacations.

"Eileen is my research assistant," I explained. "She's a librarian and one of my biggest fans. I just couldn't manage without her." I knew I was laying it on a bit thick but I felt pretentious about having an assistant.

Sandy Steelman served as the Hamlin Group's office manager. Her thick blonde hair was cut in feathery layers that we called a shag back in the seventies. Farrah Fawcett made the look famous when she starred on *Charlie's Angels*. Sandy's black slacks and blouse worn as jacket minimized her apple shape, the kind health professionals cautioned as posing a risk for any number of health problems. But nothing could minimize her impressive height of at least six feet, maybe more. Her brown eyes sparkled as she took my hand. I noticed the contrast between her nails, polished with a creamsicle orange shade, and my own bare ones. Oh well, later I'd dress them up with the sparkly red paint for my bar adventure.

"Hazel!" Sandy gushed. "I can't *wait* to read your books. I don't read a lot of romances but everyone just *raves* about your stories. You see, I'm in this book club and we read some really long books and I don't have time to read anything else. I'm thinking of taking a break from the group just to get caught up on my TBR list. And when I heard you were coming here I looked at your website and now you're at the top of my list."

"Thanks so much, Sandy." The acronym TBR stood for any number of phrases, and in this context I took it to mean "to be read."

"And I'm Nichole St. Clair. Nichole's with an 'H.'"

"Nichole's our membership specialist," Sandy explained.

Nichole's pale blonde hair, milky white complexion, pale blue eyes, and white top made her virtually disappear into the white wall behind her. I assessed her age as somewhere between twenty-five and thirty-five. The ethereal creatures of the world were blessed with a timeless quality. Her specifying that she spelled her name with an "H" seemed familiar. From her knowing look, I guessed that I seemed familiar to her as well. Perhaps we'd met somewhere along the line.

"My mom's a huge fan of yours as well." Nichole herself was too young to be a fan, but if I lived long enough, she might become one.

"Nina says you're doing research for a book," Sandy said. "Tell us about it. Oh, and help yourself to more coffee any time."

I glanced at Eileen. I already saw that she was going to get short shrift in the attention department, relegated to the echelon for servants. She was usually at the forefront of anything, but she gave me a smile and a shrug that signaled her acceptance of her temporary demotion.

We wedged ourselves into chairs at the conference table. This office space seemed designed for the Munchkins of *The Wizard of Oz*—assuming any of them were office workers. Eileen set up her laptop in preparation for note-taking for my faux book— but, if I heard enough interesting material, it could end up in a future story.

Sandy prompted, "So, Hazel, tell us about your story."

I gave a brief description of my book idea—middle-aged sex in the workplace.

"Sex in the workplace?" Sandy and Nichole both laughed. Nichole covered her mouth with her hand. She could have been ten years old. I always found it interesting that we tittered about sex in junior high and we continued tittering as adults.

Sandy went on. "I don't know what we can tell you about sex in the workplace. There's no sex going on here. Unless . . . there's something I don't know about." She glanced at Nichole, eyes twinkling.

I laughed and explained that I was researching workplaces, and the sex part I could make up. I wasn't looking for testimonials.

When we'd last talked on the phone, Nina said her plan was to leave the office on some pretext, figuring that Sandy and Nichole would speak more freely about Rox with her gone. So I wasn't surprised when she finished her coffee, stood, and announced, "Well, I have some errands to run. I'll be back in a couple of hours or so."

Once Nina left, Sandy said, "That Nina's a nice woman."

Except to Eileen. Nina had ignored Eileen during her hasty goodbyes.

Sandy turned to me and asked, "Did she tell you about her sister Roxanne?"

"Yes, she did. Roxanne was the ED here, is that right? And she was murdered?"

"Yes, she was." Sandy's voice took on a sober tone.

"Really sad," I said. "It must be maddening for Nina that the police never arrested anyone."

Sandy nodded. "She's really torn up about it. It was a terrible business—Rox was stabbed to death in the parking lot of that awful bar."

"Rox could have told you a lot about sex in the workplace," Nichole said.

"Really?" I tried for a wide-eyed look, hoping to encourage a sharing of details.

Nichole waved her hand and amended her statement. "I don't mean here, I mean at that place where she used to work. The Alzheimer's Association."

"No," Sandy corrected. "It was the Alzheimer's Research Society. And you're right, Nichole. She toned down when she came to work here."

Nichole said, "This one woman, Tracy, worked at the ARS and Rox got her so mad she up and quit. Then she, meaning Tracy, came here and told us all sorts of wild tales about Rox, about how mean she was. Other stuff, too. When Tracy heard Rox was coming to work here, she beat it out of here, said she wouldn't work for that woman for a minute."

"Fortunately, we didn't find her that bad," Sandy said. "Not great, mind you. Just not as bad as she'd been before."

"Yeah, she kind of ignored us most of the time, but she didn't yell or anything."

"So where did Tracy go from here?" I asked.

"I forget the name of the place," Nichole said. "But then she died. Car accident."

"Oh, I'm sorry." Eileen murmured her agreement.

"What were some of the wild tales she told about Rox?"

"Oh," Sandy laughed. "Like getting it on with that intern who was about a hundred years younger than she was."

I exclaimed in my best open-mouthed, incredulous manner, "Really!"

Sandy looked uncertain. "You know, we really shouldn't be talking about Rox like this. She's *dead*."

Oh, no. I stifled a groan. Just when I was about to be thankful for their forthrightness, Sandy has to suddenly realize that she was supposed to say only nice things about the dead. I had enough problems with Patty and her refusal to dish dirt.

Nichole rolled her eyes and groaned like a long-suffering teenager. "Oh, Sandy. We've come this far, we may as well finish. Besides, Hazel needs material for her book." She shot me a look that made me think she doubted that I was there for research purposes. But why would she question my intentions? Had I done or said something to give myself away? "Besides," she added, "Rox will still be dead whether or not we talk about her."

My sentiments exactly.

Sandy made a go-on motion with her hand. "Okay, Nichole, you tell Hazel and Eileen about the intern." I silently thanked Sandy for including Eileen.

"Rox and one of her interns had a fling. Lots of closed-door meetings, sometimes after work, sometimes *during* work."

Sandy shook her feathered locks. "No discretion at all. And they fought openly at the office."

"I bet the other folks in the office weren't too happy about that," I said.

"Tracy sure wasn't," Nichole said. "She was very professional."

"Sexual harassment at its finest," Sandy said. "Maybe you remember reading about what Rox did at that movie theater? It was in the papers."

I knew exactly what she was talking about, but made a show of trying to remember and falling short. "I *think* I read about that, but ages ago. When did it happen, anyway?" They didn't have to know that ages was three days. I wanted to encourage any conversation that could offer up unexpected tidbits of information. So I listened, all agog, as Sandy and Nichole took turns relating the theater story that had happened about five or six years before. Eileen took copious notes on her laptop, and Nichole jumped up periodically like a jack in the box to answer the phone.

By the end of the story, I hadn't learned anything that I hadn't already read on my own, but I said, "Fascinating story. I'm already picking up lots of inspiration for my writing. But you said she didn't bother with any of the men here? That's curious."

Nichole smirked. "At least not in the office. As for the association members, I don't know if she had any relationships with them. Harold Hamlin—he's our board president—I can't see him having sex. He'd have to take that stick out of his butt—"

"Nichole!" Sandy admonished, but she laughed as she did so. "Really!"

"But you're laughing, Sandy, so you know just what I mean."

Sandy explained, "Harold's very strait-laced."

"There was the lunatic who came charging in here one day," Nichole said. "I know he didn't work here, but I bet there was something sexual going on there."

I put on my now well-honed expectant look. "What did he do? Or she?"

Nichole refilled our cups and launched into a tale that was indeed new to me.

"This man charged in here one day, demanding to see Rox. The guy was so angry, clenched jaw, the wildest eyes I ever saw. Our then-receptionist, Audrey was her name, asked if Rox was expecting him, and he just took off back to Rox's office. Audrey called after him 'Sir, Sir, you can't go back there.' But he kept on going, yelling out names, oh my, the *names*." She put a hand over her heart. "His language would have curled your *hair*.

"He was like a wild man, acted like a real nutcase. We didn't know if he had a gun, if he'd start mowing us down. Rox slammed her office door and I guess she locked it. She yelled, 'Call the police!' Thankfully Sandy was here. When she showed up, this guy backed down. He continued to yell and swear, and assured us he'd be back, but he lost no time in beating it out of here."

I had no trouble believing that the imposing Sandy could make even a lunatic back down. "So you didn't call the police?" I asked.

"No. No need to." Sandy said.

"How long ago was this?"

"Oh, a year maybe." Sandy added, "We never found out what it was all about. Rox never mentioned it, just acted like it never happened. I'm guessing they were lovers and she had dumped him."

"Or," Nichole continued the speculation with a twinkle in her near colorless eyes, "They had makeup sex."

"Some makeup sex that would have been. Had he been here before?" I asked.

"No. I'm just glad he wasn't some wacko with a gun," Sandy said.

Yes, if you must be a wacko, be the type who supports gun control. Aloud, I asked, adding a cringe for effect, "So . . . do you think that guy did it—*killed* her?"

Sandy threw up her hands. "Well, who knows? The police questioned all of us after Rox's murder and we told them about him, but we didn't know his name or anything—"

"—And we didn't think to see if he had a car," Nichole interrupted. "But who knows where he parked? It's hard to find a space downtown during the day."

I wondered if this incident had made the papers. Probably not, since Rox hadn't pressed charges. There was nothing about it in Vince's folder, but he hadn't started in-depth research on Rox's death, so he may not have everything that had been reported about her. Nina hadn't said anything about this. Either she didn't know about it or didn't think it was relevant. Or maybe . . . she had another reason for holding back.

Nichole seemed impish. "Maybe Evangeline killed her. Let's tell Hazel about her."

Sandy looked dismayed and raised her hand in the stop position. "Nothing about that."

"Sorry," Nichole said, but with little sincerity.

With false cheeriness, Sandy said, "All this gossip isn't helping these ladies learn about an association management firm."

I was all ears. What was that about? Who was Evangeline? I hoped that Sandy would relent and enlighten us, but she became all business and proceeded to brief us on the workings of her firm, complete with history, mission, etc. This was not as riveting as sex in the workplace, but apparently we'd heard all we were going to hear on that subject.

I hoped the vigorous nodding of my head would keep me awake. Eileen continued to key away on her laptop—whether her notes concerned the firm's business model or her shopping list, I wasn't sure.

How much more would we have learned if Evangeline's name hadn't come up and put the kibosh on further conversation? Aside from the nameless lunatic, I'd learned little about Rox, at least nothing new. I'd hoped to hear about her relationship with Brad. I bet Sandy and Nichole even harbored ideas about who might have killed her. Since Rox had worked at Hamlin for five or six years, they must have gleaned something about her life that could be helpful. There was always the ARS—maybe that would bear more fruit. Sarah was good at pumping people for information. She had a persistent quality that could be annoying, but would prove useful in this case.

Even after Sandy ran out of steam, Eileen and I stayed for a while. We slapped labels on brochures and collated mailings for an upcoming retreat. When we finished, we looked for the two women to see if we could help further. Nichole had gone to the bank and post office. Sandy thanked us for our help but declined further services from us. Her manner was cordial but cool. I wondered if she'd keep my books on her TBR list.

• • •

When we got in the car, Eileen and I looked at each other and laughed. "What was that all about?" she asked.

"Beats me. I hope Nina can tell me something about these

murky people." I concentrated on the task of backing out of the parking space without colliding with a person or object.

Eileen said, "I'll do some research and see what I can turn up on Evangeline and anything else about the Hamlin Group, including the lunatic."

Car maneuvers successfully completed, I said, "Thanks, Eileen. You know, I'm thinking that the folks who are on vacation could offer something useful. But I guess we won't get to talk to them."

"Unless it's offsite."

"The way these people zippered their lips about Evangeline means something."

What it meant was the real question.

TEN

"HI NINA, IT'S Hazel. We have to talk. At the Hamlin Group, they told me about this lunatic who stormed the place one day and got booted out by Sandy. And there's someone named Evangeline. Her name stopped all conversation and I learned nothing further. The lunatic and Evangeline certainly sound like, as the police would say, 'persons of interest.' Call me." I left my number.

In less than five minutes, Nina called back. Dispensing with a greeting, she said, "It sounds like you got something useful."

"I did. *Maybe*. What's this about a lunatic?"

After I ran down the story as I'd heard it, Nina said, "I don't know. When did you say this happened?"

"About a year ago."

"Hmm. Well, Rox was living in Westover Hills then. I met some of her neighbors, in fact I think Rox drank with them. I could go over there and ask around. Someone might remember a lunatic. In fact, I would think a lunatic would be hard to forget."

"Speaking of drinking, Vince and I are going to the Moonshine Inn tonight."

"Oh, great, I'm glad you decided to do that. You should be able to pick up some information there."

"Okay, so what's the deal with Evangeline? As soon as her name came up Sandy became all business."

"Yeah, I heard about that. Sorry." Nina sighed. "Evangeline was our accountant. Rox had to fire her. Evangeline had all sorts of health problems that required taking meds. She started falling asleep a lot at her desk. When she was awake, she made a lot of mistakes. Rox warned her a number of times, and then had no choice but to let her go. I think Evangeline threatened her."

"Threatened? How?"

"I'm not sure. It couldn't have been with bodily harm. Probably just idle stuff. The woman weighs about three hundred pounds and she's riddled with arthritis. She can barely move."

"Why didn't you mention her before?"

"I didn't think it was relevant. The whole thing's a touchy subject, as she's now suing the association for wrongful termination. The board is trying to reach a settlement and they want to keep everything hush hush. So the lawyers have cautioned everyone not to mention it. I'm not surprised that Nichole brought it up. She likes to provoke things."

"Yes, I got that from her."

"So, anyway, that's why Sandy stopped talking to you this morning."

"But Nina, Evangeline could be a suspect."

"Yes, she could. But, like I said, she can hardly move. She uses a cane and even then she doesn't get around very well."

Unless she faked it, I thought. Scores of movies and books featured a physically handicapped person who turned out to be anything but. And Evangeline could have hired someone to carry out her revenge against Rox. "Where there's a will there's a way" served as more than an adage; many a person has overcome seemingly intractable obstacles to obtain a desired end. Was Rox's death a desired end for Evangeline? Time would tell.

When Nina asked if I learned anything about Andy or Foster, I said, "Nothing about Andy. As for Foster, I learned pretty much the same stuff I already knew, like the movie incident."

After a pause, Nina said, "I'm just *sure* it's one of those two."

Maybe, I thought. Or maybe Nina's tossing red herrings

around to distract me from her and Brad.

"Nina, Rox had a couple of DUIs. Did she go to AA meetings?"

"Yes."

"Do you know which one?"

"I don't. Is there more than one?"

"Well, yes. They're all over the place."

"Huh. Well, I don't know where."

"Oh, and one more thing, Nina—if you want me to find Rox's killer, you have to be upfront with me. And nothing is irrelevant."

"But Brad—"

"Brad's the number one suspect. If you're involved with him, you have to tell me. It *is* my business."

"We're involved. *Okay*?"

I didn't know if it was okay or not, but there was little I could do about it. I kept my response to a simple "Thanks for telling me."

"Anyway—let me know how things go at the Moonshine. It should be interesting."

I didn't doubt that for a minute.

• • •

When Vince came back from the gym, I described my morning at the Hamlin Group and my conversation with Nina. When I told him about Evangeline he seemed to remember the police questioning an Evangeline.

"It's not a name you hear much."

"Oh, and Vince—" I paused, unsure how to phrase my next bit of news.

He did the cop trick of remaining silent until I had to fill the void. "Brad thinks I'm investigating. And that I'll expect money for it." I described the exchange with Nina as I remembered it.

Vince sighed. "Be careful. He could be a loose cannon. I hope you have your phone with you at all times. Charged. And on."

"Of course I do. It's our *phone*." We'd ditched our landline in 2008 and relied on our cell phones and Skype. "I'd love to question Brad. Wouldn't that be a coup?"

I ignored Vince's warning look and went on. "Maybe I could woo him with flowers, chocolates, or a subscription to Omaha steaks."

"Forget your coups and wooing. Brad's the top suspect. Consider yourself lucky that he wants nothing to do with you. Let's hope he continues to feel that way."

"I'm just thinking out loud," I said to placate my husband.

After lunch I worked on my next baby-boomer adventure. I heard Vince guffawing with Dennis Mulligan, his former partner on the Richmond police force. When he appeared in the hallway outside my den, Vince said, "Evangeline Goudreau was indeed a disgruntled ex-employee of the Hamlin Group and she was questioned. Her mother, Harriett Goudreau, corroborated her daughter's alibi. Dennis knows nothing about a lunatic, but I think we need something more specific than 'lunatic'."

"Well, yes, we do. Any ideas on how we run him down?"

Vince shrugged. "Maybe Rox's boozer neighbors can help with that one."

"Hmm. Hope so. I'll tell Eileen about Evangeline. She's going to research her. Is Goudreau spelled the French way?"

"Uh, yes, it is. One of those 'eau' endings." Vince spelled out the name.

I sent an e-mail to Eileen with Evangeline's name. But I wasn't content to wait for her and so I tried Googling. I could see that this investigation would curtail my writing, and I already had enough challenges resisting the draw of social media and e-mail. It was a good thing I was more or less on a break.

The only results for Evangeline Goudreau showed a LinkedIn entry without benefit of a photo. Her profile indicated current employment as an accountant with the Hamlin Group. Any other mention of the woman appeared on a host of sites offering people searches and background check services—for a fee. Maybe Eileen could do better with library resources. When Eileen eventually got back to me, she had found pretty much the same information I had, but she was at home and could learn more the next day at the library with its better resources.

• • •

After dinner, Vince and I got ready for our field trip to the Moonshine Inn. It took me half an hour to achieve a passable redneck look. When I emerged from the bathroom, Vince and I surveyed each other.

"Wow!" His appreciative look said he liked the redneck me.

"It's just for tonight. This is way too much work."

"It's the top I like. Hair's for the birds. Literally."

Vince referred to my Harley Davidson two-sizes-too-small tank top that revealed an impressive display of cleavage. I had a Victoria's Secret contraption that I employed for the thankfully few occasions when I wanted to play up my assets. The jeans that I'd slashed in strategic places molded my bottom half, and Eileen's boots fit well with the help of thick, albeit unsexy, socks. As for the hair, I may have gone overboard with teasing and spraying my chestnut waves into something like an exploded mushroom—or a birdnest. But, as long as I fit in, that was the main thing: frosted blue eye shadow and plenty of it streaked across my eyelids, and my nails sparkled with scarlet polish.

"You look pretty good yourself!" I countered. Vince's tight jeans and Confederate T-shirt attested to his frequent gym attendance. His scuffed cowboy boots almost matched mine. An old pair of plastic-framed glasses and a baseball cap finished the look.

I hoped we were unrecognizable. If pressed by an observant neighbor, we could say we were invited to a summer Halloween party. We drove down Forest Hill Avenue, and passed the usual shopping centers alternating with residential areas. After turning on to Westover Hills Boulevard we came to the Moonshine Inn.

"Okay, before we go in, let's review some grammar. I checked this website and—"

Vince waved his hand, dismissing my preparation attempts. "It'll all come naturally. Just leave the *g*s off words that end in *ing*."

"Yes, but there's more. Time is *tahm*, fine is *fahn*, and for is *fer*."

"Fahn," Vince said. "The men will all be looking at your lovely assets and won't notice if you talk like a Harvard professor. Let's go in and get this show on the road."

I gave my husband—rather, my *old man* in redneck parlance—a look and got out of the car.

When casing the place the day before, I'd seen few vehicles in the parking lot, but tonight the sizable lot was full. A large white sign warned that parking places were only for customers of the Moonshine Inn, Jeremiah's restaurant, or Buck's Bar.

The Moonshine Inn was hopping when we walked in. The establishment served food as well as drink, and a waitperson with a name tag id-ing her as "Elvira" bustled about with plates laden with hamburgers and something that might have been chicken-fried steak. Elvira wore her straight blonde hair parted in the middle and anchored behind her ears with bobby pins. An inch-wide band of black roots showed at the part. Her half-opened eyes suggested an insomnia battle. Elvira's short, round figure was encased in snug-fitting jeans and her tiny feet shod in sneakers. Her T-shirt invited one and all to "Do It at the Moonshine Inn."

Black-and-white tiles covered the floor, and dark leather booths lined the perimeter of the space. Grime streaked the windows. The ceiling came up short on its allotment of tiles. Apparently the Moonshine Inn had a special dispensation to allow smoking, as a thick fog made the TVs positioned throughout the bar hard to see. I saw a Florida room, all white with ceiling fans and clean windows, attached to the front of the building. A prominent sign proclaimed it a non-smoking section. I looked at it longingly but, as not a soul populated the space, I figured I'd best sit elsewhere so I could get information.

The patrons caught up on the news via ESPN and Fox News amid much yelling and derogatory jokes about Obamacare. For those disinclined to watch the news, one TV offered *T.J. Hooker* reruns. But we weren't there to catch up on the news or '80s-era cop shows.

A pony-tailed man wearing flip-flops stood and stuck his half-smoked cigarette in his mouth as he collected the change that Elvira slapped down on the table.

"See ya later, hon," Elvira called to him in a smoky voice.

"That a promise?" he bantered as he walked towards the door.

I perched on a barstool. A man with a buzz cut, who was the size and general shape of a refrigerator, stood behind the bar holding a cigarette between his thumb and index finger. I guessed he doubled as the establishment's bouncer.

"What kin I git fer y'all?"

I ordered a Budweiser. Vince echoed my choice. I got some appreciative looks, or rather, my bosom did. I'd gotten carried away with slashing my jeans and hoped the snug fit didn't cause further ripping. Tiny shaded lamps on the wood-paneled wall provided little light, and they obscured my age so I could get away with the giggly and ditzy bit I'd decided was my best bet. Vince pulled his cap lower, in case someone recognized him from his days on the police force.

The female clientele had that same blowsy, hard-bitten look I'd seen in photos of Rox. A few had big hair, but I felt a bizarre sense of pride that my own blown-up tresses could win hands down in a big-hair contest. Baseball caps were the number-one fashion accessory for the male contingent with Confederate bandannas running a close second. Beer bellies predominated. Even in our getups, Vince and I looked way too healthy to be in this place.

A woman with platinum blonde hair took the stool next to mine. Her leather mini-skirt rode up her thighs.

The bartender said, "Usual, Susie?"

"Usual, hon." Her voice told a tale of a longstanding tobacco habit.

Susie glanced at me and behind me at Vince. "Ain't seen you two here before."

"We're here visitin' in-laws. Had to get away fer a little bit, ya know how that goes." I giggled and rolled my eyes, happy that I was already getting into the swing of the jargon.

"Yeah, know just whatcha mean." She extended a ringed hand. Her short nails sported dark, chipped polish. "Susie McCool."

Good redneck name, I thought. "Nice to meetcha, Susie," I shook her hand and added a giggle. "Ahm Shelby Austin and this here's my husband, Ricky." As Vince had been so anxious to get out of the car, I hadn't had a chance to brief him on the names I'd chosen for us from an online database devoted to redneck baby names. So I said "Ricky" distinctly enough for him to hear and get the message that he was to use the name as his alias during his time as a customer at the Moonshine.

"*Chahmed,*" Vince assured Susie as he in turn shook her hand. Apparently he chose a strong, silent demeanor to counter my "golly-gee" one. Susie gave him an admiring up-and-down look.

"This here's Duane," Susie pointed to the bartender. We repeated the handshaking using our pseudonyms. Duane placed three Mason jars full of beer on the counter. Foam slopped over on the scarred wooden surface. Susie, Vince, and I claimed our jars.

I started: "My sister-in-law tells me a woman got herself killed here, right out in the *pahkin'* lot. Maylene, that's my sister-in-law, she don't 'member if the woman was here or at that restaurant next door." Out of the corner of my eye I saw Vince, beer in hand, moving toward the pool tables.

The bartender said with a wry tone, "She'd been here. Miss Roxanne."

"Yeah, Roxanne come in here all the tahm," Susie said.

"*All* the tahm," Duane said with a grimace. He wiped down the counter with a sopping wet cloth, splashing a few drops down my cleavage. "Sometahms she'd be gone fer a while and then, like a bad penny, she'd turn up agin."

Susie said, "She'd get herself a DUI and have to go to AA meetins." Duane lit Susie's cigarette. After exhaling an impressive plume of smoke, she went on. "The courts sent her. Didn't do much good, though."

"Like we said, she come in here a lot, usually alone." Duane took a drag on his cigarette. "Even after she got herself hitched, she come here by herself."

I kept my wide-eyed look. "I bet her old man didn't like that."

Susie said, "Don't think so. They had a lot of loud fights on the phone. Usually he'd come pick her up, but sometahms her sister did. Guess she'd come back fer the car next mornin'."

Duane sniggered. "All we heard was 'Brad Jones, don't you tell me what to do. Don't try to run my life. I won't have it. I'll call Nina.' She'd get off the phone and complain to anyone who'd listen, usually me. 'Jerk thinks Ahm the "little woman." Thinks he can boss me around.'"

Duane looked like he had more to add, but only managed, "Dang broad was a pain in the butt."

Susie said, "Well, yes, she was. But she didn't deserve to be murdered." Duane said nothing but his smirk suggested disagreement. Susie tossed a napkin at him. A woman inked up with tattoos draped herself across the bar, an empty Mason jar in her hand. She groaned, "Duane, Duane."

Susie said, "You must think we're turrible. But she wasn't the nicest woman in the world. Drunk or sober."

Duane said, "Come in here all decked out in high-dollar suits and heels. Dunno what she was doin' in this dive." He refilled the groaning customer's jar. She treated us to an *a capella* rendition of *Feelings*.

"Come to think of it, both Brad and the sister, name was Nina—I think it was Nina—they both showed up the night she got killed. The cops questioned everyone here. The folks at Jeremiah's and Buck's got themselves grilled, too."

"Did Roxanne get all flirty with the guys here?"

Susie stubbed out her cigarette in a black plastic ashtray that advertised a football team. Shrugging, she said, "She did, and left with quite a few. Not so much after she got herself hitched to that Brad. Most of the guys here wouldn't have nothin' to do with her. Too much trouble. But when a stranger come by—"

"You guys talkin' 'bout that broad who got herself stabbed to death?" The singer, now finished singing *Feelings*, interrupted. Her hair hung in limp strings to her shoulders—definitely not the "big" style. Her tank top revealed so many tattoos that I couldn't pick out just one.

"Yeah, we are, Tanya honey." Susie rolled her eyes at me, belying her affectionate tone. "Why doncha go on over and play pool with the guys?"

"Tanya honey" wandered away towards the pool tables. "Poor Tanya, she's a bit off, bless her heart," Susie explained with the "bless her heart" euphemism favored by Southerners to suggest that someone was an idiot, but without using such harsh words.

Duane said, "That night Rox got herself killed there was that one dude all innerested in her."

"That's right! That guy in the baseball cap and the glasses. Longish dark hair." Susie placed a finger on her collarbone to measure the hair length. "I only noticed him 'cause Rox did a double-take, then said, 'Thought I knew you.' He tried to flirt with her but she wasn't havin' it, kept rollin' her eyes."

"Yeah, guy had the hots fer her," Duane said. "But she was too busy fightin' with her old man."

"Finally he left and Rox curled her lip." Susie curled her own lip in demonstration. She stuck another cigarette in her mouth and the gentlemanly Duane lit it for her. The smoke was getting to me, but I resisted the urge to make fanning motions with my hand. I sipped my beer. It tasted like urine—rather, how I imagined urine would taste.

Nina had mentioned a guy in the parking lot with a baseball cap—a description that fit any number of males in the bar as well as the general population. I looked out at a sea of baseball caps. She'd also mentioned seeing a glint of metal on the same guy. That could have been from a belt buckle, a gun—or a knife. Likely guns served as a fashion accessory with this crowd.

Duane said, "You ask me, her old man did her in. She pushed the guy too far."

"So you don't think the flirty guy did it?"

"Dunno. Whoever did it deserves a medal."

"Duane! Yer just awful." Susie wadded up another napkin and tossed it at the bartender. I suspected that Duane and Susie's sparring was a regular occurrence, not unlike in a marriage.

"Anyways," Susie went on, "Rox had her usual fight with her old man, in fact worse than usual. She was madder than a wet hen. Then she called her sister and asked her to come pick her up. She said, 'Well, Ahm goin' out to wait fer Nina.' She walked okay, a little off kilter. Last we saw of her." Susie gazed into the distance, perhaps reflecting on the brevity of life.

Amid the growing din I heard the F-word interspersed with the cracking of pool balls. A commotion behind us made us turn around to see a man with one shoe off, hopping around on his other foot. In between screaming expletives, he informed one and all that he'd spilled his drink in his shoe.

"Hey, Dawn," Susie bellowed in my ear. Dawn appeared, cascades of red frizz framing her round face. Her T-shirt offered a long message that started with "The problem with men . . ."

"Tell this nice lady—" Susie waved her cigarette at me. "What's yer name agin?"

"Me? Oh, Ahm Shelby." I added that inane giggle.

"Shelby here was askin' 'bout that woman who got herself killed here in the pahkin' lot? You know, Roxanne somethin'? You was here that night. 'Member that guy here at the bar who was tryin' to get all friendly with her?"

"Yeah, he tried to get friendly with me, too. But Wade was givin' me looks, so I brushed the guy off. Wade's my old man," she explained to me. Maybe Wade had inspired the T-shirt.

"Was this guy a regular?" I asked.

"No, but he come in another tahm, 'bout a week later. He asked 'bout Rox and I told him what happened. Haven't seen him since. You might—Rodney!"

Rodney was a cheerful man with a fire-plug physique and beetle brows. His lack of a baseball cap made him stand out. Susie and Dawn squealed with delight.

Susie swept her hand out, narrowly missing singeing my arm hair with her cigarette. "Rodney, this here's our new friend, Shelby." Her speech was slurring. "We was just tellin' her 'bout Miss Roxanne."

"Oh, ho! Miss Roxanne. May she rest in peace." He held his hand over his heart like he intended to recite the Pledge of Allegiance. That caused more giggling and yelps from the two women. "Miss Roxanne was a rose among many thorns," he intoned like a preacher.

"She sher thought so." Duane looked sour as he handed Rodney a long-necked bottle and Rodney slapped some bills on the counter.

"Gotta git back to the game, little ladies." In a flash I was alone as Susie and Dawn left to cheer on the guys at the pool table. I turned back to my odious beer and looked around. Soon three men surrounded me, all seemingly impressed with my enhanced bosom. I kept up my ditzy act.

I spotted Vince by the pool table in conversation with a lanky man with hair falling to the middle of his back and, of course, a baseball cap. Tanya, the *Feelings* singer, lingered nearby.

We stayed for another hour. In the meantime, more beers appeared before me as I laughed and flirted with a bevy of admirers. When I left with Vince, they told me to ditch my old man and get myself back real soon.

Laughing, I assured them that I'd be back—real soon.

• • •

At home, I pulled off my boots and socks. "Pew! I smell like I've smoked two packs of cigarettes."

"Yes, we're pretty aromatic."

I told Vince about my barside conversations. "Did you find

out anything interesting? What about that skinny guy with the long hair?"

"Yes, Wade."

"Wade. That must be the guy with problems." I explained about the T-shirt Dawn wore. "So go on."

"I heard much the same as you did, but a little more. The guy said, 'Tanya here says they're yakkin' over there 'bout that woman who got herself killed.'"

When Vince started to explain who Tanya was, I stopped him. "I know Tanya." I described her brief appearance at the bar. "By the way, you do redneck well."

Vince rolled his eyes and went on with his story. "So I asked, 'What woman?' and Wade says, 'Roxanne. The one who got herself stabbed out in the pahkin' lot.' Then I had to listen to Wade and Tanya sing *Roxanne.*"

I smiled as I imagined the duet's rendition of the song originally performed by The Police. "Yes, Tanya likes to sing. She did *Feelings* for us."

"Thankfully, they only knew a few lines. When they finished, I said, 'Didn't that happen a few months ago?' When Wade nodded, I asked him if he was in the bar at the time."

"'Sher was. Someone always tryin' to take that one home. Not my type. Too loud. I like my women quiet. Roxanne was one of them nasty drunks. Woman could start an argument in an empty house. And sometahms she and some poor sod would leave together. One guy, I heard she blackmailed him, threatened to tell his old lady on him. Some of these women are downright violent. We all 'member that Bobbitt dame'.'"

I recalled Lorena Bobbitt, a Virginia woman who gained notoriety years earlier after separating her husband from his penis. "Ah ha! Motive. Did he mention the guy's name?"

"No, and I couldn't grill him without blowing my cover."

That bar was an easy place to be anonymous or to use an alias. It was easy enough for me. The *Cheers* lyrics sprang to mind: *Sometimes you want to go where everybody knows your name.* Sometimes, maybe. But not always.

"Maybe she blackmailed other guys as well," I said.

Vince shrugged. "Anyway, he said everyone noticed the guy those women told you about. Noticed because most of the regulars avoided Rox. They didn't want their old ladies mowing them down with guns or cutting off vital parts. The fact that this guy was chatting her up indicated that he was new and didn't know her. They were placing bets on how soon they'd wind up leaving together.

"And, like you heard, apparently the same guy came back another time and Wade's wife told him about the stabbing. And he never showed up again."

"So, how are we going to find this guy who was flirting with Rox?"

Vince laughed. "Not an easy task."

"Especially with that generic description: dark hair and baseball cap. I never saw so many baseball caps in one place. Of course, someone up to no good would try to fit in as well as possible. Still and all, I maintain that Brad and Nina did it. Susie said that Rox was mad as a wet hen after talking to Brad."

Vince smirked. "I doubt that her being mad as a wet hen gives us the proof we need."

"Yeah, yeah, yeah." I put my hand out, palm forward, to stem his words. My sparkling nails caught the light like a Christmas tree. "Stupid proof."

We sat in silence for a few moments. "Well, after tonight I've come up with ideas for an upcoming book. In fact, Lucy gave me an idea the other night—redneck baby boomers having torrid sex."

"Need a research assistant?" The invitation in Vince's blue eyes was unmistakable. "*Shelby.*"

"Sure thing, *Ricky*. Research is the best part of writing. For starters, want to join me in a shower?"

We stood and I took his hand. We walked upstairs.

ELEVEN

NICHOLE ST. CLAIR'S e-mail asking me to call her didn't surprise me. I figured—hoped would be a more accurate way to put it—that she wanted to continue the aborted conversation of the day before at the Hamlin Group, away from the cautious Sandy.

"Hi Nichole, it's Hazel. How are you?"

"I'm fine. Do you remember me from the RWRC place? I temped there for a while and I remember you volunteering. I looked a little different back then. And my name was Nichole Irving."

"Oh, yes, now I remember. You did seem familiar." Nichole was right about looking different back in the days when she'd worked for the Richmond Women's Resource Center. I tried to reconcile her Goth persona—black hair, black clothes, miles of black makeup—with this present-day ethereal creature, a study in pale tones.

"Back then, everyone was all aflutter about your solving a murder. When I saw you yesterday I figured you were investigating Rox's death. Maybe Nina asked you to do it. The sex in the workplace bit was kind of lame. I mean really, our place?"

"Well—"

"It's okay, I won't tell your secret. Look, I'm sorry about yesterday. I should have known better than to bring up Evangeline's name. She's suing the Hamlin Group for wrongful termination. Rox fired her because she was falling asleep at work and messing up the accounts."

That squared with what I'd learned from Nina. "That sounds like a good reason—"

"She had a note from her doctor. She has arthritis really bad and has to take a lot of meds. They make her sleepy. The rest of us would nudge her awake but we couldn't be at her desk constantly."

According to advertisements for arthritis medication, drowsiness was only one of a host of unwelcome side effects. And Evangeline's obesity had to contribute to her health problems.

"Anyway, the Hamlin Group doesn't like to talk about it because of the lawsuit. Sandy was really mad at me yesterday for even saying Evangeline's name. After you guys left she reamed me a new one."

Nichole took a breath before rushing on. "There was a huge scene the day Rox fired her. You could hear them all over the office, with Evangeline yelling about something she had on Rox and she'd let the Board know about it. And Rox said she had her own information on Evangeline that she was all too willing to share. Look, Evangeline is disabled and probably can't get another job. Plus she's in her *sixties*. She can't collect unemployment because Hamlin fired her. She lives with her mother, who's about ninety and really mean."

I ignored the sixties remark. "Tell me more about the scene. And did you ever find out what Evangeline had on Rox?"

"I did, but—why don't I let Evangeline tell you about it? They don't know this at work, but Evangeline and I go out for pizza every Monday. I bring her books and stuff. Gets her away from her mother. She'll tell you all about the lawsuit and working for Rox. She and Rox used to go out drinking sometimes, so she has lots of stuff to tell."

That sounded promising. Stories over drinks could be gold.

"Evangeline isn't the least bit shy about talking about any of this. She'd love a new audience. You'll find that it's not what you think at all."

Did she know what I was thinking? She was one up on me, because I didn't know what I was thinking. "But why would she talk to me? She doesn't know me."

"I've seen your books in her house. So she must like you. Everyone likes you."

Doubtful. I had my fans, but more than a few looked down their noses at what they deemed my drivel with no redeeming social value. Thankfully, scores of folks were fine with non-redemptive drivel.

"Hasn't she been cautioned by her lawyer to keep her mouth shut?" I didn't want to show up for a meeting with the woman, only to have her zip up her lips.

Nichole laughed. "If she has, she's ignoring the cautions."

Evangeline could be a person I needed to talk to. She might not be doing herself any favors with her reckless, no-holds-barred attitude but she could certainly put some momentum in this investigation.

"I mean, I know she seems like a suspect, but she couldn't possibly have killed Rox. She can't *move*."

As I had with Nina, I kept my skeptical thoughts about Evangeline's physical challenges to myself. I said, "You said Rox had something on Evangeline. Did you find out what that was?"

"No. I tried to ask Evangeline about that in a roundabout way, but she claimed Rox was just bluffing. Oh, well . . . I know: Come to Italian Delight on Monday about six. Act like you just happened to be there and sit with us. Please say yes. It would be a treat for Evangeline to meet you."

"Can I bring someone with me?"

"Of course. Who? Eileen?"

"Maybe, I'm not sure." I had Trudy in mind, because so far she hadn't played an active role in the investigation.

"Just don't let anyone in the Hamlin Group know about this. I need to keep this job. Getting older, you know."

I rolled my eyes at that one. The woman must be all of thirty, thirty-five, tops.

Nichole went on. "Plus, my mom lost her job last year and hasn't found a new one. So my salary helps a lot. But I just feel so *bad* for Evangeline."

Before I pressed the red button to end the call, Nichole said,

"Did you know that the RWRC folded a few months ago?"

"Yes, I did. I was still volunteering there. So sad." We spent a few minutes discussing the RWRC's rise and decline.

I told Nichole I'd see her on Monday at the appointed time and place. Then I called Trudy and told her about my visit to the Hamlin Group and to the Moonshine Inn. When I invited her to Italian Delight for pizza and a chance to interview an emerging top suspect, she readily agreed. I said I'd pick her up about five forty-five.

I sent an electronic version of the report I'd given Trudy to the rest of the group, including the upcoming visit to Italian Delight. Their consensus had it that "we have a lunatic and we have a flirty guy in a bar—two persons of interest. But how do we find them?"

How indeed?

• • •

Vince decided the weather was cool enough for yard work, so he ventured outside. After making sure he donned a hat to protect himself from the sun's rays, I continued working on my new novel.

Just as I was wondering when Nina would call with a report on her visit with Rox's former neighbors, I saw that she'd left a voice mail. When I called her back, Nina launched into an account of a friendship that had gone off the rails.

"At one time Rox and her next door neighbor, Teresa, drank together. Then, according to Teresa, Rox got all high and mighty when she started going to AA, so Teresa sought out new drinking buddies. She remembers a guy Rox was seeing for a while last year. He wasn't around for long, a few weeks, a month maybe. Teresa never met him and didn't even know his name because, like I said, she and Rox were on the outs. But she thought they might have met in AA. Apparently the guy had a red Harley." I thought about how much Vince had admired my snug Harley Davidson tank top the night before.

Nina continued. "According to Teresa, Rox and the Harley rider had some loud fights, real doozies. One night Teresa heard some commotion outside, breaking glass. She thought they might be re-enacting that scene from *Body Heat*. You know the one, where William Hurt and what's-her-name—"

"Kathleen Turner," I offered. I'd seen *Body Heat* a number of times and enjoyed the remake of my favorite film noir, *Double Indemnity*. Who could forget that scene with William Hurt smashing the glass door of Kathleen Turner's house while Ms. Turner stood in the hall inside, sizzling with seductiveness? They satisfied their lust right there in the hall. Now that kind of scene goes well for my type of books or for a *Body Heat*-type of movie. In real life I'd be worrying about slivers of glass getting embedded in private parts. I winced.

"Right, Kathleen Turner," Nina said. "Anyway, Teresa says it wasn't long before the Harley roared off so she figured it was a quick sex scene. But a few minutes later the police arrived, and when Teresa went outside to see what was going on, she saw that Rox's windshield was smashed. So that accounts for the breaking glass." The romance writer in me would have preferred if the glass breaking heralded a re-take of one of the cinema's steamiest sex scenes. "Another neighbor told Teresa that Rox claimed she didn't know who did it. Put it down to random vandalism."

Likely story, I thought. Did she feign ignorance to avoid pressing charges? I marveled at the number of assaults and property damage Rox and Nina and even Foster endured without pressing charges.

"What time of night was this? Or was it daytime?" Not that it mattered, but I asked anyway.

"Don't know for sure. It was dark, anyway. Teresa said it was around the time of the summer solstice because she'd been to a solstice party the night before. So I guess about this time last year. And would have been later than nine or nine-thirty if it was already dark."

About the same time the lunatic threw his tantrum at the Hamlin Group. So it had to be the same guy. Not that lunatics were in short supply.

"Did Teresa say what the guy looked like?"

"No, she only saw him from a distance. Well, she did say he was bald. Anyway, the next morning she saw a windshield repair van in front of Rox's house."

"Did the lunatic show up again?"

"No. Teresa was definite about that." Likely Teresa coveted

some excitement in the 'hood and kept her eyes peeled.

"And Rox married Brad when? In December?"

"Yes, December," Nina said, and switched subjects: "So did you make it to the bar?"

"We did." I told Nina about my various conversations, including the one involving the man who'd seemed interested in Rox. "He made me think of the guy you told me about, the one in the parking lot. I'm not sure why, because baseball caps and longish hair aren't exactly distinguishing features. It's not like he was hanging around bankers."

"Damn, I wished I paid more attention to him at the time," Nina said in a regretful tone. "By the way, what's going on with the ARS? Did Sarah find out anything?"

I told her about Sarah's plans to approach the former executive director when she returned from vacation.

"Maisie?"

"Yes, Maisie Atwater."

"She's funny. You'll enjoy her. And she's been there for a long time so you should be able to find out something useful."

I didn't share my upcoming pizza get-together with Evangeline on Monday. Since the lawsuit was supposed to be so hush-hush I figured it best to keep the meeting under wraps.

TWELVE

ON SUNDAY, VINCE and I lingered over coffee after a late breakfast. Vince did most of the cooking but on Sundays I fixed omelets with whatever was on hand.

"So now there's this Harley-riding lunatic to hunt down, in addition to the guy from the bar." I sighed. "It would sure make it easier if they were the same guy."

Vince snickered. "Don't expect efficiency in a criminal investigation. You know, it's interesting that this Teresa's memory is so clear when she's a drunk."

"She may not always be drunk. Oh! I don't know why I didn't think of this before—Kat's in AA and may have known Rox. Maybe even the lunatic . . . Teresa thought maybe Rox met him in AA."

"It's worth a shot. Give Kat a call."

"I haven't seen her at the gym lately. She's usually there on Saturdays, but I didn't see her yesterday. Maybe she's on vacation." Kat worked as a personal trainer at the gym where Vince and I worked out. She specialized in post-menopausal women. Yesterday was the first time this post-menopausal woman had been there in a week and I was starting to feel sluggish—a clear signal that a trip to the gym was in order. I hoped I wouldn't have to make a return visit to the Moonshine Inn, but if I did I'd have to squeeze myself into tight garments again. Not the time for a weight gain.

While Vince cleaned up, I went to my den and called Kat.

I'd known Kat Berenger for many years. She was Carlene Arness's step-sister, and she'd been at the Murder on Tour book group on the night Carlene died eight years earlier. After that night, she'd never returned to the book group or to the intermittent film group, but I still saw her at the gym and we often had coffee next door at Starbucks.

Kat had accumulated many years of sobriety in AA. I knew there were a number of meetings in the Richmond area but I imagined that the recovering community was small enough that Kat might have run across Rox and the lunatic. I hoped to get a name for the lunatic as I hated labeling people, no matter how deserving.

The disease of alcoholism figured prominently in Lucy's and my families. Some members made it into recovery and others weren't as lucky. Fortunately, Lucy and I had escaped the clutches of the insidious disease. I simply had no taste for anything alcoholic.

When Kat answered my phone call, I heard ambient noise in the background. "Where are you?" I asked.

"Macy's at the Chesterfield Towne Center. How are you?"

"Pretty good. Look, do you have time for coffee sometime today?"

"Absolutely."

"I need to pick your brain about some AA people." I grimaced at the unsavory visualization my unfortunate turn of phrase conjured up.

"AA people? You know we're anonymous."

"Yes, I know. But this is important. I'll explain when I see you."

"Okay, how about the Barnes and Noble café in half an hour?"

I looked at the clock. Eleven-thirty. And still in my jammies. "How about an hour? Twelve thirty?"

"No problem. I can always find more stuff to buy. See you then."

• • •

I found Kat sitting at a round table by the window in the Barnes and Noble café, waving gaily at me. Surely she was visible from space with her electric blue top and skintight pants, the color of the carnation pink Crayola crayon. Her signature leopard print was evident in her flats and oversized satchel bag. She'd piled her mass of blonde curls on top of her head. I felt downright dowdy in my black top and denim capris.

After a quick hug, Kat tossed her Macy's bag on the table to save our place and we approached the counter. I limited my order to coffee in my usual ceramic mug and refrained from indulging in one of the tempting pastries. Kat opted for iced green tea and also eschewed the food selection. We weren't big money makers for the mega chain but surely the price of our drinks compensated a little.

Once seated, I said, "I haven't seen you at the gym lately. Of course, I haven't been there much myself."

"I'm just back from vacation. Myrtle Beach." She stroked a tan arm. "Like it?"

I thought her skin was taking on that look of an old leather handbag. I murmured a "Very nice," but added, "You need to be careful in the sun, Kat."

"Yeah, yeah, yeah, I know." Kat waved her hand, nails painted a blue shade that matched her top. "So, what's this about picking my brain?"

When I told Kat about Nina and her pleas that I find her sister's killer, she said, "Roxanne Howard, huh? So you're investigating her murder?"

"Sort of. I told Nina I'd ask around. Actually, I have the whole book group involved." I summarized what I knew of Rox's murder, the family connections, and what I'd learned so far in the early days of our inquiries. Kat howled with laughter when I told her about our visit to the Moonshine Inn. Heads turned. Between her flamboyant appearance and often boisterous manner, Kat attracted attention wherever she went. "And so here I am, asking *you* for information."

Kat thought a minute and then answered. "Rox came to meetings for a while, went out, came back again, went out. I'm not sure how many times she repeated the cycle. And if she was at the Moonshine Inn the night she was murdered, I guess she was drinking again and would eventually have been back at meetings."

"I understand she got two DUIs."

"Probably. At least two." Kat leaned closer to me and muttered, "The guy next to us keeps turning around and scowling at us."

I tried to appear nonchalant as I turned my head to see a man decked out in a suit and tie, engrossed in something on his tablet screen. I turned back to Kat and shrugged.

"Well, he *was* scowling before," Kat said. "Getting back to the matter at hand, I do remember one night after an AA meeting, Rox had a big row with some guy, not someone from the meeting. He was screaming and yelling, using the F-word, the C-word, he went through the alphabet. The F-word was his personal favorite."

"When was this?"

"Oh, I don't know. Last year sometime. It was hot. Maybe about this time of year."

"Then what happened?"

"Just more yelling, cursing, and the like. Then the guy roared off on a red Harley."

A frisson of excitement ran through me. This had to be the lunatic! "And you hadn't seen this guy before?" I asked.

"No. Neither had anyone else. My guess is that he was a spurned lover or something and tracked her down at the meeting."

"I wonder what she did to incite such rage. How was she reacting?"

"She was screaming right back at him. But I had the idea that she didn't know him. No, not exactly that."

"You think maybe she was pretending to not know him?" Somewhere in my brain I realized I'd split an infinitive. Oh well.

"That's it. She was playing a part. A game."

"Hmm. Weird. Have you seen him since?"

Kat shook her curls. "But I bet he's a drunk. A dry one, anyway."

Out of the corner of my eye, I noticed the suited man at the next table turning and looking at us. Was he fascinated by our conversation? Or annoyed by it? The tables were full of chattering people, so why single us out for his annoyance? I decided to ignore him and asked Kat, "What's a dry drunk?"

"That's someone who no longer drinks but behaves like he, or she, still does. May still be seething with anger and resentment and vent in an out-of-control way."

"Much like this guy was doing?"

"Much like he was."

Kat looked daggers at the man next to us. "Got a problem, buddy?" He turned around and didn't turn back. After a few minutes he finished his coffee, grabbed his tablet, and left. "Must be one of those dry drunks," Kat noted in a wry tone.

"So," I continued. "I'm wondering if the lunatic I told you about before, the one at the Hamlin Group, is the same one you just described. And the same one who smashed her windshield."

"Could be." Kat grinned. "But lunatics are probably much the same. And Rox may have been drawn to that type." Was Brad that type? It wouldn't surprise me if he was.

Kat asked, "So, are you thinking that one of these crazies killed Rox?"

"Do you see it?"

"From what I saw that night after the meeting, I'd say it's a possibility. Rox was probably a provocative type and the guy was provoked, no doubt about that."

"Did you ever talk to her? What was your impression of her?"

"I never spoke with her. She wasn't serious about getting sober, she just did what she had to do to satisfy the court. She hung with the guys at the meetings. They sure enjoyed her, especially the rougher types. She was loud and bawdy." I knew Kat could be loud and bawdy and tried to imagine her back in her drinking days. I felt sure she'd entertained those "rougher types," too.

"Do you think—"

"Do I think one of the AA guys killed her? Who knows?"

I decided to deal with the slew of suspects I already had before adding more to the roster; Brad, Nina, Andy, Foster, the lunatic, and Evangeline were more than enough.

"What did this guy—the lunatic—look like?"

"Oh," Kat reapplied her lipstick, a sizzling shade of pink.

"Bald. And a bushy mustache." She pressed her lips together and put the tube back in her satchel and touched her left ear. "Earring. Grizzle on his face."

I now realized that I never got a description of the lunatic at the Hamlin Group on Friday. I'd ask Nichole when I saw her. Or I could text her. I hadn't reached the point on my path to technological sophistication where I automatically thought to text.

We spent the rest of our visit catching up on each other's lives. "What are you working on now?" Kat asked.

"I sent off my manuscript last week and I'm waiting for my editor to get back to me." I summarized that plot, and the new one I'd started about women who get sun, fun, and romance while cruising the Greek Islands.

"Didn't you guys go to Greece a few years ago?"

"Yes, I'm modeling it after that cruise."

Kat's blue eyes sparkled. "I can help you with your research." She proceeded to rave about the sexual prowess of her latest lover, a singer named Demetrios. "He's straight from the Greek mainland."

"He sounds fabulous, Kat. I'll keep you two in mind."

• • •

When I left Kat, I sent a text to Nichole, asking her to describe the lunatic. Within sixty seconds, she responded: bald head, bushy mustache, and grizzly short beard. She didn't mention an earring but I felt confident she and Kat had witnessed the same lunatic in action. Once again I updated the group on my findings.

I devoted Monday to my writing, adding a sensual Greek lover named Demetrios to the cast of characters. Lucy sent me a text asking if Vince and I wanted to join her at O'Tooles's that evening. Lucy's musician husband Dave often performed at the Irish pub. I checked with Vince and texted Lucy back that we'd love to be there, but it might be eight-thirty or so, after our meeting with Evangeline. I added that Trudy might join us. Lucy responded with a smiley face emoticon.

At four o'clock I got a call that I needed to return for a follow-up mammogram due to a shifting pattern in my breast calcifications. Stunned, I made the appointment. I was plunged into a pit of anxiety, and the Greek Island adventures flew from my mind.

Several years earlier I'd been advised to have a breast biopsy, also due to calcification changes. At the time I'd done extensive research and learned about the two types of calcifications: the macro type that resembled large white dots and were considered noncancerous; and micro calcifications that appeared as white specks on the mammogram. They were usually noncancerous, too, but the aforementioned pattern shift could, just *may*, indicate precancerous cells or early breast cancer.

I had the micro kind.

Everything had been fine back then and I advised myself to be optimistic, as did Vince when I shared the unsettling news with him.

"Everything will be fine," he assured me as he held me close and stroked my hair.

THIRTEEN

A LITTLE LATER, I drove over to Trudy's house to pick her up for our "surprise" meeting with Evangeline and Nichole.

Trudy opened the door. "Be with you in a sec."

I wandered into the den. Trudy was a casual housekeeper. I'd grown up in a chaotic, disorganized home so Trudy's place didn't bother me, but the rest of the book group had had to adjust to the piles of papers, magazines, and mail. Plus, cat hair everywhere from her shedding pet, Sammy.

I petted the purring Sammy while I waited for Trudy. When she appeared, looking cool in a pink linen shirt, she gathered her purse and we were off for our rendezvous at Italian Delight.

Italian Delight on Jahnke Road served good food at moderate prices. It was wedged in an unpretentious neighborhood strip mall that catered to a diverse clientele.

When we walked in, an older couple looked up from their salads and smiled at us. I spied Nichole and an enormous woman in a booth in an adjacent room. When Nichole saw us, she feigned surprise. "Hazel Rose, is that *you*?"

"Nichole!" I exclaimed. "How nice to see you."

"This is Evangeline Goudreau. Evangeline, meet Hazel Rose." She looked at Trudy. "And you are . . . ?"

"Trudy Zimmerman," I completed the introductions.

Evangeline wore a floral-patterned housedress with snaps instead of buttons down the front.

I guessed she had once been pretty before weight and arthritis took a toll on her health. She wore her blonde hair short. Her eyes looked like she'd wrung the blue color out of them. Nichole's eyes were also a pale blue, and it felt eerie having two sets of arresting eyes fixed on me.

After a round of hand shaking, Evangeline asked, "Are you Hazel Rose, the *romance* writer?"

"Yes, I've written a few romances." I tried for a modest tone. After all, I didn't count myself in the same league as Danielle Steele or Nora Roberts.

"Oh, I just *love* your books, Hazel. They're so, well, *romantic*." She held a swollen-looking hand over her heart and I half expected her to swoon.

"Sit with us," Nichole invited.

"Yes, please do," Evangeline seconded the motion. "We'll scooch over." Evangeline's scooching left scant room for Trudy, leaving half of her hanging over the edge of the booth. I'd picked the better seating, next to the slim Nichole. The wait person appeared, informed us that her name was Avila, and took our drink orders.

"Want to share a couple of pizzas with us?" Evangeline asked.

"Sure." Trudy nodded her agreement.

We gave our orders to Avila when she delivered our drinks. We had the whole room to ourselves. I traced a low hum of voices to a CNN broadcast on a TV mounted on the wall in one corner.

"So, how do you two know each other?" Evangeline looked first at me and then at Trudy.

"We're in the same book group," I said.

"Romances?"

"No, mysteries."

"That's surprising, Hazel, since you write romances."

"I like to read both. And I'm thinking of starting a romantic suspense series." I'd toyed with the idea for a while but up 'til now had never voiced it.

"Cool." Evangeline regarded me with admiration.

Nichole began, "Evangeline, Hazel was at the Hamlin Group the other day." Evangeline's lip curled at the mere mention of the place. "She's researching sex in the workplace for her next book."

A smile of delight replaced the lip curl. "Sex in the workplace? In *that* workplace?"

"Well, I do write fiction—"

Evangeline chortled. "It would have to be fiction if you're using the Hamlin Group as a setting. Now if I were you I'd go to the Alzheimer's Research Society where our dearly departed VP used to work—and *play*. God rest her soul." Again, the pudgy hand crossed her heart, likely in a mock tribute to the memory of her former boss.

"She's talking about Rox Howard," Nichole explained. "We mentioned her the other day."

"But there was some excitement the day that guy showed up, screaming and yelling like he'd just lost his nuts. Remember that, Nichole?"

"Oh, yes. We told Hazel about that."

"Guy sure had his shorts in a bunch." Evangeline and Nichole giggled at the memory.

"We figured they'd had a lover's tiff. The makeup sex must have been something." Evangeline waved her hand in a parody of fanning out a blaze.

As if on cue, Trudy's phone burst into a rendition of *Whiter Shade of Pale* and Nichole's into something I didn't recognize.

"Crap! it's my ex," Nichole cried. "Excuse me, Hazel." I stood to let her out of the booth. She stomped into the next room and outside to take her call.

"I have to take this," Trudy said. "Should just be a minute or so." Trudy retreated to a booth by the window where she could still see me and fulfill her bodyguard duties.

So it was me and Evangeline. Unless the woman managed to poison my drink, I didn't have much to fear.

"You started to say something about the Alzheimer's place?" I made a "please begin" gesture with my hand.

"Oh, yes." Evangeline told the now familiar story about Rox Howard at her former job, a woman who belittled and marginalized her employees. But her real legacy was in her ultra-dramatic relationship with Foster Hayden. Evangeline ran down the movie theater incident as well.

"How did you get along with Rox?" I asked.

"Fine for a while. She surprised me by asking me to join her for drinks a couple of times. It was flattering at first, because I don't think she asked anyone else. The woman liked to drink but I wasn't used to it. I thought she had an agenda, was trying to pump me for information about myself and the other employees. I didn't tell her anything. Truth is, there wasn't much to tell. I lead a boring but exasperating existence with my mother." Evangeline started tearing her napkin into strips.

Trudy remained in her booth, a serious look on her face as she listened to her caller. I saw Nichole outside, walking by the window. Even though blinds and a potted plant partially obscured my view, I could still make out her teal shorts and milky white legs. Were the two deliberately staying away to enable me to "bond" with Evangeline? Likely Trudy preferred to stay where she was and not have to settle for a sliver of space next to the corpulent Evangeline.

"So, I take it you're not still at the Hamlin Group," I said to get Evangeline talking about her termination.

"Oh, lordy, no. Did they tell you about my last day there?"

"Uh, no. They didn't."

"Probably the lawsuit's got their lips zipped up. The lawyers don't want any of us to talk about it." Evangeline waved a hand, dismissing the cautious lawyers. She was clearly eager to tell all and no one would cow her into submission.

"You see, Hazel, Rox fired me for falling asleep on the job. I'd just had some minor surgery and was on pain meds. She had warned me about it, saying she didn't know how much longer she could pay me. I had a note from my doctor so I wasn't too worried. But one day she called me into her office. Harold Hamlin was there, he's the chairman and CEO of the Hamlin Group. Guy's a weasel. Anyway, she *fired* me. I was devastated and, well, I threatened her. I said I had some items that I doubted she'd want going public. 'Remember the day I helped you clean out your friend Marcie's place?' and as soon as I mentioned Marcie's name, Rox went white, the blood just drained from her face. And the weasel's lips puckered up like the place smelled like that smelly cheese."

"Limburger?"

"That's it, Limburger. So then he went to the door and told Sandy to call security. I said, 'Don't bother, Harold honey, I'm going.' Harold and Sandy hovered over me while I collected my things. And Harold hauled boxes out to my car.

"What did they think I was going to do, anyway? I did have my cane and I guess I could've started whacking everyone in sight. In fact, that's what Mother did later, but I'm getting ahead of myself." Evangeline's tone turned mischievous. "I have to admit that the whole time we were clearing out I never stopped yelling about the pictures I was going to send to John-Boy and to Rox's husband, showing them what Rox was *really* like. Needless to say, I got hustled right out of there."

With the cane and arthritis, it must have been a slow hustle.

Evangeline carried on, her tone arch. "Later, at home, Brad Jones—do you know who he is?"

"Sounds familiar." I tried for my best figuring out look. "They might have mentioned him the other day."

"He was Rox's husband. They just got married last Christmas. At the time I got fired they were engaged. Anyway, he showed up at my house that night, threatening me if I showed anything about Rox to the Board, or to anyone else for that matter. 'You'll deeply regret it, you fat cow,' he yelled as he shook a finger very close to my face."

I had such classy relatives. I considered deleting Brad from the family tree.

"Mother came to my rescue. She swung her cane at him, smacking him right across the back. I thought he was going to pop a blood vessel, he was so mad. She swung again, but he caught the cane before it hit him again.

"'Get out of here, Sonny. How dare you come here and threaten my daughter.'" Evangeline gave a fair imitation of the creaky, raspy voice so common in the elderly.

"'I'll have you arrested for assault, you nasty old woman.'

"'And I'll sue you for trespassing and harassment. See you in court, sonny. Now get out of here before I crack this over your head.' She had the cane poised to do just that.

"And he left. He never filed charges. I guess he didn't want to admit he'd been bested by a ninety-one-year-old woman." I joined Evangeline in a titter over that one.

"So your mother was your hero."

Evangeline's face darkened. "Yes, briefly. No sooner was Brad gone than she was all over me. I hadn't yet told her about being fired, so I had to do that. That unleashed a heap of verbal abuse. Then it was 'What was that nincompoop talking about?' I left that vague, just said I made some idle threats to Rox but I didn't actually have anything on her."

"But you did have something, didn't you? You mentioned pictures."

"Ah! There I go again, getting ahead of myself." Evangeline leaned forward, eager to keep dishing about Rox. "Rox had this close friend named Marcie who died from pancreatic cancer. And Marcie and Brad were cousins, but Marcie picked Rox, a non-relative, to be her POA. Rox was cleaning out Marcie's house and invited some folks from work over to help. Said she'd get us pizza and gift cards. She did follow through on the pizza, but I never saw any gift cards." Evangeline tore confetti-sized squares from the napkin strips.

"The room she assigned to me was full of clothes, knee-deep in clothes, piles of clothes everywhere. Rox wanted everything folded and separated out so she could see if she wanted to consign stuff or just give it to charity for a write-off. I started in on the piles and discovered that the piles weren't just clothes: underneath a top layer of clothes were dishes, jewelry, loose photos, outdated bills, books, more clothes. I found the same assortment in the other piles. I found a book, get this, *Lesbian Erotica*. As you can imagine, I was *quite* curious. Inside Rox had written 'To Marcie, a gift to you and to me! Love, Rox.'"

"Are you sure it was the same Rox?" I knew as I asked the question that it sounded stupid.

"Absolutely. I knew the woman's handwriting—she signed the checks at the Hamlin Group. I can show you the book, I have it at home."

"No, I'll take your word for it."

"I also found a photo of Rox and Marcie. *Kissing*." Evangeline looked at me meaningfully. I caught a nasty gleam in her washed-out eyes.

This revelation signaled questions that I left unasked: How do we know you didn't forge Rox's name on the book? As for the photo, there was Photoshop. Evangeline could well have the photo editing skills needed to combine separate photos of Rox and Marcie into one.

"I guess Rox didn't know these books and pictures were there in Marcie's place?"

"Guess not." Evangeline sounded proud of her accomplishments. "I tucked the book and photo in my bag. Just in case I ever needed them. Later I found a similar book and took that as well. If some of those board members ever found out that Rox was a lesbian, she could have kissed that job goodbye."

"In this day and age?"

"Oh, some of those board members don't live in this day and age. Pretty conservative folks, believe me. Especially Harold the weasel." Evangeline shook her head. "But I don't know why Rox was even worried. She could have sweet-talked her way into another job. Although she *was* over fifty, so she might have been worried about age discrimination."

"I think non-profits are more open to older employees." I didn't digress into a discussion about the laws protecting older job seekers against age discrimination. I suspected that employers found ways to sidestep the laws.

"I'm sure she didn't have to work," Evangeline said. "Wouldn't Brad rake in plenty of dough from his dental practice?"

My feminist side bristled. "Possibly she didn't want to rely on her husband for money. Plus she sounds like someone who liked the power she got from working."

"Could be. She did like her power."

Evangeline fumed in silence for a moment before going on. "According to Nichole, Rox didn't say a thing about my leaving. Just went on like nothing happened."

"Unbelievable," I said. But apparently Rox had done the same hiding-her-head-in-the-sand thing over the lunatic.

"Speaking of Nichole, where did she go off to?"

I pointed towards the window. "She's right outside."

Evangeline tried to turn to see her friend, but the effort was too much so she took my word for it.

"When did all this happen?" I asked.

"I was fired last November." Evangeline pushed away her pyramid of napkin squares and burst into tears. "Now I have no job, no prospects, and I'm stuck with Mother who constantly ridicules me about losing my job."

The pizza arrived. Avila asked Evangeline if there was anything she could do for her. But Evangeline managed a tremulous smile and said she was fine. She grabbed the nearest pizza slice and set to battling a network of hot cheese strings and about every topping Italian Delight offered. Avila looked unsure but moved away.

Nichole and Trudy magically appeared in time for the pizza. This time Trudy perched sideways on the edge of the booth and turned her body to face me.

"What a jerk!" Nichole exclaimed, adding a few expletives for good measure. I took it she referred to her ex. Her look of anger transformed to one of concern when she saw the tears streaming down Evangeline's face. "Evangeline! Are you all right?"

"I'll be okay. I was telling Hazel about that last day at the Hamlin Group."

"Unbelievable!" Nichole commiserated. "Well, let's enjoy our pizza and forget all about that."

We took time out to eat. Could Evangeline have killed Rox? Probably not by herself, not if she was *really* disabled. But getting fired gave her a powerful motive. And hadn't Nichole said that Rox claimed to have something on Evangeline? If Evangeline had shared a shameful secret with Rox—I thought it might have happened over drinks—I didn't know how I'd worm it out of her. I shelved the idea. But if Rox had resorted to blackmail, it supplied Evangeline with yet another motive to kill.

"I know I'm making myself out to be a suspect. But can you see me stabbing someone in the parking lot of a bar?"

No, but you could have hired someone.

"And I didn't hire someone, if that's what you're thinking." Evangeline gave me a smug smile that made me want to squirm. I didn't feel comfortable with a suspect echoing my thoughts.

Evangeline went on. "I certainly had a motive. But someone beat me to it. I'm glad. Believe me, I didn't shed any tears when I heard about her death. Anyway, the burden of proof is on the police. The D.A. *Whomever.*"

Was arthritis one of those diseases brought on by bitterness and negative emotions? Who knew what the stress of living with an abusive mother could do?

Avila presented our checks and we busied ourselves with fishing for debit cards and figuring out tips. Evangeline scrounged through her purse and found enough change to pay her bill in coin.

When we finally left, getting to Nichole's car was a laborious process for Evangeline. Once she settled in the passenger seat I pressed one of Lucy's business cards in her hand. "This is my cousin, Lucy Hooper. She runs a placement agency and has lots of temp jobs. She specializes in people who are difficult to place." I ad-libbed that last part, but it sounded good. "She can't guarantee anything and probably can't get you a job handling money."

Evangeline thanked me profusely as she took the card and said she wanted me to sign some books for her. I assured her that I would. Trudy and I waved until Nichole's car left the parking lot.

Trudy said eagerly, "So tell me what Evangeline said."

"Wow," Trudy said when I finished. "That's some story. Especially about Rox and Marcie. But we only have Evangeline's word for any of it. Rox isn't here to say anything different."

"True."

"Evangeline definitely needs professional help. And as for her murdering Rox or getting someone to do it for her—it's pretty unlikely."

"Who were you talking to over there?"

"My sister." Trudy grinned. "I prolonged the conversation to give you quality time with Evangeline."

I rolled my eyes. "Want to come to O'Toole's with me and hear Dave perform?"

"You bet. We need some entertainment after that experience."

• • •

It only took a few minutes to reach O'Toole's, a neighborhood Irish pub and restaurant that featured a sports bar and musical entertainment. Lucy's husband, Dave Considine, often participated in the monthly Songwriters Showcase, playing his guitar and singing. As always, we enjoyed his performance.

At home, Vince and I sat on the screen porch with the cats.

"Did you tell Lucy about your mammogram?" Vince asked.

"Yeah, I did." I didn't want to talk about my mammogram. Or think about it. "And I told her about my conversation with Evangeline. Wait'll you hear this."

"That's sure a lot to take in," Vince said when I finished.

"So, Evangeline had motives galore, but means and opportunity not so much. Maybe her mother did it. She sounds pretty spry."

"All we need is proof," Vince said.

I ignored the relentless proof reminder. "I didn't know that Marcie was a lesbian. I wonder if Nina knew. Or Patty. And did either of them ever see that erotica book, or anything else like it? Assuming there even was such a book."

"Being Rox's sister, Nina might have known about her relationship with Marcie. As for Patty, I don't have the impression that she was close to Marcie, despite their being cousins."

"No, I don't think so," I said. "Still, she might have known or at least have wondered about it." I didn't know Nina or Patty's views on same-sex relationships. Would it have been bad news or ho-hum news? Knowing Patty, she'd cloak any negative feelings with assurances that it was all fine and dandy.

"They probably kept their relationship hidden," Vince said. "Marcie was a stockbroker and they're a pretty conservative bunch. Her being a woman in a traditionally man's field would have made her even more cautious about standing out from the crowd. She'd want to appear as conventional as possible. And Rox might have had to consider her career as well. Even today, not everyone's on board with same-sex relationships."

"Yes, Evangeline indicated that the Hamlin Group is especially conservative." We were making a good case for Rox and Marcie remaining deep in the closet.

"It kind of threw me for a loop, hearing about this relationship. I mean, Rox has had so many affairs with men. There's Foster. And Brad. Maybe the lunatic. And some of the guys from the Moonshine Inn."

Vince started, "Was Marcie—"

"Oh," I cut in, "And Rox was married before Brad. To that guy who lives in Australia. They had a daughter together."

"Was Marcie ever married?"

"Yes, according to the family tree that Ruth gave me, Marcie was married long ago when she was quite young, still in college. No children."

"Lots of gay folks marry to mask their sexuality, to bow to social expectations."

"Or maybe they're in deep denial, even to themselves."

"Did Marcie know about Rox's other relationships? What did she think about her affair with Foster? And with Brad?"

"I'm not clear on whether Rox and Brad were just friends or if they were lovers before they got married. As for Marcie, maybe she had her own diversions."

"And maybe the intimate part of her relationship with Rox didn't last long, so they ended it and became friends. Do you know how long they were lovers?"

"I don't," I said. "But they must have been very good friends for Rox to be Marcie's POA."

"We can only speculate at this point," Vince said. "And Evangeline could be making up the whole thing—the book, the photos, Brad coming to her house and threatening her. We don't have an easy way of verifying any of this. And didn't those women at the Hamlin Group say Rox had something on Evangeline?"

"Yeah, but I don't know what. According to Evangeline, when they went out for drinks Rox tried to pump her for information, but she had nothing to spill. Said her life was boring. Now I wonder." Olive jumped in my lap and I petted her soft, silky fur. "It seems to me that Evangeline would have been so thrilled to be invited for drinks by her boss that she'd have willingly shared secrets about herself, even if she had to make up something."

"Well—".

"Evangeline offered to show me those books and photos, but a clever person could fake them. And I think she's clever enough. Her threatening Rox when she got fired is probably real—she was overheard making threats—but it could have been just hot air. Evangeline could well be delusional, what with her situation and all—the health problems, her mother, the whole bit."

Vince considered. "It's all possible."

That was the problem. Too many possibilities.

FOURTEEN

ON TUESDAY I e-mailed the book group about my meeting with Evangeline. Then I started researching my calcification issue. I found nothing new since my last round of research years before. There was still that 80 to 90 percent chance that the biopsy would produce benign results. Was there a way to prevent or reverse this calcification, stop it in its tracks? I saw nothing that said there was, or wasn't. I was still looking for answers when Sarah called.

"I talked to Maisie Atwater. When she heard that you and I are in the same book group she got all excited, saying how much she loved your books, how she has your latest and would love for you to sign it. Can you come by later? She lives nearby so she'll run home and get the book."

"Okay. What time?"

"How about noon? And if you go for a walk with her I think you'll learn some interesting tidbits about our Rox."

"Well, I'm not much for walking in this heat, but if she has some worthwhile information, I can sweat it out. Do you think she does?"

"She's bound to. I told her that you met Nina recently. When Nina talked about her sister is when you started thinking about writing a romance about women in the non-profit world. Which means you need to interview people. She said she'd not only love to talk to you but she could tell you plenty about women and non-profits."

"Excellent. Good job, Sarah." I felt my spirits lift.

"Maisie says it's cooler by the lake. That's where she wants to walk. It's right across the road from here. She wants to lose weight and is starting this new regime. So is noon okay?"

"Sounds good to me." That was an understatement. I was getting nowhere on my breast cancer research, and I was eager for a firsthand account of Rox's stint at the Alzheimer's Research Society.

After writing down the ARS address in the Innsbrook office park, I changed into something business-casual but still cool enough for a hot and muggy midday walk. It was only eleven, too early to leave, so I scanned Facebook and Twitter to kill time. Thinking I might record my talk with Maisie, I did a practice session with the voice recorder app on my phone. To be safe, I also charged my phone.

Nichole called, asking about my conversation with Evangeline. "Did she tell you anything useful?"

"Yes, she was certainly interesting. But I'm not sure she was entirely truthful."

To my surprise, Nichole got huffy and hung up on me. I stared at the phone for a minute like I expected it to explain the young woman's attitude.

En route to Innsbrook in Glen Allen, a suburb northwest of Richmond, I crossed the falls of the James River on the S-shaped Edward E. Willey Bridge, glancing out my window at Bosher Dam. Thick stands of trees hid from view a number of high-priced homes that overlooked the dam. Mr. Willey was a Virginia politician and the father-in-law of Kathleen Willey, a former White House aide who once alleged on *60 Minutes* that Bill Clinton sexually assaulted her during his presidency.

The Innsbrook office park included residential areas and boasted three lakes, walking trails, and high standards in landscape design. I had no trouble finding the ARS, housed in a wood-shingled building with large glass windows. After parking under a tree, I donned a hat and sunglasses and locked my purse in the trunk.

Sarah and another woman sat on the front patio at a wooden table, a wide umbrella shading them. They leaned close to each other, deep in conversation, and didn't see me until I hovered over them.

"Hazel!" Sarah looked up. She wore her long hair in a single braid that trailed down her back. "I didn't see you drive in. We're so glad you could make it. This is Maisie Atwater. Maisie, Hazel Rose."

"Hazel!" Maisie effused in a charming British accent. "Oh, I just *adore* your books." Maisie had a cloud of jet black hair and blue eyeshadow streaked across her eyelids, recalling my Moonshine Inn getup. Her glittery blue knit top looked hot, despite its short sleeves. "I have your latest with me, it's right inside. Will you sign it before we leave?"

When I assured her that I would, she went on, "I love how you have us old folks enjoying a good roll in the hay."

I regarded my characters as mature, not old. But I preferred the tell-it-better-than-it-is approach to the tell-it-like-it-is one.

Maisie stood. "Sarah says you're up for a walk around the lake."

"Oh yes, I love to walk."

"I can't say I like it too much, not yet anyway. But I have to get rid of these love handles." She pinched a roll that circled her midsection. "Too much fish and chips," she said cheerfully. "Let's go over to the lake."

"Sarah, are you coming with us?" I asked.

"No, I have a lot to do here. Besides, those walking paths are too narrow for three people."

Maisie and I crossed Cox Road and started along a path that wound around a small lake. We briefly discussed Maisie's recent trip to visit her family in Leeds. That segued into a back-and-forth on the *DCI Banks* TV series, set in Yorkshire and inspired by the novels by Peter Robinson.

Small talk over, Maisie said, "So, Sarah tells me that you met Roxanne Howard's sister, Nina."

"Yes, I did. She told me she's not happy with what the

police are doing and wanted to know if I knew of any private investigators she could hire to solve Roxanne's murder. I guess she figures that since I'm in a mystery group I might know about such things." I assumed a look of deep regret. "Unfortunately, I don't."

Maisie shook her head. "Yes, the whole thing was tragic. Rox used to be our executive director. She was first the development director and then she got promoted. And her husband is one of our board members."

"I'm thinking of using someone like Rox in my next novel, something about women and romance in a non-profit."

Maisie looked delighted. "Yes, Sarah said that. Well, I could tell you some stories. True ones."

"Really?" I prompted.

"Rox was a quite a character. If you want to learn about romance in the workplace you've come to the right source. She had quite a thing going with one of our interns, Foster Hayden."

"Well, this sure sounds interesting."

"Foster was, I imagine still is, a *very* attractive gentleman. Quite dishy. And *much* younger than she was."

"You're kidding?" I held up my phone. "Mind if I record this? For my story?"

"Not at all." I started the app and put the phone back in my pocket.

Maisie picked up her tale. "They were attracted to each other the minute he walked into the office to start his internship, and one thing led to another. Foster was a nice young man, I always liked him. Unfortunately, no matter how nice, men are men— they're *prone*. My oh my, you could have gathered some good story material when they were around. Lots of fighting, very public. And making up, *if* you know what I mean. Behind closed doors. Most unprofessional." She *tsked* but her delighted expression told me the unprofessionalism hadn't bothered her a bit.

"She used the office like a hotel room. After all, there's a nice sofa, small refrigerator, wet bar, you name it. You could *live* there. And she kept a supply of wine, beer, and champagne in the refrigerator."

"Why didn't Rox and Foster just go to a hotel?"

Maisie shrugged. "Maybe they did sometimes. But with all

these amenities, why pay for a hotel room?"

"How often did she, um, entertain Foster?"

Maisie thought for a moment. "Evenings mostly. One night I left my phone at work and had to go back. My first hint that they were in the building was their cars in the lot. And the sounds coming from Rox's office . . ." She trailed with a do-I-have-to-draw-you-a-picture tone in her voice. "I found my phone and tiptoed through the rest of the office. I saw Foster's jacket in his cubicle, his monitor still on.

"If one of us shagged in the office she'd have booted us out the door pronto." Then, thinking I may not be up on British slang, she asked, "Do you know what shagging means?"

"Yes," I smiled. "Sex. I think most Americans are familiar with the term."

"Just want to be sure. Anyway, one time they didn't even wait until everyone left for the day. I'll never forget hearing those sounds from her office. A board member was there and heard it as well. I couldn't make eye contact with him. He was waiting to talk to Rox about our fundraiser."

"When was all this going on? What time period?" We crossed a small bridge. I tried to imagine the tranquil-looking setting without the constant hum of traffic.

"Oh, we're talking six, maybe seven years ago."

"So then what happened?"

"Rox started acting really crazy and possessive and Foster quit. She said she'd see to it that his career was over."

"Was it?"

"Not at all. The Public Policy Director who was there at the time helped Foster get a position with the ACLU. Later we heard he was working for a large legal practice. Do you want to walk over to the other lake?"

"Okay." We headed that way. Maisie was right—the lake lowered the temperature by several degrees, making for a pleasant walk.

"Didn't Rox go over to his house or apartment one time and cause a scene?" I asked. "I think I read something about that."

"Yes. She banged on his door, yelling and screaming. He wouldn't let her in. He finally came out and they wound up wrestling and rolling around in the hall. That was all in the paper."

"Did he ever file a sexual harassment complaint?"

"No, at least I never heard that he did. He was probably too embarrassed to file a complaint. Besides, he gave in to her. And he didn't want to damage his career."

Did he think that dallying with the boss would further his career? Did Rox give him any indication that such a move would be successful? Or had hormones been the deciding factor and ambition forgotten?

"So, anyway, after Foster left the ARS, Rox calmed down for a while. Then there was that scene at the theater."

"Oh, I think I read about that too," I said. "A long time ago. I'm fuzzy on the details." It couldn't hurt to hear Maisie's perspective of the incident. I might learn something new.

I didn't. Maisie related the same information I already had—the dramatic showdown in the theater and the car damage. Car damage was a common theme in Rox's relationships, I thought, thinking of the crazed windshield smasher—only this time, she was the damager.

A gaggle of geese greeted us at the next lake. A number of office buildings surrounded a body of water twice the size of the one we'd just left. I counted three fountains shooting geyser-like sprays. A bridge spanned the water at its midpoint.

Maisie wiped her brow. "It's sure getting hot out here."

I handed her a tissue from my pocket. "You might want to wear a hat if you keep up your walking routine."

"I hate hats. But back to Foster. There was that whole thing with his father." Maisie was on a roll and clearly enjoying herself.

"Father?" My ears perked up like a cat's. I hadn't heard anything about Foster's father.

"Not long after the movie incident, Foster's father showed up, wanting to see Rox. The two of them met behind closed doors and I don't know what they talked about. But a few weeks later Foster stormed into the office. He called Rox every name in the book. Told her to stay away from his father. I took him outside and tried to calm him down. He showed me pictures of Rox and his father. In some they were leaving the office building; in others, they leaned against a car with their tongues shoved down each other's throats and his hand hiking up her skirt. Right in the *parking* lot. Foster's mother had hired a private detective to follow her husband. The date and time stamps on the pictures were for different days over a period of a month. Always in the office or the parking lot, late in the evening."

"How cheesy," I said. "First the son, then the father. Maybe the father was a trophy."

"He certainly was a coup," Maisie agreed. "And the man was running for some kind of office. State senate, I think. Rox didn't say a thing about Foster's tirade when I returned to the office, just acted like nothing had happened." Those words echoed what Nichole had reported about Rox's behavior in the aftermath of Evangeline's termination. "But I caught a hint of a pleased look. I think Rox really liked upsetting people and actually took a perverse pleasure in it. Like that woman in *East of Eden*."

"Funny you should mention *East of Eden,* because we were just talking about it at book group last week. But you probably mean Cathy Ames, and Rox must have been *pretty* bad if you're comparing her to Cathy. Cathy was the devil incarnate. I read somewhere that John Steinbeck modeled her after one of his wives."

"If that's true, he was lucky she didn't kill him."

Figuring we were getting off track, I said, "So what happened next with Rox?"

"Soon after that, the father died. The paper just said he died, no cause. Rox showed up at the funeral. So did Pamela, Foster's girlfriend from the movie incident. His mother started screaming when she saw Rox. There was a terrible scene and Foster reminded Rox that he had taken out a restraining order on her and that he wouldn't hesitate to invoke it. Rox held up her hands in mock surrender"—here Maisie demonstrated by raising both hands— "and left with an amused look on her face."

"He took out a restraining order?"

"That's what Foster said. And he told me that he and his family blamed Rox for his father's death. All the stress, especially when the mother got hold of the pictures."

And all that gave Foster a powerful motive to kill Rox, I thought.

"Even with all her hijinks, Rox could put on a professional face when she needed to. She raised money, she gave good talks, knew how to schmooze with the donors. The board loved her results. But they couldn't take the publicity and ultimately had to fire her. After that we kept up with her antics via the paper."

We fell silent. As I admired the scenery and stepped around goose droppings, I tried to process the information Maisie had shared. The part about Foster's parents was quite a revelation.

"So Hazel, is this giving you some inspiration?"

"Sure is. And it makes me wonder . . . do you think Foster could have, you know, *killed* her?"

"Oh I don't know. He certainly had a motive, but it was so long ago."

I considered his alibi of being in Atlanta. But alibis weren't always reliable. How long would it take him to get here from Atlanta? Eight hours? Ten? Not inconceivable that he made the trip with an intent to kill. However, it seemed unlikely. I couldn't wait to hear what Lucy had to report after her lunch with him.

"What about Rox's current husband? Widower, rather? How did he come into the picture? Didn't you say he was on the ARS board?"

"Ah, Brad. Yes, he's on our board. He got Rox the job at the Hamlin Group when the ARS canned her. Brad knew one of the members and got her in there. Then she started getting DUIs. The woman was a train wreck.

"Brad had been in a relationship with Nina, Rox's sister. Nina's a nice person. And so was that other woman who used to come in the office to visit Rox. What was her name? Oh, I'm having a senior moment."

Interesting that Rox associated with such nice people when she herself was not so nice.

"Marcie. It was Marcie. I think she and Brad were cousins." Maisie offered nothing more. If she knew of a relationship beyond friendship between Rox and Marcie, she wasn't sharing. And I felt sure she would have.

"You know, Brad's had his share of tragedy as well. He was happily married, then his wife disappeared." Maisie described how Veronica Jones' body was found on the banks of the James River in Lynchburg.

I acted like it was news to me. "When was this?"

"Oh, four years ago. Maybe five. It's hard to keep track of time. We went to her funeral, as well."

I thought back to my conversation with Nina at Joe's Inn. Brad's son Andy suspected Rox and his father of killing Veronica. Again, Rox sounded like Cathy Ames. Or was this a case of insurance fraud, a la Fred MacMurray and Barbara Stanwyck in *Double Indemnity*? I reined myself in. I was getting carried away with the movie parallels.

"What was Rox like as an employer?"

Maisie made a waffling motion with her hand. "Okay. For the most part she had little to do with the employees and left me to deal with them. I was the office manager then." That echoed what I'd heard at the Hamlin Group. "Of course, she paid a lot of attention to Foster."

"So she didn't have any run-ins with her employees?"

Maisie thought. "There was this one woman, Tracy. Hard worker, but not much personality. One day she noticed a candy bar missing from her desk and said something about it. Rox admitted that she'd taken it the night before when she'd been working late. Probably working late with Foster. Anyway, the woman got indignant and actually yelled at Rox. You can imagine how well that went over. Tracy didn't last long. Rox took advantage of any opportunity to criticize her in front of the others. One day Tracy left in tears, yelling that she didn't have to take this crap anymore, and she wound up at the Hamlin Group." Maisie repeated Nichole's account of Tracy's tragic death in an accident.

"We'd better head back," Maisie said.

. . .

Wood, glass, and plants created a pleasing interior at the ARS, unlike the gray cubicles of most workplaces. Sarah sat at a computer, checking off names on a printout. Maisie retrieved her book and I signed it, thanking her profusely for her interest.

"You think you have some good material there?" She asked, a twinkle in her eye.

"No doubt about it." I took my phone out of my pocket and waved it. Remembering that the app still ran, I ended the recording. "You'll have a top spot in my acknowledgments."

"I'll walk out with you," Sarah said.

"Did you get my e-mail about Evangeline?" I asked on the way to my car.

"Not yet. I haven't checked."

"That Rox was a piece of work," Sarah said when I caught her up on my visits with both Evangeline and Maisie, adding, "So is Evangeline."

"I recorded the conversation with Maisie." But when I played back the recording all we heard were strange sounds, like thumping or squishing. And heavy breathing.

Sarah and I looked at each other and laughed. "Sounds kind of obscene," she said.

"Guess I shouldn't have left the phone in my pocket. Oh well, I remember everything."

"We'll have plenty to talk about tomorrow," Sarah said. "And hopefully Lucy will too, after her visit with Foster."

"We're not in danger of running short on conversation any time soon."

. . .

At home I fixed a salad and looked up Foster Hayden on LinkedIn. Maisie was right, the young man was quite "dishy." He'd earned his degree from VCU in communications. What did that cover? Phones, television, radio, Morse code, carrier pigeon? Currently he worked for a legal firm. On Facebook, I hunted through his postings for indications that he'd been in town on the night Rox was killed. But nothing said "I did it! I did it!" Foster had chatty, friendly postings, many of the "I'm drinking coffee now" type. He also ate a lot of attractive food and shared the pictures with his friends, who numbered in the hundreds. I found Pamela Barry, Foster's companion and fellow victim from Rox's movie theatre drama. Pamela smiled for the camera, her face framed by a mop of curls. Her few postings had to do with church activities.

Vince came home laden with groceries. After I helped him put away the items we sat with cold drinks while I recounted my walk with Maisie.

"It sounds like you got a lot of information."

"I had never heard all that about the father and the PI. All I'd heard about Foster was the movie incident . . . nothing beyond that." I sipped my cold cider. "So maybe Brad and Nina didn't kill Rox, and Foster did. He could've made a quick trip to

Richmond and hightailed it back to Atlanta."

"Remember, he has an alibi. As I recall, a nurse vouched for him. His mother was close to death in the hospital. He was there the whole evening with her and his brother."

I sighed. "You know something, Vince? Rox gets worse with each telling."

FIFTEEN

AT THE BOOK group's next Skype session on Wednesday, we fairly burst with eagerness to share the fruits of our detective work. Even though we'd been updating by e-mail, more information was bound to come out in actual conversation.

We launched into our accounts, covering the visits to the Hamlin Group and the Moonshine Inn as well as our conversations with Nina, Kat, Evangeline, and Maisie. Despite the fact that this was a group effort, so far I was the only one involved in every interaction, and so I did the bulk of the reporting.

When at last we wound down, Eileen said, "Whew! Lunatics, feisty old women, lesbian erotica . . . and Evangeline sounds like a mess."

Lucy said, "I've been thinking about what Hazel said about Rox being in a same-sex relationship with Marcie, or at least Evangeline's saying she was. Maybe Rox latched onto anyone who had money, regardless of their gender."

"Could be," Trudy agreed. "Anyone who could give her a meal ticket."

"I imagine Brad does well enough in his dental practice to make him appealing to a gold digger," Eileen said. "But back to

Evangeline—I apologize for not doing the research on her that I said I'd do. But my mother's been acting up at the assisted-living place and I've been in meetings with the staff there. I hope they don't throw her out."

"Would they do that?" I asked.

"I hope not." Eileen sounded rueful. "Anyway, I'll see what I can find on Evangeline."

Sarah said, "So Lucy, tell us about your meeting with Foster."

"Okay. I have some notes here." We heard the sound of paper shuffling. "I've tried to arrange all of this in chronological order. I stopped by Foster's office and invited him for coffee. I frequently do visit my clients to touch base, see if they need anything and check on the employees I placed. So it didn't seem at all unusual that I did so today.

"I told Foster that a couple of people from my book group had met Rox Howard's sister and that she wanted to hire a PI to find out who killed Rox."

"He said, 'Who cares who killed her? Whoever did it should get a medal. Unchristian of me, I know.' In no time he was off and running with a list of Rox's various transgressions."

"Good job, Lucy," Trudy cheered.

"We've already heard, or read, about the movie incident countless times, so I won't rehash that. Foster seemed especially incensed when Rox, during her tirade in the theater, asked if Foster and Pamela had been intimate yet, and then proceeded to recommend Foster's services. In detail."

We laughed at the sheer audacity of the deceased woman. "I'm sure the audience won't forget that performance," Eileen said. "But they probably forgot all about the movie."

Lucy continued. "To quote Foster: 'Pamela's very religious and doesn't believe in intimacy before marriage'."

"Quite a departure from Rox," I said.

"Okay, you know about Rox going to Foster's place and causing a scene in the hallway. After that, Foster's father suggested that he get a restraining order. And—this you heard from Maisie—his dad went to see Rox, to try to reason with her. They wound up having an affair."

Interesting. Mr. Hayden advises a restraining order against the woman and he winds up sleeping with her. I remembered

Maisie saying that he was running for political office. Why did politicians so often seem to have their own brand of logic?

Lucy went on to describe how Foster's mother hired a PI to follow her husband, the PI's damaging photos, and the father's suicide.

"Suicide?" I said, surprised. "Maisie didn't say anything about suicide. She just said he died."

"As far as the public was concerned, he died of a heart attack," Lucy explained. "But Foster told me his father overdosed on sleeping pills. And he told me the same account of the funeral that Maisie told Hazel."

Lucy went on. "After the funeral, Rox faded from the scene—".

"—and moved on to other prospects to torment," Sarah snorted.

Lucy ignored the interruption. "Foster's mother and brother went to live in Atlanta. The rest of his family eventually followed and Foster's the only one left in Richmond. He goes to Atlanta a lot and is trying to get a job there."

"Well, that's his alibi, visiting his sick mother in Atlanta," I said. "So Foster said Rox was gone from the scene after his dad's funeral?"

"Pretty much, at least from his life. She showed up in the paper on a regular basis, what with the DUIs and all. And with some good reports concerning her work at the Hamlin Group."

"But one day Foster saw Rox and an older woman in the parking lot of the office building where he works."

"What was that all about?" I asked.

"He doesn't know. He was leaving to go to lunch, and Rox and the older woman had just arrived. There are a lot of lawyers in the building. Foster works for a group specializing in employment law."

"Maybe one of Rox's employees was suing her," Trudy suggested.

"Evangeline was," I said.

"Foster said they didn't go to the firm he's with," Lucy said. "But there are other lawyers in the building who practice employment law."

"Interesting," Sarah said. "But without canvassing all the lawyers in the building, how would we find out what Rox and the woman were doing there?"

"And the lawyers wouldn't tell you anyway," Trudy reminded Sarah about client confidentiality.

"And I don't think the whole building is lawyers, just a lot of them," Lucy said. "Besides, it may not even matter. Okay, that takes us to last New Year's Day when Rox once again showed up at Foster's place."

"What happened?"

"He says he didn't open the door and she eventually left."

"Hmm. What was she doing there?" I asked. "Why wouldn't she leave the poor guy alone? She'd just married Brad."

I heard the shrug in Lucy's voice. "Foster couldn't say."

"Or wouldn't," Sarah said with a wry tone. "Did she show up again after that?"

"No. Foster claims that's the last time he saw her. I asked him if he had any idea who killed Rox. He didn't, but suggested that she had probably tormented others besides him—maybe someone at that redneck bar."

"So," I said. "Rox wreaked a lot of havoc in Foster's life. He lost his father and his family moved away—motives galore."

"We've certainly covered a lot of territory," Eileen said.

"Yes," I said, "But so far it's all puzzle pieces. We're hearing Rox's story in layers. Maybe we should find out who this PI is that Foster's mother hired and recommend him to Nina."

"We're sure not getting anywhere," Sarah sounded as rueful as I felt.

"Maybe the lunatic will turn up," Lucy tried to inject a note of optimism. "Or the parking lot guy."

Maybe.

• • •

"Vince, if Foster killed Rox, why did he wait all this time? All that drama happened way back in 2007. Did it have something to do with her visit on New Year's Day?" I'd just summed up my book group's meeting for Vince.

"You keep forgetting that Foster had an alibi. As did his brother. They were at their mother's bedside in an Atlanta hospital." Morris jumped in Vince's lap and circled a few times before settling on the perfect spot.

"Couldn't they fake alibis and have someone cover for them?"
"Unlikely."
"We're at a standstill, aren't we?"
As it turned out, we weren't standing still for long.

SIXTEEN

"HAZEL, I HAVE really bad news." Trudy's voice sounded ragged. "It's Nina. She was murdered last night."

"Murdered? You're joking. Please tell me you're joking."

"Someone stabbed her multiple times, right in her own *house* . . . Can you come over?"

"Absolutely."

"I'll be at Mrs. Ellbee's house, that's right across the street from Nina's. The neighbors are gathering there." She sighed. "We've been up all night being questioned by the police."

"Which house is Nina's?"

"Two doors down from mine. You can't miss it with all the crime scene tape."

"Are they still processing the scene?"

"No, they're done. For now, anyway."

"I'm be there in about thirty minutes. Don't say anything to your neighbors about our investigation."

"I won't."

While I dashed around to make myself presentable, I told Vince the news.

"I'll find out what's going on," he said.

"Let me know when you do." I grabbed a banana. "Oh, I'd better call Patty and cancel our lunch."

When I told Patty about Nina, she exclaimed, "Oh, no. How awful. What happened?"

"I don't know any details yet. I'm going over to Trudy's now. I'll call you later."

If not for the swamp-like weather, I'd have walked the short distance. I parked in Trudy's driveway and made my way to Nina's house. Trudy was right—the crime scene tape made Nina's house easy to spot. I stood by her gravel driveway and took in the Colonial-style house, white, with black shutters. A magnolia tree provided shade. Tall azalea bushes bordered the front of her property.

Across the street, Mrs. Ellbee's yard blazed with color due to a variety of annuals and crape myrtle trees. Monkey grass, its spidery tendrils bordering the flagstone walkway, promised more color in a few weeks.

As I started up the steps of Mrs. Ellbee's Cape Cod-style house, a middle-aged couple with matching scowls came out the door. The man's beach ball-sized belly strained the buttons of his Hawaiian shirt. The woman's identical shirt didn't fare much better. They ignored my nod of greeting.

Trudy held the door open. Her face looked drawn, and dark shadows under her eyes told of her sleepless night. A brown and white dog of indeterminate breed leaped on me, causing me to trip over a hole in the worn carpet. I caught myself on the arm of a chair. A man sitting on the sofa assured me that Elmer wouldn't bite.

"Dear me. Carl, you have to do something about that carpet. And do something about Elmer. I've told you a hundred times." The woman I presumed to be Mrs. Ellbee spoke with a birdlike quality. Her high-pitched voice was not unlike a tweet—and I didn't refer to the one hundred and forty character kind that characterized the social media titan, Twitter.

"Okay, Mom." Carl sounded like a long-suffering teenager.

"You don't want this nice lady to fall and hurt herself, not at her age. Why, she could sue us for everything we have. She could—"

Mrs. Ellbee might have gone on predicting what an aged, infirm, and litigious person like myself might do, but Trudy broke off the dire speculations to introduce me to the woman and her son, Carl Ellbee, adding, "Hazel is a good friend of mine and she recently met Nina."

Mrs. Ellbee presided over the room from a recliner in front of a picture window. She not only sounded like a bird, but she resembled one as well. A tiny woman whose small eyes darted here and there, she accessorized her pink sweats with a chiffon scarf and pearls. She wore slippers that looked like ballet shoes and matched the pink of the sweats.

The end table next to her held an assortment of prescription medication bottles, a pile of mail, and two TV remotes. A pair of reading glasses sat atop a stack of books. A copy of *Gone Girl*, the bestseller thriller by Gillian Flynn, topped the stack.

Carl Ellbee appeared to be in his early fifties. He sported a Moody Blues T-shirt, shorts, and athletic shoes. A wad of adhesive tape over the bridge of his nose held his glasses together.

Mrs. Ellbee waved a hand towards the dining room. "Help yourself to those things, tell me again what you call them?"

"Bagels, Mom," Carl answered in a tone that suggested his mother had asked the same question several times. To me, he added, "My sister and brother-in-law brought this stuff over. They just left." I figured they were the scowling couple in the Hawaiian shirts.

"They made some coffee as well," Trudy said. "The neighbors have been in and out of here all morning. Most left to go to work. Can I get you something, Hazel?"

"I'd love some coffee." My coffee ritual had been interrupted by the unwelcome news of Nina's death. The few bagels remaining didn't look too appealing.

I took the cup Trudy handed to me and sat in the same tattered chair that had broken my fall during my ungainly entrance. The loveliness of the Ellbee yard did not carry through to the inside of the house. Cracks in the wall and peeling woodwork called for a major paint job. The faded and scratched furniture in the dining and living rooms had seen better days. The widescreen television and Mrs. Ellbee's recliner lent an incongruous note with their newness.

"Mrs. Ellbee has quite a story to tell," Trudy said. "She might have seen Nina's killer."

"I would have seen more if she didn't have all those bushes and trees in the way." I looked out the window. The tall bushes and the magnolia tree did a good job of obscuring the view of all but the upper story of Nina's house. I suspected that Nina, or the previous owner, had planted the foliage to block their curious neighbor's view.

Mrs. Ellbee went on, "But I do have a good view of the street and that's where the car was, waiting. Of course, it was dark."

After a pause, I prompted her, "Waiting for what?"

"The woman. The woman who got out of the car and walked up the driveway. A few minutes later she came back and got back in the car."

"Could you see what she looked like?"

"Well, like I said, it was dark so I couldn't see much. She was tall. When she opened the car door, I saw that she had dark hair, down to here." She put a finger on her shoulder to measure a length of hair. "Close to her scalp, much like yours." She cast a critical look at my head. "You'd look younger with some lift to your hair, dear."

I bristled at her repeated references to my age. Did she think I should emulate her and get a once-a-week wash and set? Granted, her hair had "lift" and with all the hair spray I doubted that it could ever collapse. Smiling, I asked, "Anything else you remember about her?"

"She had trouble walking. Either she'd had a bit too much to drink—or she had on those silly high heels that girls teeter around in these days. They're going to pay a price one day." Mrs. Ellbee went on to predict grim consequences for the wearers of sky-high heels. As I seldom wore heels anymore and, when I did, they measured a mere three inches, the woman was preaching to the choir. "Oh, and she carried a tote bag."

Toting a bloody knife, perhaps? Or was the knife left at the scene, like with Rox's murder?

I asked, "What time was this?"

"Nine-thirty." Mrs. Ellbee sounded firm on the time. "My show had just ended."

"Did you see the driver?"

"Yes. It was an older woman. I couldn't see her well. But she had white hair. Curly."

"Did you see what kind of car it was?"

"No. But Carl was out walking Elmer and went right past the car," Mrs. Ellbee twittered. "He says the car was from Florida."

"Did you get the license number? Or the make of the car?" I asked.

Carl shrugged. "All I remember was that the car was green and there was an 'IT' in the license number. I work in IT so that's why I noticed."

"But you said it was dark out—were the car lights on?"

"No, but I carry a flashlight."

Mrs. Ellbee went on with her story. "About eleven, that man who's always coming around and staying all night arrived at Nina's. He left a few minutes later and the police arrived soon after. He must have found the poor woman, dead. Can you imagine? The man has no moral fiber, just runs away like a scared little boy."

She must be talking about Brad. It sounded like he found Nina's body, made an anonymous call, and split. Or did he kill her before making the call? Was Brad a murderer, or just the victim of bad timing?

"Believe you me, I told that detective about him. I couldn't see his license plate, though. Maddening."

"So how—"

"I told the police it was probably Brad Jones," Trudy said.

Mrs. Ellbee sniffed. "This Brad was around a lot when Nina went down to Florida. There was a lot of activity—house painted, inside and out. Landscaping as well."

Trudy looked at her iPhone and said, "Well, I have to get going. I said I'd be at the library before noon."

"Yes, I have to go as well," I said. I thanked Mrs. Ellbee and Carl for their time and hospitality, such as it was.

Once outside, I stopped to admire the landscaping. "Oh, Trudy, I wish Vince and I had green thumbs. Our fathers were both fabulous gardeners, but they didn't pass the talent down to us."

Carl and Elmer bounded out of the house. When I complimented Carl on the yard, he said, "Yes, my dad was a gardener, he designed this. I try to keep it up." I wondered if Carl's gardening zeal—and maybe his dad's as well—came from needing to escape the twittery Mrs. Ellbee.

"So, you live here with your mom?" I asked.

"Oh, God, no! I live at the end of the block, next to Eileen." He waved his hand in a direction to the left. "My sister lives next door." Again, the hand waved to the left at a house that mirrored Mrs. Ellbee's, minus the lush plantings. "We help Mom out," he added with little enthusiasm.

Apparently Mrs. Ellbee's children regarded her as an obligation. Carl didn't offer further insight on his family dynamics. I'd seen enough to judge for myself.

"Speaking of Eileen, was she here earlier?"

"Yes, but she had to leave," Trudy said. "She had a meeting scheduled with the staff at her mother's assisted living place."

"She's having a really bad time with her mom," I said.

"Yeah. I have a feeling she'll wind up living with Eileen. We might be acquiring another neighbor, Carl."

He snickered. "What's one more cranky old lady?"

"See you later, Carl," Trudy said. She and I crossed the street to stand by the crime scene tape barring access to Nina's driveway.

• • •

"So who do you think did it, Trudy?"

"Who knows? Probably Brad."

"Probably. I have to call Vince. He was going to find out what happened."

"I told the police about Phyllis, about how she acted that day at Panera. They might ask you about it."

"So you think Phyllis might have killed Nina?"

Trudy shrugged. "She's as good a suspect as anyone."

I thought. "She has all that wild hair. But she could tamp it down somehow, plaster it to her head, so she'd look old, like me." I still smarted over Mrs. Ellbee's unsolicited beauty advice.

Trudy grinned. "Yes, Mrs. E. is free with her opinions. She often tells me I'm too old for long hair." Trudy put a hand up to her long white mane. Mrs. Ellbee had a point, but I didn't voice my agreement with the woman.

"And Phyllis is fairly tall," I mused. "At least five eight or nine. I don't know Mrs. Ellbee's criteria for describing someone as tall."

"And if the woman wore heels that could raise her up by several inches."

I looked at the gravel driveway. Anyone wearing heels would have a hard time walking on this driveway. Especially if she wasn't used to them.

"The difficulty in walking could point to a man as well," I said. "A man wearing heels."

"Yes. We can't eliminate a man trying to pass as a woman. The driver could have been a man as well. Height and hair length can so easily be altered."

I wiped away a bead of sweat that ran down my cheek. "At Nina's funeral, let's be on the lookout for a tall woman, possibly someone with another woman. And a car with Florida plates. Long shot, I know."

"We have to e-mail the book group. Hopefully we can all go to the funeral. Whenever it is."

"I'll send out the e-mail when I get home."

"Let's go to my house. It's too yucky out here."

I welcomed the coolness of Trudy's house. I didn't see Sammy in the den—perhaps the cat had a favorite morning spot. I cleared copies of the *Washington Post* from a chair and called Vince. He verified that Nina was stabbed multiple times in the neck, chest, and arm. Brad had found her in the front hall and called 911.

"A neighbor told the police about Brad and he was brought in for questioning. He said—"

"That was Mrs. Ellbee," I interrupted. "Trudy and I were just at her house."

"Brad said he arrived at Nina's house and found her dead. He called the police from Nina's landline. He's being questioned now. He has his lawyer with him."

Vince took a breath and continued. "Phyllis was questioned as well. She was at a fundraiser at the museum." That must mean the Virginia Museum of Fine Arts, referred to locally as "The Museum." "She was there until ten o'clock."

"What time did Brad call the police?"

"Eleven."

"So Phyllis could have hot-footed it over to Nina's after she left The Museum. And then there are the two women in the green car from Florida—Mrs. Ellbee said they showed up at nine-thirty."

"Yes, well, there's not much to go on yet with them. By the way, the police want to question you about Phyllis. When you get home we can go to headquarters."

"What about the knife? Was it left at the scene?"

"Nope."

"Hmm. Well, that's different from Rox's stabbing."

After ending the call I told Trudy what Vince said. "Was Nina going to sell her house? Is that why Brad was getting it all spruced up for her?"

"I think so. She talked about downsizing. She'd been in that house for about ten years. When she split with her husband he moved to Arizona."

"Were they in touch?"

"Not as far as I know. But that's not very far."

Hmm. An ex made a good suspect. But I told myself to concentrate on the suspects close at hand. At least for the time being.

"Maybe Nina and Brad were going to set up house together," I said.

"Maybe."

"So, Trudy—what about those women in the green car?"

Trudy repeated Vince's statement that there was nothing to go on yet. "Besides, the couple didn't necessarily have anything to do with the murder. They could have arrived before the killer did. Maybe the woman was dropping off something. Or she was a real estate agent."

"Or, how's this?" I spun a different scenario. "The couple gets there *after* the murder. The woman sees Nina lying on the floor, dead. Does Nina have those little windows on the side of her front door?"

"Probably. I do."

"So the woman looks through the windows and panics at what she sees. I know I would. And that could explain her stumbling on the driveway. She wanted to get away from the scene as soon as possible."

"Maybe she wanted to get away because she—or *he*—just killed Nina."

I nodded. "Either way could get a person fleeing."

"If the woman saw Nina dead and ran, wouldn't she have called the police?"

"You'd think so. Unless she didn't want to get involved. Possibly she'll hear about it on the news and come forward then."

"Remember that Nina went to Florida for a while after Rox's funeral. The two women could have been people she knew from there."

"You're right." I chided myself for not thinking of that. "Maybe one was the friend she stayed with."

We fell silent for a moment, considering the possibilities. I asked. "How reliable is Mrs. Ellbee?"

"Oh, probably reliable enough. Granted, she's nosy as all get out and revels in being the center of attention. That's why the neighbors didn't stick around. Get the story, get some free food, get out. But I don't think she makes up stuff."

"Could she be in danger if whoever killed Nina saw her watching?"

"She probably turned out the lights. She's been known to do just that."

When the phone rang Trudy got up to answer it. "Phyllis," she mouthed, unnecessarily. I could hear Phyllis ranting from across the room.

"Phyllis, I didn't 'out' you, as you put it. But your behavior at Panera that day was outrageous. I felt an obligation to tell the police." Phyllis carried on some more until Trudy said, "Phyllis, if you didn't kill Nina you have nothing to worry about."

Obviously Phyllis was using a land line because I definitely heard the phone slam down.

Trudy grimaced. "That Phyllis sure knows how to ratchet up the drama."

Trudy and I continued considering suspects until she had to leave for work. As we parted, I laughed and said, "If we don't watch out, we'll find ourselves drowning in speculation."

SEVENTEEN

VINCE ACCOMPANIED ME downtown to police headquarters where I gave a statement to the detective in charge of Nina's murder, Thomas Fischella. Despite the detective's goofy manner, I knew from Vince that he was as sharp as they came. Many a suspect had learned that too late. I provided all the Nina-related information I had. Whether any of it could nail her killer was anyone's guess.

"Leave the investigating to us," Detective Fischella advised me in parting.

Vince chatted with some of his former colleagues, hoping to pick up more information. Not much yet. Apparently Nina's laptop was missing and presumed stolen. There was an APB out for a green car with Florida plates and "IT" in the plate number. That sounded like the kind of grunt work they'd assign to a rookie cop.

Back at home, I said to Vince, "I wonder if I could have prevented Nina's murder if I'd taken the investigation more seriously. Maybe the book group has been treating this whole thing like a game."

"Hazel, that's a slippery slope. Besides, it's looked to me like you've all been taking this very seriously."

But I wasn't convinced. I resolved to double my efforts and rev up the rest of the group. How I'd do that was another matter—Brad still looked like the culprit and I couldn't come up with a way of finagling a meeting with him.

Did Brad kill Nina? Why would he? Because Nina knew that he killed Rox? Perhaps going in for some blackmail? *Romantic blackmail*—intriguing concept and a possible story premise.

Leaving Brad aside, what could we do to nail the killer or killers? I considered the lunatic—but why would he kill Nina? Because he might have killed Rox and her death was intertwined with Nina's? Not unless we were looking at a killer who specialized in sisters. *Niche killers*. The latest trend in killing? Another twist on the Cain and Abel story.

Using my fingers, I ticked off suspects: Brad, Andy, Evangeline, Foster, and possibly the still-unnamed lunatic. All connected with Rox. And Nina might have killed Rox—but who killed Nina? The police had given no indication that her wounds were self-inflicted. As things stood, Brad and money looked like the common denominators in the sister killings. If Nina was selling her house and moving in with Brad, she might have been pressing him for marriage with his bounty from Rox as a nice fringe benefit. Did Nina have a will? I wondered what its terms were.

I e-mailed the book group, summarizing what I knew of Nina's death. When Patty called she said that on the news they mentioned a car that had Florida plates with an "IT" in the number.

"I heard that as well. One of the neighbors was out walking his dog but he didn't get the license number. Not much to go on."

"I wish Brad wasn't involved in all of this." I pictured Patty wringing her hands in consternation. "First he finds Rox's body and now Nina's."

"Have you talked to him?"

"No, I left a message on his voice mail. The poor man must be devastated." I murmured my agreement as to Brad's possible emotional state and kept my suspicions to myself. Patty said, "Between you and me I always thought Nina was Brad's true love."

Did Patty know that Brad and Nina were back together? It sounded like she didn't.

"Patty, let's reschedule our lunch. I have a doctor's appointment tomorrow. Do you want to go to Frank's on Saturday?" I didn't feel up to going into the details of the follow-up mammogram.

She agreed and I said I'd pick her up. "I'll bring those titles with me, the cozies set in the ancient world."

"Okay, thanks. And let me know about the funeral arrangements. I don't know if Brad will get back to me."

"Will do."

I saw that Kat had left a voice mail asking about Nina.

"This has to be connected with Rox," Kat said once I recounted my morning with the Ellbees and the Richmond Police Department.

"You're right. It's way too coincidental otherwise."

That was the prevailing sentiment of the book group once the responses to my e-mail trickled in. "It just has to be connected," Sarah said. "Let's all go to Nina's funeral. No one has to know that we didn't know her. Not all of us, anyway."

"Yes," Lucy put in. "If anyone asks, we'll say we're there to support Nina's dear friends, Trudy and Eileen."

I wrote, "Let's be on the lookout for anyone from Florida fitting the vague descriptions of the two women. And check the parking lot for Florida plates." It occurred to me that if the women were real estate agents, they might attend the funeral with cards in hand, hoping to find someone to buy Nina's house.

"I'd think that if the women hear about this they'll contact the police," Eileen wrote.

"That's *if* they hear about it," I said. "Maybe they don't keep up with local news."

The e-mails fizzled out. I felt at loose ends and needed to busy myself. Hoping to put mindless activity to good use, I decided to look for Brad's son, Andy, on Facebook. Andy Jones—nothing like an easy task. This was a project better suited to Eileen or Trudy, but I needed the diversion. I didn't know if I should start with Andy's home state of Virginia or his adopted one of Kentucky, but I tossed a mental coin, called tails, and Kentucky came up.

The Andy Jones profiles that appeared featured Andrea Joneses, African-American Andy Joneses, and other Andy Joneses who didn't bear the remotest resemblance to the Andy Jones in the photo that sat atop Patty's bookcase. No one had long dark hair, glasses, or a mustache. But those styles were all changeable. The Andys didn't all provide profile pictures of themselves—many chose to hide their mugs behind those of their pets. Others used cars, motorcycles, rifles, and gardens. Extremely shy folks preferred the Facebook-provided silhouette. Besides Andy, I tried Andrew, Anders, and Anderson. I found the Facebook privacy settings to be another hurdle. Some Andys closely guarded their privacy while others revealed all in sometimes shocking detail.

Vince came into my den and kissed the top of my head. "How are you doing?"

"Not too well. You wouldn't believe how many Andy Joneses there are in Kentucky. I'm about to start on Virginia."

"Why are you looking for him?"

"I'm hoping to find some indication that he was in Virginia in March. And last night. He might have posted something. If I can see his postings, that is."

"The police check social media, you know. Besides, he might not even be on Facebook. Not everyone is."

"Yes, well, *almost* everyone is."

Before starting the Andy-in-Virginia search, I looked at Foster Hayden's Facebook page. I silently thanked him for having a searchable name. A picture of his dinner from the night before in a Richmond eatery proved that he was in the area, but I found no proclamations that he'd killed Nina. Not that I expected any. I couldn't imagine why he would kill her anyway, unless she'd spotted him in the Moonshine Inn parking lot holding a bloody knife over her sister Rox's body.

I returned to the Andy hunt. I didn't fare better in Virginia using the same search terms.

I had to agree with Vince—not everyone was on Facebook.

EIGHTEEN

VINCE AND I arrived at the imaging center on Friday afternoon for my mammogram followup. I checked in and took my clipboard to a seat between Vince and a priest reading his Yahoo e-mail on his tablet. In this digital age, did churchgoers seek counsel for their various life problems and crises of faith via e-mail? I tried, and failed, to resist the urge to peer over his shoulder. He turned and bestowed a beneficent smile on me. Sheepishly, I smiled back and busied myself with my paperwork.

Paperwork completed, I flipped through a *People* magazine. But the highs and lows of celebrities' lives failed to grab my attention. I snuck another look at the priest's tablet. He was firming up plans for a golf outing. So much for the pressing problems of his flock. Vince was involved with his own tablet. In fact, everyone in the waiting area gazed fixedly at their devices so I joined the crowd and pulled out my own phone. I found little to engage me and soon returned to the magazines, looking for articles on turning back the hands of time. I told myself that I looked fine for my age and that Mrs. Ellbee was just jealous. Not surprisingly, that tactic didn't work and I kept on the trail of the fountain of youth.

After fifteen minutes, a large woman with a voice to match announced my name, making me jump. Vince and I exchanged a quick hug and kiss and I was escorted to a dressing room. The large woman told me her name and that she would be my technician. I promptly forgot her name. In a dressing room I donned a cape that was black and short. The usual mammogram garb was a wrap-around smock-like affair in either pastel colors or white with unappealing designs, much like the ones on men's boxer shorts. The technician reappeared and led me to a roomful of women wearing identical black capes. I felt like I was being inducted into a science fiction coven. Was this a movie set? All the scene lacked was a film crew and lights.

The anxiety in the room was so palpable I felt like I could reach out and touch it. One woman had been waiting three hours for her biopsy. The staff explained that they were behind schedule and would be with her shortly. Plus, she murmured that she was starving. Figuring that it was cruel to pile starvation on top of anxiety, I rooted through my bag for a snack. I came up with a Balance bar that the woman accepted gratefully.

Conversations swirled around me. Women shared their diagnoses and prognoses. This medical center provided other services besides breast imaging. Every two years, I had a bone density test here: the most recent one had showed me shrinking in height at an alarming rate; and my neighbor recently had a vascular ultrasound at this center. But my present companions, like myself, anticipated breast-related procedures, like mammograms, biopsies, and ultrasounds.

I picked up the magazine I'd brought in from the waiting room and turned to an article on antioxidants, only to find that someone had ripped out the pages. Nothing else in the periodical piqued my interest, so I took my Kindle out of my bag and tried to engross myself in a mystery for the next book group—assuming we'd even talk about books. We now had two murders to deal with. But I couldn't shut out all the chat, and couldn't concentrate on the story. I suspected it wouldn't hold my interest under any circumstances. I knew I should feel a sisterly bond with these women, but sadly I didn't. I was accustomed to the mammogram process being a quick and solitary experience.

In one corner of the room, a couple of women, well-endowed

in the breast department, railed against the unwelcome attention they had received from men over the years. While they'd enjoyed having men ogle their assets when they were young, over the years they'd come to be repelled by it. One was considering reduction surgery, but her husband was trying to talk her out of it. Having nothing to contribute to that conversation I turned back to my Kindle.

I overheard someone else say that every woman on her family tree had had breast cancer. She was considering following the actress Angelina Jolie's example and having a double mastectomy to significantly lower her chances of becoming a victim of the dreaded disease. Some in the room said it was all well and good for Angelina to choose that option, as she had the resources. But what about middle- and lower-income women? Would the insurance companies cover the procedure for them?

Their conversation gave me an idea, but not related to breast cancer or to Angelina. It was the thing about the family tree. Why hadn't I thought to look up Andy on the chart my sister had sent? That way, I'd have his full legal name. Maybe it wasn't even Andy. I remembered learning during the Carlene Arness investigation that many people used their middle names. Or they renamed themselves, possibly not liking their own names. Or they were running from something—like the law.

Eventually I heard the sweet sound of "Ms. Rose." I stood, relieved to be leaving this hotbed of anxiety. In five minutes I was back in the waiting room, this time fully dressed.

In fifteen minutes a young woman escorted me to the desk of a doctor with a round, beaming face. Like with the technician, I instantly forgot his name. He informed me about the two sites on my left breast that required further investigation. "Investigation" translated to biopsy. They could schedule the procedure in three weeks.

"Three weeks!" I exclaimed in dismay.

"I'm sorry, Ms. Rose, but we're very backed up."

"But *three* weeks?"

He assured me that chances were the biopsy would show no problems. It was simply a precautionary measure. I sighed and made the appointment for exactly three weeks into what looked like an eternity.

On the way out, I said goodbye to my "sisters," wishing them good luck. A couple of them asked how I'd fared. When I said I needed to return for a biopsy, they wished me luck as well.

Vince was sitting in the same chair, finger swiping at his tablet screen. The priest was gone.

Was that an omen?

NINETEEN

TO CHEER ME up, Vince treated me to gelato at Deluca Gelato. Picking a flavor was hard, but the bubbly woman who served us was generous with the samples. I settled on coconut and Vince couldn't choose between pistachio and espresso so he compromised and ended up with both flavors.

"I talked to Dennis earlier," Vince said. "Nina's laptop was stolen—I think I told you that—along with her purse and probably cell phone. The police checked her Verizon e-mail account. Just messages to Brad and people at the Hamlin Group. And you. She didn't pay bills online. Didn't shop online."

"One of those careful people," I noted.

"She also didn't make or receive many calls. They found a few bills, utility and such. She had a MasterCard that was paid off. Plane fare to Florida and restaurants. Nothing unusual."

When I told Vince my insight that Angelina Jolie had unknowingly given me about the family tree, he looked thoughtful for a moment. "Andy's name's in his mother's obit. And I don't think it's Andrew, it's something else."

"Oh, that's right. I forgot about the obit."

Two heads were indeed better than one—depending on the heads, of course.

Back at home, I lost no time fretting about my upcoming biopsy and turned to the Internet for the latest statistics. Nothing had changed in the past four days, there was still that 80 to 90 percent chance that the biopsy would prove benign. But what about the other 10 to 20 percent? I reminded myself that I was an optimist.

Trudy informed the book group by e-mail that Nina's funeral was scheduled for Monday at eleven o'clock at the Lamalle Chapel. She gave us an address in the West End. Sarah almost immediately replied that she had a doctor's appointment scheduled for Monday morning and wouldn't be at the funeral. But she knew we'd be hyper observant.

Remembering that Patty wanted to know about the funeral arrangements, I called her. She sounded like she was writing down the details as I recited them. Had she touched base with Brad?

"No, he hasn't returned my call," she said when I asked.

I found Andy's name in his mother's obit. Alexander M. Jones. Alexander, huh? I hadn't noted that unusual parsing of Andy out of Alexander during my initial perusal of Vince's articles. No matter, I still couldn't find him on Facebook. He didn't appear to have much use for Twitter or LinkedIn either, either as Andy or as Alexander. Thinking that he might use his middle name, I turned to the family tree to see what the "M" signified.

I located the folder labeled "Family Tree" on my hard drive and looked up Andy. Alexander Michael Jones, born February 10, 1973. Again I turned to social media and again social media failed to come through. While the Alexander Michael Jones and Michael Jones names appeared countless times, the ones that interested me remained elusive. If I got desperate I could search out the ones who hid their visages by displaying their pet's photos. But I didn't plan to get that desperate.

• • •

On Saturday, I arrived at Patty's apartment to pick her up for our lunch date. When Patty, clad in white capris and a red knit top, opened the door, we exchanged our usual hugs. I waved a hand at a number of half-full boxes placed around the living room and asked, "Does this mean you *are* going back to Pittsburgh?"

"It does." Patty smiled but I noticed the strain around her eyes. "I didn't realize we had so much stuff."

"It accumulates in the blink of an eye. I hope Vince and I don't have to uproot ourselves. I shudder just thinking what packing up our place would be like."

I noticed a copy of *Greater Tuna* in one of the boxes. I had seen the play years before in New Orleans. Two men played the entire cast of characters, male and female, of various ages. I exclaimed in delight when I saw *The Woman in White* by Wilkie Collins. "I loved *The Woman in White*. I just read it a few months ago."

Patty smiled. "Yes, it's one of my favorites. Have you read *The Moonstone*?"

"No, but it's on my TBR list." When Patty looked askance, I explained, "To Be Read list."

"Hazel, I don't feel that great. Do you mind if we don't go to lunch?"

"Oh no, not at all. Is there anything I can do?"

"No. I'll make some herbal tea and we can sit and chat here."

"Okay. Do you want me to fix the tea? Since you're not feeling well . . . "

"I'm fine, just not up to eating anything. Have a seat." I sank into one of the ugly chairs and Patty stepped into the kitchen for the tea preparations.

"Where's Paul?" I asked.

"Either at the storage unit or the library. He planned to stop at both places."

"Any more news on Nina?" Patty asked after a pause.

I shrugged. "As far as I know, they don't have any suspects. It could be a robbery. Her laptop is missing." I didn't mention Brad. To my knowledge he was the only suspect—at least the only one they could pinpoint. I thought of the two women in the Florida car.

"Oh, I almost forgot—" Patty went to a table by the door and took a folded sheet of paper from her purse. "Here's that medical history you wanted."

I scanned the handwritten list. Aside from Patty's father's cardiac issues and our cousin Marcie dying from pancreatic cancer, deaths on my father's side of the family appeared to be from natural causes. "For the most part our relatives die in their sleep. And at advanced ages."

I nodded. "Good to know. Thanks." When I refolded the sheet and tucked it in my bag I saw the list of cozies set in the ancient world that I'd printed from the online *Cozy Mystery List*. I handed it to Patty.

"Oh, thanks, Hazel. I'll take a look at this later." She placed the printout on the counter that divided the kitchen from the living area.

"So, are you two going to live with Paul's mother?"

Patty nodded. "She's due to leave rehab and won't go to assisted living. Her house isn't conducive to an elderly, frail person. There's just one bathroom and it's on the second floor. There are no handicapped accommodations, like railings and such. But she insists on living there. The place is a mess so she doesn't want any health care there."

So she gets her dear son and daughter-in-law to do her bidding, be her unpaid slaves.

Patty placed a tray laden with a teapot, mugs, and a plate of cookies in front of me.

"So it would help Mom to have someone there," Patty said as she poured tea. "And she's such a nice lady." One corner of Patty's mouth tightened, belying her words. Patty's mother-in-law sounded like a self-centered shrew to me. Would a "nice lady" expect her son and his wife to uproot themselves? Granted, the two hadn't really settled down in Richmond. Still.

Did Patty and Paul have financial difficulties? This tiny apartment. Even if the place was meant to be temporary, I felt sure they could afford something bigger. Patty must have a good pension from her years of teaching. And Paul—I still didn't know what he'd done for a living. Maybe they were big spenders—or had been, until reduced circumstances forced them to cut back. And reduced circumstances could be driving the decision to take care of Mom, especially if Mom was providing free room and board.

An uncomfortable pause followed. I sensed that Patty left whole paragraphs out of her account. But it was their business.

"So when are you two actually leaving?"

"Tuesday, right after the truck's loaded up."

"Truck?"

"Paul's brother from Pittsburgh is coming down with his truck."

Why couldn't the brother care for the mother? Likely one of those inexplicable family deals. Maybe the son and/or his wife had more backbone. Aloud I said, "Oh. I thought you'd wait until the end of the month. Isn't your rent paid through then?"

"We'd hoped to stay until then, but Mom's getting out of rehab sooner than we thought, so we had to move things up a bit. But we'll be back to visit. And you can visit us."

I didn't see that happening. We hadn't sufficiently bonded. And from all appearances, she and Brad weren't close enough to bring them back here to visit him. "Have you told Brad?"

She looked startled almost like she was thinking "Brad? Who's he?" Then she collected herself. "Not yet." She looked down at her steaming mug. "We'll be at the funeral on Monday. It's the least we can do for Nina."

"Vince and I will see you there."

Patty looked puzzled. "I didn't realize you knew Nina well enough to attend her funeral."

"I'm friends with her neighbors, Trudy and Eileen. We're going to support them."

"And I guess Vince is going to see if the killer shows up. Isn't that what they do? But Vince is retired, isn't he?"

"Yes, but he's going with me. I imagine the detectives in charge of the investigation will be there."

"Well, I'll miss our lunches," I said after a couple of beats. In truth, I felt relieved, but decency dictated that I express regret. Much as I'd enjoyed meeting a newfound family member, I didn't really find Patty interesting, and more often than not our conversations were tough going. We had little in common beyond our love of books. That was something, but not enough.

"Me too," Patty agreed. I wondered if she felt as relieved about the end of our lunches as I did.

"Maybe you'll find a book group in Pittsburgh. Or you can start your own."

She looked alarmed at my suggestion. Was starting a book

group that daunting? How does one reach her age without developing some initiative? Or self-confidence? What kind of English teacher had she been? In my experience, teachers in general had take-charge personalities. And she'd taught high school English for many years, probably needing the hide of a rhinoceros to endure those challenging adolescents. How had she coped? Unless she harbored a facet of her personality reserved for her students.

Patty stood. "I want to take a look at this reading list you gave me." She grabbed the printout from the kitchen counter and returned to her chair.

"Oh, Lindsay Davis—I've heard about her." As we discussed the titles and authors on the list Patty's face and shoulders visibly relaxed—she was clearly more at ease than she had been when talking about Paul, her mother-in-law, and the apparently alarming notion of starting a book group. That's what going back to the ancient world will do. No wonder some people liked to live in the past.

But this investigation had me rooted in the present so I couldn't tarry in antiquity for long. "Can I ask you something about Marcie?"

When Patty nodded, I went on. "I'm curious about her decision. I just read about a former college classmate who became a teacher and then founded a chain—franchise, I guess—of gyms. So I wondered what prompted Marcie's decision to become a stockbroker?"

"Money, I guess. And she had a bad experience with her early investments, so she educated herself about investing. That led her to becoming a stockbroker."

"Tell me, maybe you told me this before . . ." She hadn't said anything before about what I was about to ask, so that was for form. "Did Marcie go to any of the major cancer centers, like Sloan-Kettering, or Duke?"

"No, she didn't." Did I catch a flash of anger in Patty's usually mild eyes? If so, the flash was truly a flash and disappeared as quickly as it appeared.

"Just wondered." That prompt netted me nothing.

Patty picked up the teapot to freshen our mugs. But instead of the tea landing in my mug, it flooded the cookies and splashed on the legs of my slacks.

Patty profusely apologized and stood wringing her hands. I assured her that it was all right, accidents happened, and dashed to the kitchen for paper towels. A large carton of newspaper-wrapped items took up most of the space in the small kitchen. My own moving experiences had taught me that smaller boxes were much more manageable than large ones.

Back in the living area, Patty and I mopped up the spill. I regarded the tea stain on my slacks. Normally I wore dark colors but that day, as luck would have it, I'd chosen a lighter palette. Obviously, a return home was in order before I continued with my errands. I laughed to myself at the unlikelihood of being involved in two beverage incidents in less than two weeks. Of course, Patty's spill didn't match the drama of Phyllis's flinging Nina's coffee in her face.

"I'm so sorry, Hazel. I don't know how I missed your mug like that. I guess I'm . . . well, I'm kind of discombobulated. Moving always does this to me."

"Oh, I totally understand. Moving's the worst. You should have seen me when Vince and I moved in together." Actually, our move hadn't been that bad, but Patty needed empathy. Plus I intuited that moving in with her mother-in-law wasn't an item on her bucket list.

As I prepared to leave, it occurred to me that I should do something for Patty and Paul, not just let them go off. But I really didn't relish time alone with them. Even with Vince present, the conversations weren't enjoyable. And so I found myself saying, "Come over tomorrow night. We'll invite some friends over for barbecue. Let's say . . . five o'clock?"

"Oh. Well . . . okay. Thanks." She smiled.

Now I'd have to rustle up some people. And food.

TWENTY

AT HOME I changed clothes and grabbed a quick lunch before tackling my impromptu guest list. Vince invited his former partner Dennis Mulligan and his wife, but they couldn't make it. Lucy, Dave, and Kat could. I suggested that Kat bring Demetrios, the lover who had her all aflutter, but she said he was out of town.

I spent the rest of the day running errands, including buying items for the next day's do. I came home with fixings for hamburgers, all-beef hot dogs, salads, chips, buns, drinks, and so on.

On Sunday Kat called. "Is it okay if I bring Tammy? You know, my step-mom? I guess she's still my step-mom." Kat's father had died the year before and Kat remained close with his widow.

"Sure."

"She has some information about Nina and Brad that you might find useful. But since Patty's Brad's cousin, we don't want to mention it when she's there. So can we arrive a little early?"

"Of course. But Patty called and said they'd be five or ten minutes late."

"Great. Oh, and a word of warning. Tammy never stops talking. *Never.* She'll hog the conversation."

"That's okay. If she has useful information she can talk all she wants."

Lucy and Dave arrived first. "I know we're early, but I thought you might need some help," Lucy said.

"We brought baked beans," Dave indicated the pot he carried. "Vegetarian."

"One of Dave's specialties," Lucy added. "They're really good."

Dave was a handsome man with dark hair showing gray at the temples. His warm brown eyes and ready smile lit up a room, to coin an oft-used phrase. I knew he was ten years younger than Lucy but her youthful appearance made the age difference unnoticeable.

"I'll put these in the kitchen," Dave said as the doorbell rang. Kat and Tammy.

It took a moment for my eyes to adjust to Kat's hot pink top and prison-orange capris. Tammy stood out as well, with her neon pink lipstick, matching nails, and hair sculpted into short white spikes that didn't so much as quiver.

After rapid-fire introductions, Kat said, "Tammy wants to tell you her story before Patty and Paul get here."

Tammy started. "I heard about poor Nina. I find it most interesting that Brad was married to Rox and apparently was the one who found Nina."

"Yes, it *is* interesting," I agreed.

"Vero's mother and my mother went to the same hairdresser for years. On the same day, at the same time. Vero's mother hated Brad. So did Vero, for that matter. She even went to a different dentist."

"Oh, I forgot that Brad was a dentist," Lucy said.

"Nina said that's how she first met Brad. He was her dentist." I waved my hand at Tammy. "Go on, Tammy. You were going to tell us something about Vero."

"Wait"—Lucy held up her hand—"Who's Vero?"

"Veronica Jones, Brad's first wife," Tammy said.

After Tammy described Vero's death by drowning, I asked, "So, why did Vero and her mother hate Brad?"

"He was unfaithful. He had flings with his patients. His

hygienist walked in on him once. He and his patient were 'doing it' right in the chair."

"Talk about uncomfortable," Lucy commented.

Kat's bawdy laugh filled the room. "Did the patient still have that paper bib clipped to her?"

Was Nina the patient who had benefitted from Brad's bedside manner? Years earlier, I had read a Susan Isaacs tale of a dentist who not only preyed on his female patients but took photos of them while they were asleep in his chair. Did Brad carry sleaziness that far? If so, he'd better watch out—Ms. Isaacs's fictional dentist ended up dead.

"One of his conquests turned into a long-term fling," Tammy said. "The hygienist told Vero about everything that went on." Again, I thought of Nina.

"Why did Vero stay with him?" Kat asked.

Tammy waved a hand. "Despite all her education, Vero had no interest in supporting herself. I don't think the woman worked a day in her life."

The peal of the doorbell cut off further discussion. "That's Patty and Paul," I stage whispered, unnecessarily.

"Well, I pretty much finished with what I had to say, anyway," Tammy said.

Patty and Paul Ratzenberger both greeted me with a kiss on the cheek. Paul combed his white hair straight back with no part, like some of the Fox News anchors.

Sunday's steamy weather made staying indoors for the festivities more appealing than going out on the patio. Vince tended the grill and chatted with Paul and Dave. From the few words I caught, I gathered they were discussing Nina's murder.

In stereotypical fashion, the women stayed indoors and set the bowls of salad and condiments on the large dining room table. The chatty Tammy gushed over the soft green theme of the dining room.

I smiled. "When we first saw this house, Vince said the whole interior matched my eyes."

Green prevailed throughout, especially in the dining room with its mint-green wrought iron furniture and floral wallpaper. I thought back to decades before when school blackboards gave way to "greenboards," the restful and refreshing color expected to enhance learning. I had no idea if the expectation was met, but greenboards had to be easier on the eyes.

"Speaking of green eyes," Tammy said, "Hazel and Patty look so much alike around the eyes."

At that moment the men burst through the door, laden with platters of grilled meat, cutting off commentary about the family resemblance between me and Patty.

During dinner, Tammy regaled us with anecdotes involving her two greyhound rescues. She made a number of impassioned speeches on the importance of rescuing animals. My attempts to get the other guests talking were overpowered by the relentless Tammy who had an endless supply of dog-related stories to share. I made brief eye contact with Kat, her lips arranged in a Mona Lisa smile. I remembered her warning about Tammy, but since she'd provided potentially useful information about Brad and Nina, I overlooked her nonstop chatter. We wedged into the conversation occasional compliments on the deliciousness of the food, especially Dave's vegetarian beans.

When I presented the cake I'd bought for Patty and Paul, everyone exclaimed, asking them about their plans. About all they managed was "We're going back to Pittsburgh." Tammy grabbed the opportunity to tout the Steel City Greyhounds, a Pittsburgh area rescue organization dedicated to finding homes for the animals no longer deemed fit for racing.

"So, is Nina's funeral tomorrow?" Kat asked when Tammy finally paused.

"Yes, tomorrow," I confirmed.

"Anyone here going?"

"Vince and I are. And Patty and Paul." I waited for someone to comment about the funeral. When no one did, I smiled and asked, "So—anyone seen any good movies lately?" Still trying to include them in the conversation I turned to Patty and Paul and asked, "How about you two?" But my cousins hadn't seen a movie in five years so it wasn't long before Tammy, who apparently binge-watched movies, listed and fully described her own favorites.

As everyone was leaving, I said to Patty and Paul, who'd been virtually mute throughout the evening, "I guess I'll see you two tomorrow."

. . .

"Vince, I've decided that Brad killed Nina. And that both of them killed Rox."

Vince looked amused. "You've said that before, more than once. Why so adamant about it now?" Guests gone, cleanup done, Vince and I relaxed in the family room with Morris.

"The way I figure it is this: Brad and Nina wanted to get back together. Brad only married Rox for the money she might have got from Marcie. Nina wanted to kill Rox to get back at her for marrying Brad. And Brad and Nina were always actually an item, probably had this plot brewing for years. But maybe Nina got too demanding and Brad didn't want to share his wealth. Maybe Nina even blackmailed him. So he killed her."

"Could be. But, like I said, we've gone over all this before."

"Don't the police ask suspects the same questions over and over?"

Vince laughed and allowed that repetition often worked because the police might get different answers to the same questions. "The police still think it was Brad. It may look like him, but we don't have proof."

"Don't forget, he may have killed before. Remember his first wife?" I ran down Tammy's tale about the philandering Brad with a wife who loathed him. "It's not a good idea to be married to Brad. Or hope to be, considering Nina's fate." I admonished myself to presume the man innocent until proven guilty.

Vince let me go on airing my views. "It'll be interesting to finally lay eyes on the man."

"But you've seen pictures of him, haven't you?"

"Yes, he has a website." I recalled Brad's smile—a smile that didn't reach his hard-as-marbles eyes. A rictus really. But the smile allowed him to advertise his even white teeth, promising a similar look to anyone who walked into his office.

"I haven't seen an obituary for Nina," I said. "I've been on the lookout but all I've seen is the article about her murder."

"Possibly no one had any information. Brad may not have known much about her. And they're expensive now, too."

"Brad could spring for an obit." I fumed at the injustice of the poor woman exiting the world obit-less.

"She didn't have much family, did she?" Vince asked.

"No, she didn't. She mentioned some distant cousins. That's it, unless Nina forgot about some of her relatives."

"So what did you guys talk about outside?" I asked.

"The investigation, what else? Dave and Paul asked about it. They probably thought I knew all about it, being a true crime writer and still with close ties to the force and all, and that I was being tight-lipped. But there's little to tell at this point."

Later, I sat up in bed reading *Aristotle Detective* by Margaret Doody. I'd given up on the one I'd labored to read at the imaging center. Morris stretched out on my lap and I propped up my Kindle on him. The famed philosopher Aristotle becomes a reluctant investigator when one of his trainees needs to defend a family member suspected of murder. I identified with Aristotle—not with being a famed philosopher, but as a reluctant investigator. It would be interesting to see how much book discussion went on the next night.

Vince watched something on PBS with his headset so as not to disturb me. My mind wandered to the cruise Vince and I had taken a few years before—we sailed from Istanbul to Athens, and stopped at a number of islands in between. My musing made me want to return to Greece and visit the places we'd missed, but the thought of my upcoming biopsy rudely broke into my reverie.

I started praying.

TWENTY-ONE

ON MONDAY MORNING Vince and I got gussied up for Nina's funeral. For me, that meant my *femme fatale* outfit—a fitted black suit that I was proud to still be able to wear. Vince wore a navy blue suit that brought out the color of his already blue eyes. He secured his burgundy striped tie with a sapphire pin I'd given him for our fifth anniversary. Too bad the temperature and barometer readings weren't a good match for our finery.

"When we die, let's do it in better weather and not put our mourners through this misery."

Vince snickered. "I'll keep that in mind."

The parking lot of the funeral home was half full, more than I'd expected. I knew that Nina didn't have much family but I had no idea how many friends she had. As I got out of the car I muted my phone.

A somber undertaker greeted us at the entrance to the chapel and invited us to sign the guest register. I signed for myself and Vince, noting the tasteful arrangements of flowers and candles on the table with the register. In fact the whole place was tasteful with its intimate furniture groupings in restful peaches and soft greens. A box of tissues topped each table. I scanned the page of the register, seeing several familiar names, including those of Nina's neighbors.

Inside the chapel an older woman pounded on the keys of an organ, putting her whole body into the effort. A closed coffin blanketed with multi-colored flowers presided over rows of tufted pink chairs.

Vince and I planned to sit in one of the back rows so we could see everyone. Several people waved and I waved back. I saw Sandy and Nichole from the Hamlin Group. Nichole turned her nose up at me. I recognized Mrs. Ellbee and Carl in funeral-appropriate garb, not pink sweats or Moody Blues shirts. On second glance, I realized that Mrs. Ellbee sported black sweats, tastefully accessorized with pearls.

Patty and Paul sat in the front row next to two men. I recognized one of the men when he turned and did a double-take when he saw me. If looks could kill—well, I'd be in a convenient place. He stood and bore down on us. None other than my dear cousin, Brad Jones. He wasn't flashing his pearly whites as he'd done for his website photo, but it was him all right. Brown eyes blazed in a face as red as an overripe tomato. The redness extended to his scalp, visible through his brush cut.

"Out!" He pointed at the door.

"Excuse me?" I looked him in the eye.

"Out!" He thundered. "It's your doing. It's completely *your* doing and I want you out of here!"

Honestly, the man wasn't even a blood relative of Nina's. But apparently they were in short supply. I stood my ground in my too-high heels (not that high by today's standards, about three inches—but at this juncture in my life span, anything over an inch was tantamount to stilts).

"Is there a problem, Mr. Jones?" The undertaker approached in his smooth-as-butter voice.

Brad ignored him and repeated his demand that I make my exit. "Get out! You've no business here. It's your fault that she's dead."

Vince touched my arm. "Let's go."

Brad shook his finger dangerously close to my face. "You killed her. If it wasn't for your meddling—"

I could feel twenty-five or so pairs of eyes glued on us. We could have been actors in a play. I lowered my voice, trying to defuse the situation. "Brad, I'm sorry for your loss, but perhaps we could discuss this privately?"

Brad went on as if I hadn't spoken. "You couldn't keep your nose out of our affairs. You had to investigate my wife's murder, probably hoping to get money—"

A man who had been hovering interrupted Brad's rant. "Mr. Jones, that's enough." I recognized him as Detective Fischella, the one who had earlier taken my statement. He'd abandoned his goofy manner for a stern one.

I felt like shushing the detective. Something interesting could come out of Brad's considerable rage. "Brad, I'm not investigating anything. I'm a writer. A romance writer."

Was his snort of derision a commentary on my writing? I doubted that he knew it firsthand. If I had to depend on men for my sales I'd be doomed from the get-go. Likely anything I did nettled Brad.

"According to Nina, you were making so-called discreet inquiries. Well, we all know how discreet you are *not*! You killed Nina!" He stepped closer to me.

"Mr. Jones," Vince said as he stepped between Brad and me. He used what I called his cop voice, a voice he reserved for criminals and unruly citizens. As I didn't live in that world, I had rarely heard that hard-edged, no-nonsense voice. Brad backed off, but still fumed.

"Let's go, Hazel." Vince took my arm.

"Again, our condolences, Brad," I said as I turned to leave. I wanted to add a sarcastic "Nice to meet you, *cousin*." But so far in this unfortunate exchange I'd maintained a semblance of dignity and didn't want to stoop to Brad's level.

"And keep your nose out of our business. Let the police do their jobs."

I felt tempted to say that Nina hadn't thought much of the job the police were doing, but as the police were present, I kept that rejoinder to myself and let Brad have the last word.

But that wasn't his last word. "I said to Nina, 'Let the police handle things.' And they did. They have. They are." I let Brad work out his tenses.

I'd managed to hold my own and remain calm, but by the time we reached the car I shook like the temperature had dropped fifty degrees.

"The nerve of that man. The unmitigated *gall*."

Vince shook his head. "He certainly has it in for you."

I gave a short laugh. "You think?"

"Well, to use an old cliché, every cloud has a silver lining. At least we don't have to endure an interment service in this weather."

"True. On the other hand, we're missing out on the funeral lunch. And the chance to observe people."

"Don't worry. Tom Fischella is a good observer."

"I'm sure he is, but he's a *cop* observer. Not . . . not a *regular* person observer. I mean—" I saw Vince's amused look. "Oh, you know what I mean."

"I do. But some of your book group people are there. And they're 'regular people observers,' as you put it."

"I didn't even see any of them. Once Brad started in on me . . . " I huffed and shook my head. "But you're right, they'll do a great job. But I wanted to do my own observing."

"It's the control freak in you," Vince said as he pulled me close and kissed me on the forehead. "Let's go and have our own lunch."

• • •

We picked Mosaic's for lunch. "Do you think the funeral proceedings got back on track?" I asked after our orders were taken.

"Oh sure. Those kinds of outbursts aren't unusual at funerals. I've seen fistfights. Emotions run high." Vince knew what he was talking about. As a former detective he'd attended many funerals. Cops did that because often the killer showed up and revealed himself or herself in some covert way. Sometimes even overt.

Vince continued. "That funeral director is a pro at getting things back on track. They all are."

"Did they ever find the knife that killed Nina?"

"No, but the medical examiner guesses it was a standard kitchen knife."

The server delivered my chicken salad and Vince's turkey burger.

"What's with Brad anyway?" Vince asked. "What's he got against you? It can't just be that he thinks you want his money."

"No, he's way too intense."

"He's hiding something that he's afraid you'll figure out."

"Yeah, that he's Nina's killer. He's trying to hide that he killed Nina and he wants to take any attention off of himself and put it on me." I sniffed. "I've never in my life been accused of killing someone. I hope I didn't say something that put Nina in danger." I reviewed my conversations. "At the Hamlin Group, Nina was there so of course she was mentioned. At the Moonshine people referred to Nina, but not by name, and I certainly didn't say anything about her. That leaves Evangeline, Maisie, and Foster. I don't know if Lucy used Nina's name but I'm almost positive I didn't."

"Hmm." Vince looked lost in thought. "Brad's problem with you might not be about murder—maybe it does have to do with money."

"Well, he *is* focused on money, that's for sure. And he's determined that I'm out to part him from his. The man doth protest too much, methinks." Not being an expert on Shakespeare I couldn't say which of his plays included this oft-quoted line. I felt lucky to know the quote well enough to paraphrase it. But my point was that Brad was doing much protesting.

"Hazel, you need to stay away from Brad. He's dangerous. Who knows who he'll go after next?"

"Well, there are no more sisters—"

"Hazel, this isn't funny."

"No, it isn't. I'm sorry. But I *am* staying away from Brad. Today's the first time I've laid eyes on him. And he's probably all hot air anyway."

"It wasn't hot air that killed the two sisters. Or Brad's wife."

"I won't be bullied."

"Hazel, this isn't an opportunity for you to prove how strong you are."

"I'm always with someone. I've been quite good about that."

If only I'd honored that promise.

Lucy's call interrupted the waitperson's litany of Mosaic's

dessert selections. "Are you okay?" she asked. When I assured her that the only danger I faced was being lured into dessert, she laughed. "You know that under normal circumstances we would have left the funeral with you, don't you?"

"Yes, but I expected you to stay and be on the lookout. Plus you have to go to the lunch."

"Right. That's where we're headed now, to Brad's house. We were just concerned you might think we deserted you."

I felt touched by their concern for my feelings. "Thanks for telling me that."

"See you later at book group. My house, remember."

I passed on dessert, thinking ahead to the inevitable concoction that Lucy would serve. Vince decided that he didn't need dessert either. I suspected that he had his mind on the ice cream stash in our freezer.

For the first time since arriving in the restaurant I took a moment to survey the décor. "I haven't been here for a while. It's all changed." Blown glass light fixtures shaped like exotic sea creatures hung from the ceiling, and decorative plates lined the walls. "Very pretty."

Vince followed my gaze and offered an "Uh huh" of agreement.

When we got home I silenced my phone and made feeble attempts to work on my writing, but felt bombarded by distracting thoughts. At three o'clock I gave up, switched the phone back to sound mode, and saw that I had a voice mail message.

Trudy said, "Hi Hazel. I'm glad you survived your little exchange with Brad. We just finished with the lunch. Will catch up tonight."

Two seconds later, Patty called. "I'm so sorry about Brad. He wasn't very nice to you."

I almost laughed out loud at her understatement. Instead, I tried to inject some compassion into my voice. "I suppose he was stressed." There. I could wield the understatements with the best of them.

"Hazel," Patty started, sounding tentative, "I didn't know you investigated murders."

I gave a short laugh. "I don't. I think I told you that Nina wanted to hire a PI. I don't know how Brad got the idea that I was the PI."

"But later, at the lunch, Brad said you investigated another murder."

I explained. "Years ago, someone in our book group was killed. I happened to stumble across the killer."

"That sounds scary."

"It was."

"Oh, Hazel, please be careful," Patty's voice trembled. "I don't want anything to happen to you."

I laughed to lighten the mood. "I can assure you that I'm being careful, Patty. I'm not doing anything and I can't get more careful than that." Wanting to leave the subject, I asked, "Are you still planning on leaving tomorrow?"

"Yes, we are." Patty sounded distracted. "Oh, I hope you don't mind that I gave Andy your phone number. He feels so bad about how Brad behaved."

"That's fine." I hid my elation at the prospect of talking to Andy. "Was he there today?"

"Yes, he was. I'm sorry you didn't get to meet him. Oh, hang on a second, Hazel." Two seconds later Patty returned. "Our landlady's at the door. I'll talk to you later."

• • •

My editor had sent my manuscript along with a letter that started out with "Great story, love it, etc. However . . . " and went on to list a number of suggestions to enhance the "great story." She thought an additional scene at the end between two lovers who decided to go their separate ways would provide closure for the reader. I rolled my eyes at the overused "closure" but, as always, I thought her ideas sound ones.

By late afternoon, I saw that I had another voice mail. The call must have come in when I stepped outside to get the mail. "Hi, Hazel. This is your cousin, Andy Jones. Brad's son. Look, I'm sorry about how my dad acted today. Guy can be such a hothead!" He rattled off a number in a low, seductive voice. I called him and left a return voice mail.

The phone tag had begun.

TWENTY-TWO

DAVE OPENED THE door when I arrived at Lucy's house for book group. I had a key but thought I should knock, especially since the couple were still newlyweds of sorts, having tied the knot less than a year before.

"Hi, Hazel," Dave said as we bussed cheeks. "You're the first one here."

"I have to check out the morning room," I said as I walked towards the back of the house.

"Yes, Purple Rain," Dave quipped. I assumed he referred to the song of the same name made famous by Prince.

Lucy had recently redecorated the morning room with purple flowered chintz. What was chintz, anyway? I called all flowered cloth *chintz*. The original rattan grouping remained. Plants hung from the ceiling and sat atop tables. The many windows looked out on a yard abundant with plants and colorful annuals. Two cats perched on the wide window ledges. I wouldn't have made the purple rain connection as the color didn't overpower the mostly white room, but likely musical connections came naturally to Dave.

When I'd moved from Los Angeles to Richmond in 2000

Lucy had said "Stay with me for a while." The "while" turned into nearly six years, and if not for marrying Vince and buying a house with him, Lucy and I might still be housemates.

I didn't arrive on the East Coast by myself—Shammy, my beautiful calico cat, accompanied me. Daisy, a charcoal and white domestic shorthair, had lived happily with Lucy for a few years before Shammy and I came on the scene. After an iffy initiation, Daisy and Shammy settled down and got along amazingly well—for the most part.

When Vince and I married I found it wrenching to give up Shammy but I didn't want to break up the pair. And I visited often so got to spend time with my old friend.

Lucy, looking cool in a blue linen sheath, appeared as the doorbell rang. Sarah, Trudy, and Eileen arrived at once and poured into the morning room, alarming the cats who scrammed for safer haven.

We all oohed and aahed over Lucy's redecorating success before getting down to business. At the present stage business meant a rehash and update of the day's happenings. For Sarah's benefit we recapped the funeral dramatics, starting with my exile from the chapel.

Sarah looked at me and repeated Vince's earlier comment. "Brad really has it in for you."

"Yeah, I can picture him with a voodoo doll that looks remarkably like me."

"What's with him, anyway?"

"I overheard him telling Paul that he 'wants nothing to do with that woman!' I somehow thought the woman was Hazel." Lucy looked at me and smiled as she said this.

"I'm sure. Unless he has hostile feelings toward a number of women. I wouldn't doubt it."

"Seriously, be careful of him. He may have killed Rox and Nina—and don't forget his wife who drowned. We don't know if he had a hand in that death as well. And he's so angry at you."

"Lucy's right," Eileen put in. "The guy's a loose cannon. But maybe we shouldn't be scaring poor Hazel."

Trudy piped up, "But if he was planning to kill Hazel, why would he act the way he did today? Talk about being a prime suspect."

Lucy raked her layered hair with her perfectly manicured burgundy nails. "He isn't rational."

I waved my hand back and forth. "I don't care to have my demise discussed like I'm not here. But you're right, I need to be careful. As do we all. But tell Sarah more about the funeral. And I don't know what happened after I left."

"Brad settled down and we didn't hear a peep out of him until the service was over," Trudy said. "He didn't even give a eulogy. He got Eileen and me to do it. Asked us the minute we arrived in the chapel. We didn't mind but it would've been nice to have had some advance notice. We did our best."

"They were very nice eulogies," Lucy assured them.

"The poor woman had to have a eulogy," Sarah said.

I agreed, adding, "Especially since she didn't have an obit."

"It was kind of tough because we didn't know her well at all." Trudy grinned. "I think Eileen made up stuff as she went along."

"Well, I barely knew the woman," Eileen said. "Trudy saw her more because she walks Millie right past Nina's house."

"And I only saw her once or twice a year, if that," Trudy said. "She wasn't an outdoorsy person."

Neighborhoods were funny. My own neighbors were a friendly lot but I rarely saw them. Nowadays so many people had gardeners, and homeowners didn't venture outside as much.

"Did you see any possibilities for the two women in the green car?" I asked.

Trudy, Eileen, and Lucy looked at each other and shrugged. "It was hard to tell," Lucy began. "Those descriptions are so vague and could apply to almost anyone. There were a couple of women with white hair—"

"We saw a tall woman, five-seven or so, with longish hair, flat on top." Eileen patted the top of her head. "And she wore heels."

"No trouble walking in them, though," Trudy said. "But we didn't see two women together who fit the descriptions that Mrs. Ellbee gave us." Lucy and Eileen agreed.

"Lucy, did Brad know you were my cousin?"

"He didn't know it from me. I didn't talk to him much beyond the 'sorry for your loss' type of thing. He was distracted, dismissive."

"If he thought you and Hazel were related, he'd probably have ordered you off the premises as well," Eileen noted with a smirk.

We fell to analyzing Brad's bizarre behavior, but we didn't get any further than Vince and I had at lunch. We maintained our belief that Brad probably killed Nina as well as her sister and he was happy to have the police declare it a cold case due to lack of proof.

"Apparently he thinks quite highly of Hazel's skills if he's that afraid that she'll come up with the proof."

I rolled my eyes. "All because Nina told him about Carlene."

"And then money's a recurrent theme with him," Sarah said. "He thinks you're after his. He's clearly paranoid."

"What really bothers me is what he said about me being the cause of Nina's death. I've been racking my brain trying to remember if I said something to put her in danger, but I can't come up with anything."

Lucy nodded. "I can't either. But I only talked to Foster and I'm pretty sure I didn't say anything about Nina, didn't even mention her name."

"I may have mentioned her with Maisie, but only in passing," I said. "And I don't see her killing Nina. Do you, Sarah?"

"Absolutely not."

"So I guess it was just Brad mouthing off," I concluded. "Still, it's unnerving to be accused of being the cause of someone's death."

"Eileen and I had an interesting chat with one of Nina's old friends. If we ever hear that Brad was murdered, this woman would be the likely culprit. She sure raked him over the coals."

When Trudy paused, I made a "go on" motion. "At some point, Nina got pregnant. I think this was some time ago, maybe in the late eighties. Nina didn't want her mom to know, so this friend went with her to have an abortion. Apparently Brad was the father, and Nina had been sure that he would leave his wife and marry her, especially when she got pregnant. According to the friend—I can't for the life of me remember her name—can you, Eileen?"

Eileen shook her head ruefully and Trudy continued. "Apparently, Brad wasn't keen on leaving his wife and making an honest woman out of Nina. So Nina threatened to tell his wife. That got her a black eye. Nina's friend pleaded with her not to say anything to Brad's wife. As far as she knows, Nina never did. Maybe the black eye scared her into backing off."

Eileen took up the tale. "Even though Nina eventually married—and divorced—she still pined for Brad. Her friend said she wouldn't have been surprised if Nina carried on with Brad behind hubby's back."

"And then," Trudy put in, "Almost the minute Brad's poor wife drowns, Brad marries Rox. Then she's killed and Brad goes running back to Nina."

"Sheesh," I said when Trudy finished. "And Nina claimed, more than once, that Brad was 'such a nice man.'"

"He's clearly a bully," Sarah said. "You told us about his threatening Evangeline."

"True. I was a little doubtful about some of her claims, but at this juncture I think she was telling the truth."

"Hazel, what about what Tammy said last night?" Lucy asked.

"Oh, yes. You tell them, Lucy."

Lucy detailed the conversation of the night before with the loquacious Tammy's tale of the Veronica-Brad-Nina triangle.

"Ew," Eileen screwed up her face. "The guy's a real sleaze."

"Didn't Susan Isaacs write something about a dentist servicing his patients?" Sarah asked. I had thought the same thing when Tammy regaled us the night before.

"*Compromising Positions*," Trudy supplied the name. "It was a movie as well."

"So, Hazel, Patty and Paul are moving back to Pittsburgh to care for Paul's mother?" Lucy asked.

"Yes. They're leaving tomorrow."

"Too bad," Sarah said. "Just when you were getting to know her." Had I gotten to know her? I felt like I knew little more than when we first met.

"She called me this afternoon, apologizing for Brad. And you'll never guess who else called." When no one hazarded a guess, I mimed a game show host. "Andy! He called and left a voice mail, also apologizing about Brad. I called him back but had to leave a voice mail."

"Phone tag," Eileen joked. "What else did he say?"

"Nothing. Just left his number."

"We met Andy today," Trudy said. "He came in from Kentucky. Didn't get to chat though. I really wanted to get something out of him, but lots of people were trying to talk to him."

"Well, I hope he calls back. Maybe I can get something out of him. Since he apologized for Brad, I'm guessing he doesn't share his father's hostility towards me. So, was he sitting with Brad at the chapel?"

"Yes, right next to him in the front row. Short hair, tan suit."

I nodded. "I saw him. The back of him, that is. I was expecting long hair." I described the picture in Patty's apartment.

"He's quite charming," Lucy said. "Maybe his mother was charming."

"Assuming that personalities are inherited," I said.

"Let's leave that question to the nature-vs.-nurture experts," Eileen said as she took a sheet of paper from a manila folder by her purse. "I have some information on Evangeline."

We gave Eileen our attention and she began. "Evangeline Goudreau was born in 1962, graduated from VCU in 1984, and has held various accounting jobs over the years. She went to the Hamlin Group in 1993—"

I broke in. "I didn't realize she'd been there that long. And Rox just up and fires her?"

"Hazel, employers stopped being loyal years ago," Trudy gave me a rueful smile. "Employees too, for that matter."

I shook my head. "Yes, but still."

"And she's not a CPA," Eileen continued. "At least, not according to the American Institute of CPAs."

"Well, I don't think anyone said she was a CPA," I said.

Lucy put in her knowledge as an employment counselor. "Many employers don't require their accountants to be CPAs. If she could use a computerized accounting program, she could get a job in the field."

Eileen turned a page of her notes and read: "Evangeline has lived in the same house all her life. Her parents purchased it in 1960. Her mother served on the board of the Parent and Child Foundation for many years."

"Hmm," Sarah mused. "They're very pro-life."

I snapped my fingers. "That's it! Evangeline had an abortion. Her mother would throw her out of the house if she knew.

Disinherit her as well. And Evangeline says she's mean. So I'm thinking that Evangeline told Rox about the abortion over a glass of wine and Rox, knowing dear old mom's pro-life leanings, threatened to tell her all about her daughter's deed."

"Hazel, your writer's imagination is running amok," Lucy said. "But you may be on to something."

"But if Evangeline was born in 1962 she's what, fifty-one now? This alleged abortion probably happened some time ago. Would her mother still get up in arms about it?"

"Yes, Sarah, she could," Trudy said. "If she's very committed to the pro-life cause, it wouldn't matter how long ago it happened."

"Nichole might know," I said. "But I'd have to get back in her good graces to find out. And she might not tell me if Evangeline told her in confidence."

"Still, we're speculating." Trudy looked thoughtful. "What about embezzlement? Evangeline could have helped herself to some funds."

"Would she be dumb enough to tell her boss about it?" Sarah's brows came together.

Trudy shrugged. "Maybe after enough glasses of wine."

"Now that Nina's dead, does that mean she didn't kill Rox?" Eileen asked.

"Not at all," I said. "Just because she herself was murdered doesn't mean she didn't murder. But for some reason they come to conclusions like that in books."

Sarah piped up. "And if this was a book, the murderer wouldn't be Brad, just because he seems so obvious."

Trudy nodded, adding, "Murder mysteries in books are written to be puzzles for the reader's enjoyment. In real life, it usually *is* the obvious one. Vince has said that a number of times, right, Hazel?"

"Right."

We fell silent for a moment and just looked at each other. "So where are we now?" Sarah asked. "What else can we do?"

"Good question," Trudy said. "Are we out of ideas?"

"I say we do nothing," Lucy said. "Brad's clearly no one to mess with."

"No, I'm sticking with it. I agree that we're stumped at the moment, but something's bound to turn up."

"But Hazel, you saw how Brad was today. And we've heard enough bad stuff about his treatment of women. Even if he doesn't kill them, he's very abusive."

I held up both hands as if to fend off a blow. "I know, Lucy. But after today and what I've heard tonight, I'm more determined than ever. Look, when I told Nina I'd make inquiries into Rox's death I was motivated by family reasons, thinking that I should do what I could to clear Brad if he didn't do the killings. But now Nina is dead. While I doubt that I had anything to do with her death I'm not *totally* sure of that. And I'm still not sure what hand Brad had in either death. At any rate, I want to see justice served for both sisters. I can't sit by. The stakes are doubled now."

Lucy sighed. "Okay. So are we all still in this with Hazel?"

After a unanimous show of hands, I said, "I hope to talk to Andy soon." I checked my phone but I had no messages. "If we're lucky, he'll tell me something useful. Let's still plan on Skyping on Wednesday. If there's nothing to say, we can skip it until something comes up."

"Let's continue to travel in pairs," Trudy cautioned. "And not take any chances."

"We can be cerebral," I suggested. "Like Miss Marple. I don't think she was ever in personal danger. Or the rabbi, who wrote that series?"

Eileen explained, showing her librarian stripes. "Harry Kemelman. Rabbi Small was his detective. And you're right, he solved mysteries through pure logic."

"Well, let's hope the killer is a fan of Miss Marple and Rabbi Small," Lucy said dryly. "Speaking of fictional detectives, are we going to discuss books? I know our real-life mystery is more interesting, but still . . ."

We briefly time-traveled to the ancient world, sharing our reading selections complete with thumbs-up and thumbs-down reviews. Over refreshments we went back to speculating about the triangle of Rox, Nina, and Brad.

• • •

I hemmed and hawed about telling Vince about Nina's abortion and Brad's abusiveness. I knew he'd get concerned and try to discourage me from further investigation. But Vince and

I had built our marriage on trust and full disclosure. And so I caved.

As I'd predicted, Vince issued the usual cautions and reminders to travel in pairs, preferably packs.

"There's nothing really to do now, anyway," I said. "Unless Andy gets in touch and offers something illuminating."

Vince sighed. "Aren't you glad your sister turned up those bad apples on your family tree?"

TWENTY-THREE

I SPENT TUESDAY in "do not disturb" mode. I didn't turn on my computer or even get dressed. I didn't write and I didn't detect. After the events and drama of the past two weeks I needed to shut out the world. I did keep my phone nearby in case Andy called, but my elusive cousin didn't intrude on my self-imposed hibernation. I sat on my porch in my nightgown, reading *The Last Embrace* by Denise Hamilton, set in 1949—not exactly the ancient world but not contemporary times, either.

At seven forty-five, Kat's call brought the world back, front and center.

"I'm at an AA meeting. You'll never guess who's here." Without waiting for my guess, she went on, "That crazy guy we were talking about. You know, the one who was screaming at Rox."

"The lunatic?"

"That's the one. I almost didn't recognize him, 'cause he's not bald anymore. But I did recognize the tat on his arm. I'd forgotten all about that. He has this tat of a dog, maybe a Great Dane. Or a wolf. I'm not a dog person."

Apparently not, I thought. I wasn't a dog person either but I could tell a Great Dane from a wolf.

"He seems nice, not at all lunaticky, so I chatted with him at the break. He's really *hot* and has a great voice. And—you won't believe this—his name is Andy Jones!"

"You're kidding!"

"I'm not. Isn't he Brad's son?"

"If it's the same Andy Jones, and it just *has* to be, he is Brad's son. He called yesterday and left a voice message. You're right, he has a nice voice."

"Well, come on over and make it quick. The meeting's over at eight thirty." Kat gave directions to the church that provided space for the meeting.

I dislodged Morris from my lap and rushed upstairs to get dressed. I found Vince holed up in his den, working on his true crime account of the murderous housekeeper. When I told him that the lunatic and Andy were one and the same and that he was at an AA meeting, Vince said, "I'm going with you."

"Okay, but we have to get a move on. The meeting's over at eight thirty."

"Is it an open meeting?"

"What does that mean?"

"That anyone can go. Some meetings are closed to anyone but alcoholics."

"We'll be lucky if the meeting is still going on by the time we get there." I saw Vince's appreciative look as I unbuttoned my nightgown. "Don't get any ideas," I warned with a mock stern look. In record time I assembled an outfit, slapped on some makeup, and ran a brush through my hair.

"I'm ready," I announced.

• • •

Kat was waiting outside the church fellowship hall. "The meeting's just about over," she whispered. Vince and I joined her in a circle, holding hands, while the group recited the Lord's Prayer. When the circle broke, Kat said, "There he is, in the red shirt and denim shorts."

"Yes, I recognize him," Vince said. "He was at the service yesterday, sitting in the front row."

Andy stood, hands in pockets, talking to another man. As Vince and I approached I recognized my cousin's voice from the phone, seductive and intimate. A con man voice. It was hard to imagine someone with such a voice in lunatic mode. His fine dark hair clung to his head in half-inch lengths. I noted the German shepherd inked on his arm. I could understand Kat's mistaking a German shepherd for a wolf, but a Great Dane?

Before I lost my nerve I held out my hand. "Andy, Hazel Rose. I recognized your voice from the phone."

Andy looked at me, then did a double-take. "Hazel! At last we meet. Just didn't happen yesterday, somehow." His eyes sparkled behind his tinted glasses and an earring gleamed from his left earlobe. "Do you come to this meeting?"

"Not usually," I said vaguely. "What a surprise to see you here." I introduced Vince and they shook hands.

"Do you have time for coffee?" Andy asked. "My treat."

I glanced at Vince, who nodded his agreement.

"How about the Starbucks next to the gym? Do you know where it is?"

"We do. I'll just say goodbye to Kat."

When I told Kat about our Starbucks date, she said, "Let me know what happens."

"I will," I said as I rushed off.

In the Starbucks parking lot, we saw Andy taking off his helmet and attaching it to his red Harley. The bike lent further credence to his being the lunatic. At his request, we waited while he smoked a cigarette before going into the café. Once inside, we ordered coffee drinks and oatmeal cookies and chose a table by the window that afforded a view of the Harley.

Andy started. "Again, I'm sorry about Brad and the way he acted yesterday. It's no wonder he's a top suspect."

"It's been a tough time for him." My attempt to express compassion sounded flat to my ears. "Weren't he and Nina planning to get married?"

"Beats me. I can't keep up with Dad's women."

"I'm sorry about Nina. I just met her recently." I explained how I met her at Panera, omitting the coffee incident.

"So are you investigating her death as well?"

"I haven't been investigating *anyone's* death."

Noting Andy's skeptical look, I said, "It's true. Okay, I've discussed Rox's death with a few people. But with a murder like that of a prominent woman, everyone discusses it. As for *investigating*, I told Nina no dice. She'd have to hire a PI for that. A *licensed* one."

"That's right," Vince said. "Hazel has more sense than to get involved with a murder investigation." I almost laughed at my husband's untrue assertion, but held myself in check.

"Well, you sure got Brad in a state," Andy said.

"Apparently so."

"That's not hard to do."

"What's his issue with me anyway?"

"Besides his thinking that you got Nina killed?"

When I winced, Andy said, "Sorry. I don't know what his problem is. He said once that he suspected you wanted money. He didn't understand why else you'd suddenly pop up, long lost relative and all. He's touchy about money."

"So," I tried for a confused expression, "Weren't Nina and Brad together before? How did Brad come to marry Rox?"

"I have no idea. I know that Rox and Brad were together when my mom died." At the mention of his mother, Andy's face clouded. "Do you know about that?"

"Yes," Vince and I both nodded. "We're so sorry."

"Me, too." Andy sipped his coffee. "I always thought, and still do, that the two of them had something to do with Mom's death. It wasn't suicide. But I couldn't prove anything. They were smart, those two. But then Brad got together with Nina and by the time I came back to visit Marcie when she was in such bad shape, Brad and Rox were back together. The three of them went around in circles. Maybe even together," Andy suggested with a wicked grin. "I guess Brad didn't know there were more than just those two women in the world.

"I wanted to avoid Rox as much as possible so I visited Marcie at the assisted living place in the mornings when Brad and Rox were at work. Nina came by sometimes on her way to work; she and Marcie had always been good friends. I think Nina also wanted to avoid Rox and Brad. They might have had sibling rivalry issues to begin with, and losing out to her sister probably didn't help. And Paul and Patty visited in the mornings as well."

"Were Patty and Paul trying to avoid Rox and Brad?" Vince asked.

"I don't know. Maybe. Brad told me there were conflicts. Patty and Paul never said. Patty's too sweet to say anything against anyone."

I nodded. "That's true. Did Brad tell you what the conflicts were about?"

Andy seemed to be scanning his memory. "They'd asked Rox why Marcie wasn't at one of the cancer centers, like Duke or Sloan-Kettering."

I thought back to a few days before and Patty's flash of anger when I asked about the cancer centers. "Why *wasn't* she at one of those centers?"

"It probably had to do with money. Having money wasn't a problem, Marcie was loaded but she didn't like to spend money. And my guess is that Rox didn't want Marcie to spend her money, either. Rox was her POA and wielded a lot of influence over her. Marcie said the care she was getting was good enough. She'd made a ton of money and held management jobs, but she let Rox make all the decisions about her care. And Rox got Marcie's estate when she died."

"She did?" I looked at Vince. "All of it?"

"Well, maybe not all of it. Brad exaggerates sometimes. But most of it. A lot, anyway."

Interesting. Very interesting. Money trumped medical care not only in Rox's eyes but in Marcie's as well. I was about to ask more about the will, but Andy started talking before I did.

"Marcie hated the assisted living place, so Rox tried to strong-arm Patty and Paul into taking Marcie to live with them, along with a caregiver."

"You're kidding. Their place is the size of a shoebox."

"That's what they said, but Rox didn't seem to believe them. I guess she thought they lived in a palace. Brad said Rox wouldn't speak to them for a while."

I asked, "What about Marcie's own place?"

Andy feigned horror. "Oh, my God. You never saw her place? No," he answered his own question, "you wouldn't have. It was a disaster, piled to the rafters with newspapers, magazines, books, clothes, you name it." That accorded with Evangeline's description.

Andy continued. "Every surface was covered with stacks of

paper. The place wasn't too clean either. No way they could've brought a caregiver in there.

"And Marcie wouldn't let anyone in to clean. She was embarrassed, but not enough to do anything about it."

"What about Rox? Or Brad? Couldn't she stay with them?"

"Ah, good question. Rox lived in a house that had enough space and was clean enough. But there was some reason that now escapes me why she couldn't do it. Probably would put a crimp in her love life. As for Brad, can you see him as a caregiver?"

Neither Vince nor I responded to Andy's rhetorical question.

"So what happened?" Vince asked.

"Marcie finally agreed to move back to her own place but stipulated that nothing be removed, only rearranged. Rox, Brad, and yours truly were to do the cleaning and rearranging in preparation for the caregiver."

"What about Patty and Paul?"

"Don't know. They weren't in on the cleaning. Maybe that was their punishment for not going along with Rox's idea of caring for Marcie."

"Some punishment." I snickered.

"Yeah, really. We straightened up somewhat, meaning we moved everything into some unused rooms. There were still stacks of papers everywhere. When we visited Marcie we sat on her deck. Only place where there weren't papers."

"Did you still visit in the morning?"

"Still in the morning."

"Patty and Paul as well?"

When Andy nodded, I asked, "Who was the caregiver? Probably there was more than one?"

"A couple. Nice enough people, but they had no medical training, they just cooked and cleaned. Eventually they had to bring in hospice care."

"Very sad," I said. "I wish I'd gotten to know Marcie."

Andy said, "So tell me how you found out that you had a passel of cousins you never knew about?" I told him the story of my sister Ruth and her genealogical pursuits.

"You know, Andy, I've enjoyed having lunch with Patty a number of times. But I still feel like I don't know much about her. And even less about Paul, but I haven't been around him much at all."

Andy nodded. "They're hard to get to know. I do know about Paul's financial problems, only because I'm in debt up to my eyeballs as well. So we often commiserated. He owed a lot of money to the racetrack. And the IRS."

"Really? But Patty should have had a good income from her years of teaching. What did Paul do for a living? He told me once but I forgot."

"He taught as well. What was it? Speech? Philosophy? Something like that."

Philosophy made me think of Greece. I remembered seeing some Greek books in their bookcase. Epics, dramas, and the like. So Paul could very well have a background in philosophy or some associated subject. Heavy stuff.

I asked, "Why didn't Patty and Paul move in with Marcie and take care of her?"

"I have no idea."

"Did Patty and Paul ever resolve their differences with Rox?"

"Oh sure. They were all pretty lovey-dovey at Marcie's funeral. Maybe just for show, I don't know, but there weren't any funeral fights or scenes." I thought of the scene Nina told me that an angry Andy had staged when his mother died.

"You said that Rox was Marcie's POA and that Marcie left everything to her? Why was that? She wasn't even a family member. I could see her leaving her something, being generous, but the whole shebang?" Rox sure benefitted from her moonlighting job as a POA. And my mind lit on Foster's report of Rox and an elderly woman outside an office building that housed a number of lawyers.

"I didn't say she got the *whole* shebang, Brad said that. Marcie had her pet charities, so she might have left something to them. But Rox likely got the bulk of it and sure as I'm sitting here talking to you, Brad married her for her hard-earned bucks. But probably the true explanation is in Marcie and Rox's long history. At one time they were lovers." Andy stopped to gauge my reaction.

"Marcie and Rox were lovers? I didn't know that. Did you know that, Vince?" Vince shrugged, going along with my feigning surprise at Andy's revelation.

"Oh yeah. Marcie was in the closet, but hell, you're family. We all knew. Suspected, anyway. She and Rox lived together for years."

"That doesn't mean—"

"I know, they could live together without being lovers. But Marcie told me all about it a few days before she died. She'd always loved Rox, but she knew Rox enjoyed men as well, and there wasn't much she could do about that. They parted ways and had other relationships but remained good friends. Marcie never really got over Rox and would do anything for her."

"Anything" apparently included bequeathing her vast estate to her former lover.

Vince asked, "Why do you call your father Brad?"

Andy smirked. "To piss him off." Andy had more charm than Brad—but not a lot.

I thought of the erotic books Evangeline had found. "Did Patty and Paul know about Rox and Marcie's relationship?"

Andy shrugged. "Not to my knowledge. Maybe Marcie told them the same thing she told me."

"So," I took a deep breath and took the proverbial nosedive, "Did you and Rox ever have a relationship?"

Andy gave me a long look before responding. "Yes, a brief one. Very brief. And chaotic."

"From what I've heard, chaotic is putting it mildly. Didn't you storm her place of employment and smash her windshield?" Who did I think I was, this daring me? Of course, I had the law by my side. Retired law, but law all the same.

Andy smirked. "I thought you weren't an investigator."

"Actually, I'm just guessing it was you. I've heard about someone who did what I described but didn't know who it was. So it *was* you?"

"Guilty, as charged."

"How did this start? And it wasn't long ago, was it?"

"Last year. We ran into each other at some dive. Moonshine Inn. Do you know it?"

"We know of it." I smiled at Vince.

Andy grinned. "I don't peg you as the sorts who'd spend time there."

If he only knew, I thought. "So you said you and Rox met

up at the Moonshine Inn. That's where she was killed, isn't it?"

"Right." Andy drained his coffee before going on. "She was all decked out in her business suit like she was at a board meeting. I couldn't believe I would even speak to her. But one thing led to another and—" Andy trailed off but I had no trouble finishing his sentence.

"But why would you have a relationship with her when you thought she'd had a hand in your mother's death?"

He shrugged. "I decided that she didn't do it, that I overreacted."

I gave him a measuring look. Probably a case where his brain, and perhaps heart, disconnected from other body parts. "Weren't she and Brad together at that point?"

"No, they were on the outs so I got to take up the slack. We fought a lot and had a lot of great sex. Make-up sex mostly. I smashed her windshield when she wouldn't open her door. I don't know if anyone was in the house with her. I didn't see a car."

"How did you happen to have a hammer? Do you carry one on your cycle?"

"I took a rock from her garden."

"And she didn't press charges?"

"Nope."

"And what about the incident at the Hamlin Group? What brought that on?"

"She was seeing some other dude. I followed her one time."

Foster? For all I knew, the woman had lovers stashed all over Richmond.

"But I didn't kill her. I was cleared."

"How so?"

"The great city of Owensboro, Kentucky gave me a DUI that night. Can't ask for a better alibi than that." That much was true as he was on record for having an airtight alibi.

I leaned forward in a gesture of sharing confidences. "Any ideas about who did kill Rox?"

"I sure wanted to enough times," he snorted. "The woman was mean. Laughed at me a lot. Taunted me. But I would have strangled her in the heat of the moment, not stab her in a parking lot." Andy probably had something there.

"But any number of folks besides me could've done it. There's Nina—but she's dead, so maybe, maybe not. And then, who killed Nina? Things look bad for dear old dad. First Mom, then Rox, now Nina. Rox didn't treat him very well, but he probably deserved it."

"Why would Brad kill her? For the money she got from Marcie?" It seemed shocking that a child would seriously consider his or her parent a killer.

"Sure, the money. Plus she hung out at redneck bars, besmirching his reputation."

I tried and failed to hold back a laugh at the idea of Brad being concerned about "besmirching" his reputation. He sure must have forgotten about protecting his standing in the community the day of Nina's funeral.

"Yes, dear cousin, laugh. That's all we can do."

"What about Nina? Why would Brad kill her?" Vince asked.

"Maybe Nina knew something damaging about him and let on to him what she knew. Maybe she wanted to marry him and was trying to blackmail him."

I reflected on Andy's speculations. "Perhaps Nina either knew, or surmised, that Brad killed her sister."

"That's my guess."

That wasn't the first time the idea had been entertained. I paused for a beat before redirecting the subject. "So you live in Owensboro now?"

"Yeah, my son and his mother live there. Della doesn't want to come here, she can't stand Brad. Occasionally I bring Elliott for a visit. Unlike Della, he likes Brad."

"You bring Elliott on your Harley?"

"No, I take the car."

"That's quite a drive," Vince noted.

Andy agreed. "Ten to eleven hours."

"Did you go to Rox's funeral?"

"Hell, yes. Had to make sure she was dead."

"How did you know about Nina being killed?"

"Brad told me."

"So you two are in touch."

"Oh, yeah." Andy looked surprised. "We get along okay when we're apart. Right now things are dicey, us being in the same house and all." Did Brad support him? It occurred to me that, with Brad getting a windfall via Rox, it would benefit Andy. As if Andy read my mind, he said, "My goal in life is to stay sober long enough and hold down a job long enough to repay Brad and not have to rely on him."

Vince asked, "Do you have a job now in Owensboro?"

Andy managed a sheepish grin. "No, not really." He went on to say that he had two masters' degrees, and was himself an aspiring writer. "Sometimes I work as a telemarketer." Ah, put that con man voice to good use.

"What do you write?" Vince asked.

"I'm working on a thriller. It's based on *Crash*." I recalled the movie from 2005. Well made. And dark.

Before leaving the café, Andy and I exchanged e-mail addresses. In the parking lot we hugged but made no mention of seeing each other again.

That was fine with me. I reckoned it was fine with Vince as well.

TWENTY-FOUR

"DO YOU THINK Marcie really left her estate to Rox? It's odd to leave everything to a friend. Even if she was a really good friend."

"Sometimes friends are closer than family," Vince said. "It doesn't sound to me like Marcie was close to her cousins. And if Rox was her POA, her primary caregiver—"

"And former lover," I completed the list of reasons. "That's an important consideration. I wouldn't be surprised if Rox persuaded Marcie to leave everything to her. Andy said that Marcie never got over Rox and would do anything for her. Even let her go and have relationships with men, to the point of marrying them. Even Marcie's own cousin."

"So it doesn't sound like Marcie would've needed much persuasion to leave the bulk of her fortune to Rox."

"No."

Vince and I sat on the porch, reviewing our discussion with Andy. Morris settled on Vince's lap while Olive draped herself on his shoulder like a fur stole.

"But Andy wasn't sure if she'd left everything to Rox." Vince stroked Olive's silky tail.

"Yeah, well, apparently she didn't leave anything to him. Unless he's gone through it already."

"You can always get a copy of Marcie's will. It would have gone through probate long before now."

"Yeah, maybe I will. I don't know that it would help us, though. If Marcie left her fortune to Rox, that gives Brad, and maybe Nina, a motive to kill Rox. But it still doesn't give us proof that they actually did."

After a pause I said, "You know, stockbrokers are a rough, tough lot. It's a cutthroat business and requires a lot of strength. Especially for a woman who started back in the '70s or early '80s like Marcie did. I know, I worked in the securities industry for years in IT. But she doesn't sound strong in her dealings with Rox."

"But she might have operated differently in business than in her personal life. That's not the first time I've seen or heard of that sort of thing."

"You're right." I flashed to a couple of examples I'd come across in the past. Like a former co-worker who swore a blue streak at work but wouldn't utter so much as a "damn" in her husband's presence.

"I wonder if Patty and Paul have left town yet," Vince said.

"They were supposed to leave today. Speaking of Patty and Paul, I can't believe Rox expected them to take Marcie in. And as for Paul and Patty's financial problems—well, it doesn't surprise me. It explains the teeny apartment, the one vehicle. And maybe their moving back to Pittsburgh is driven more by their own financial need than from wanting to take care of dear old mom. Mom might provide free room and board." I shook my head. "And to think of all the income they must have had from their years of teaching."

"That's what gambling can do—your income goes up in smoke."

"I'll send an e-mail to the group. I guess we won't be Skyping tomorrow. There's really nothing to talk about—the most exciting thing we found out tonight is that Andy's the lunatic. But that excitement's already fizzled out for me."

"There's the will."

"Yes, but that's not exciting. It's not even that unexpected."

We stopped talking, and for the next half hour the only sounds were the cats purring and the tree frogs singing. At eleven we went back in the house, gave the cats treats, and went through the various rituals of preparing for sleep.

• • •

The next morning, I sent out the e-mail. To my surprise, Sarah still wanted to get together, as did Lucy and Trudy. "We can't lose our momentum," they said. Only Eileen begged off, saying her mother was wringing every last drop of energy out of her.

"Lucy installed Skype on my computer and I've been visiting by video with my sister," Sarah said. "I really like it." I felt happy to have had even a small part in Sarah's technological progress.

I also sent an e-mail to Kat, updating her on what happened after leaving her the previous evening. She responded, "Well, finding out he was the lunatic is one mystery solved. Let me know if I can help out in any other way."

Once we all connected on Skype I gave a more detailed account of the meeting with Andy.

"You're right, Hazel," Lucy said. "It's interesting but also . . . I don't know . . . it's so-what stuff. It doesn't get us anywhere. But I wonder if Rox did get Marcie's estate."

"Vince checked with Dennis. Rox made significant deposits into various accounts from the estate. *Millions* of dollars."

"One thing's for sure," Sarah said. "Eileen's mother may be a trial but at least Eileen doesn't have to endure conflicts with siblings and other relatives. I was laughing when you described Patty and Paul's dealings with Rox. I've heard so many stories like that."

We all had stories to share of family conflicts. Once we exhausted our supply of them, Trudy said, "I was thinking about Pamela: what if she carried a torch for Foster and resented Rox, especially when it looked like she and Foster were seeing each other again?"

I groaned. "Pamela was in Boston and she had an alibi. Let's not pile on more suspects, please."

"Didn't Foster tell Lucy he saw Rox with an elderly woman, presumably headed for an appointment with an attorney? Do you think that was Marcie?"

"Interesting question, Sarah," Lucy said.

I thought of that group picture I'd seen in Patty's apartment. Marcie did look old, the cancer having ravaged her looks. And Foster was still young enough to deem anyone over fifty as old. Were Rox and Marcie having their wills done together? Marcie was reputedly disorganized, but if Rox wanted her former lover's estate, she'd lose no time in getting Marcie to a lawyer. Had Rox had her will done that day as well?

When I presented this scenario, everyone agreed that it rang true. "Do you have a picture of Marcie?" Lucy asked.

"I might. Let me check my phone." After my usual fumbling around and hitting the wrong buttons, I located the picture I sought. It was the one from Patty's bookcase, showing Patty, Paul, Nina, Andy, and a turbaned Marcie. "Here it is. I'm texting it to all of you."

"Oh," Trudy said. "I almost forgot—Brad asked me and Eileen to go through Nina's books. He says we can donate them to the library."

"When are you doing this?" I asked.

"Sunday. They just lifted the crime scene today and Brad's having the place cleaned up."

"Poor Marcie," Lucy sounded sad. "She looks quite elderly in this picture. How old was she?"

"She was sixty-nine when she died. But the cancer probably aged her considerably."

"I just texted this to Foster to see if it's the same woman he saw that day in the parking lot."

"How did you do that so fast? You and Trudy have lightning fingers."

"Lightning thumbs," Lucy laughed.

"Next on my to-do list is honing my phone skills so I don't look like a stereotypical technophobic old person."

"Don't feel bad, Hazel," Sarah assured me. "I'm much worse."

"Getting back to Brad," I said, "will he be there on Sunday?"

"I'm not sure. He'll let us in the house, but I don't know if he'll stick around." Trudy laughed. "Probably you should stay home, Hazel."

"Be careful of him," I warned.

"We will. I'm taking Millie with me." I wasn't sure how

ferocious Trudy's dog could be, but maybe she, like some people, showed their strength when necessary. And only then.

"There's my phone," Lucy said. "Foster says he can't tell if the woman in the picture is the same one he saw in the parking lot. He didn't take particular notice of her anyway. He was more focused on Rox."

"It was a long shot, anyway," I said.

"So," Trudy began, "Where are we as far as suspects?"

For what seemed the hundredth time, we reviewed our circle of suspects and pondered the identity of the women in the Florida car. We didn't whittle down the list but at least we didn't add to it.

"The field still looms large," Sarah intoned.

In reality, the field was quite small—the answer was right under our noses.

TWENTY-FIVE

"WE FOUND A play at Nina's! A *very* interesting play. Come on over, you just have to see it."

"Did she write it?"

"Looks like it."

"But what about Brad? Is he around?"

"Don't worry about him. He gave us a key and said to lock up and leave the key in the soil around the bird bath. I'm back home now, anyway."

For the past few days I'd found myself at sixes and sevens. I knew I should work on my writing but I was into this investigation—this *stalled* investigation. Maybe this play would revive my spirits.

Trudy continued. "Eileen had to leave. Her mother's acting up again. She kicked a nurse aide in the shins."

"Oh, dear. I don't envy Eileen. She's going to have to do something about her mother."

"And quickly," Trudy said. "I don't know how long they'll keep her there. Feisty senior citizens."

I thought of Evangeline's mother taking her cane to Brad. Is that what I had to look forward to, taking power where I could get it, even if I had to resort to physical violence?

"Anyway, come on over."

When I got there no one answered except for Millie barking inside. Figuring that Trudy might have gone back to Nina's house for something, I walked to the end of the driveway. I recognized Trudy first by her walk. It was funny how distinctive walks could be. I remembered a myopic friend who wouldn't wear her glasses out of vanity, claiming that she recognized people by their walks.

Nina had said the guy in the parking lot at the Moonshine Inn looked familiar. Or did she say *seemed* familiar? She said the lot wasn't well lit but she'd seen a glint of metal. But did she see his face? Is that when she thought he looked familiar? How clearly could she have seen it? Was it his walk she recognized? I wished I'd recorded the conversation.

"Sorry to keep you waiting. I left my phone at Nina's." Trudy had dressed for the hot weather in a cotton shirt and jean shorts, hair scraped back in a ponytail.

A rush of cool air greeted me when we entered Trudy's house. Millie leaped up on me, overwhelming me with enthusiasm. By contrast, the imperious Sammy greeted me from his favorite chair with only a baleful look.

"Want some carrot juice?" Trudy offered.

"Okay."

"Look through those boxes while I make a copy of this play." Trudy pointed to a couple of boxes stacked by the computer that occupied a corner of her den. I found an assortment of books, VHS cassettes, and DVDs. Nina favored self-help titles from the '80s and '90s—*I'm OK, You're OK*, *Men Are Just Desserts*, that sort of thing. At one time I had practically devoured this genre but they no longer held my interest. Not that I was beyond help—I just felt like I'd read enough of the stuff. The tapes and DVDs offered self-help as well.

Nina liked Susan Howatch, judging from the number of titles in the box penned by the British author. Years earlier I'd enjoyed her family saga tales. The remaining volumes related to marketing and personal finance subjects. The how-to book on rug hooking make me smile. Why would anyone need a manual for that? I'd once hooked a rug and never once felt the need for a book on the craft.

"What are you going to do with all this stuff?" I asked Trudy.

"Either sell it or donate it to the prison system. If all else fails, we'll recycle them."

"Self-help might appeal to prisoners. At least the ones who want to rehabilitate themselves. I don't see any plays here."

"No. I thought about that, too. But here's a copy of the one I found upstairs in her bedroom." Trudy handed me a sheaf of papers. "I printed one for each of us. And I scanned it to my hard drive and e-mailed you a copy. I'll send one to that detective in charge of the case, what's his name?"

"Fischella. Thomas Fischella."

I chose an uncomfortable chair—even Sammy eschewed it. Was that a smug look he gave me from his own comfortable seat? I wouldn't doubt it. I sipped my carrot juice as I read Nina's play. It only had one act, so it didn't take long to get through it. I was astounded at her subject matter: a woman who's stabbed to death in a parking lot. Only, this parking lot accommodated members and guests of a Richmond-area country club. A person who seemed familiar to her walked through the lot and got into the passenger side of a dark car.

When I finished reading, I looked up at Trudy. She was re-reading the play. "Interesting," I said. "This is the same story she told me, just with an upscale venue. Complete with the person who seemed familiar to her."

"Who could this person be? And who wrote these notes in the margins? They're not in Nina's writing. I compared the writing to notes I saw around her house—shopping list on the fridge, a few other things. Her writing is much larger and loopier. Funny thing, I didn't find a calendar. And I looked for one."

"Hmm. Maybe she carried it in the purse that was stolen. As for the notes, it looks to me like notes a teacher would make."

I glanced at the notes. The small, cramped handwriting was difficult to decipher. *Why is your character telling this story? You have no stage directions. Dialog is stiff. If she's talking to a friend, she wouldn't be so formal.* More critical comments filled the margins. The last one made me laugh: *Interesting concept. Interesting* often served as an intentionally ambiguous word, or a euphemism.

"Why did Nina write this? Was it cathartic?"

"I'd say so."

"I guess she was trying to work out who her sister's killer was—maybe she thought that if she reconstructed the scene, something buried in her subconscious would surface in her conscious mind."

"Did she succeed? Did she identify the familiar person in the parking lot? We need to find this teacher."

Trudy and I continued to talk it through. "Let's call Mary Anne," I suggested. "She was in the class and might know something."

"Good idea. I'll e-mail the play to the group. Maybe they'll have some thoughts about it. While I'm doing that, you can call Mary Anne."

It made sense that I would be the one to call Mary Anne Branch. I'd met her at a James River Writers event a couple of months earlier when I'd served on a panel for romantic fiction. She expressed interest in the book group and started attending. But I sensed that her interest had waned. She was more interested in reading plays than fiction. Despite being in her forties, Mary Anne had an innocent outlook and lack of worldliness that made me wonder what sort of play she'd write. Maybe she'd surprise us and turn out something about serial killers, psychopaths, or axe murderers.

"Do you have her number?" Trudy opened a desk drawer and grabbed a list of book group names. I tapped the number on my keypad as she recited it.

I rushed through the usual pleasantries with Mary Anne and got right to the purpose of my call: the playwriting class. "I'd like to ask you about Nina. We're all just *sick* about what happened to her." I injected as much anguish as I could.

"Oh, that was *so* sad! Frankly I'm worried that something about her play caused her death and that I might be in danger. The others in the class as well. The whole thing gives me the willies."

"Really? You think there was something about the play? What do you think it could have been?"

"Well, it was about this woman who was stabbed to death in a parking lot. Wasn't Nina's sister stabbed in a parking lot?"

"Yes, she was."

"Nina read the play with great drama and emotion. Maybe it

was—what's that word?"

"Cathartic?"

"Yes. Cathartic for her. Creepy for me."

"Who was in your class?"

"Well, um . . . there was this really sweet blonde woman. She wrote a beautiful play. A romantic comedy. She couldn't have done it—killed Nina, I mean."

Why? I thought with amusement. Because she wrote a beautiful romance? Because she was funny?

"Oh, gosh, Hazel, I shouldn't be telling you about the people in the class." Mary Anne's voice took on a note of alarm. "What if one of them did it and comes after me? Or you? I did give names to the police."

"Take it easy, Mary Anne. I didn't mean to upset you. I just thought someone I knew might have been in the class."

"Oh, I'm sorry. I didn't mean—look, I have to go. I'll call you back tomorrow." And she ended the call.

"Trudy, did Nina or Mary Anne ever say where the playwriting class was?"

Trudy sat at her computer. "I don't think so. Let me look up playwriting classes in Richmond."

"Don't spend too much time on it. Vince might know, or he could find out."

A moment later Trudy said, "There are two possibilities: The Visual Arts Center and River City Writing Center. They both started playwriting classes on May 7 and ended on June 11."

"Okay, thanks. I'm going to hold Mary Anne to her promise about calling me. If I don't hear from her by ten tomorrow I'm calling her. I'll bribe her, offer to treat her to one of those healthy smoothies she likes so much at Ellwood Thompson."

"Speaking of healthy food, want to go out for pizza?"

"Okay. Can Vince come?"

"Sure."

• • •

Vince met us at Italian Delight. As it was Sunday and not Monday, we figured we weren't apt to run into Evangeline and Nichole as we had a few weeks before. Avila, our waitperson, remembered us and asked if our friends would be joining us.

Maybe she craved the excitement of crying, angry customers.

"Not tonight," I smiled sweetly. Once we gave our orders I handed Vince my copy of the play to peruse and we bandied ideas about on the possible meanings.

"Sounds cathartic," Vince said.

"According to Mary Anne, Nina read it with great emotion," I said. "I'd love to know what the others in the class thought of it."

"Vince, where was the class? At the Richmond arts place?"

"River City Writing Center."

"Didn't you say Mary Anne mentioned someone who wrote a romance?" Trudy asked.

"Yes. But she just said she was sweet and blonde. It's kind of hard to identify someone from that generic description. When I talk to Mary Anne I'll try to get names out of her."

"Everyone in the class was interviewed," Vince said. "Including the teacher. They all had alibis."

"Still, they might offer information to one of us that they wouldn't to the police."

Vince gave me a look but said nothing further.

We enjoyed our salads and pizza, undisturbed by drama. Later, I sat at my computer reading through the replies the book group sent after reading Nina's play.

Lucy wrote, "It sounds so much like her sister's killing. She just changed the setting to something more upscale." The other responses pretty much echoed those of my cousin.

• • •

The next day Mary Anne called at nine o'clock on the dot.

"Hazel, I'm sorry I was such a ninny yesterday. I promise I won't be a ninny anymore."

I silently applauded her determination to break her ninny habit. "Well, it can't be easy having a classmate get killed."

"Anyway, I know your book group was investigating Nina's sister's murder. I really didn't see how I could help with that. And I'm not sure how I can help with Nina's mystery, either. But if you have any questions, just ask me."

"Can we get together, maybe at Ellwood Thompson? Don't you work near there?"

"Oh, yes, I'd *love* that. Oh, and Hazel?"

"Yes?"

"Maybe you could give me tips about writing? I'm thinking of writing a romance, paranormal maybe. I don't think playwriting is for me after all."

"Sure, I'm happy to help."

We agreed to meet at twelve-thirty in the eating area of the locally owned natural food store.

I remembered my promise not to be alone with anyone. This cheerful woman could be a psychopathic killer. But a public spot like Ellwood Thompson should be safe enough. When I told Vince of my plans he looked uncertain, then said, "Well, she's not a suspect. But text me when you get there and when you leave."

I arrived at Ellwood Thompson and sent Vince the promised text. The aroma of fresh produce greeted me when I walked into the store—and vitamins. All health and natural food stores were redolent of the odor of vitamins and other supplements, strange since they were sealed in their bottles. For some inexplicable reason, I found the medicinal scent pleasing.

Lots of wood created a rustic, farmhouse atmosphere, appropriate to the store's mission of providing healthy and natural food. The only thing I didn't like was the din created by the high-powered blenders that produced the smoothies—tantamount to being in the middle of a construction site.

Mary Anne Branch's sleek cap of dark hair matched shining eyes that hinted at mischief. Cheer was written all over her. The woman fairly burst with vibrant health. Even her golden tan looked healthy and smooth. Still, any tan held potential dangers. I held back the words of caution that came to me.

To contribute to the noise level, we both decided on smoothies. If Mary Anne indulged in these smoothies on a regular basis, that could account for her glow. With that in mind I duplicated her order, something involving kale, spinach, and—to quote Mary Anne—"lots of good stuff." I ignored her protestations and paid for both smoothies. We took our concoctions to a wooden booth, as far from the smoothie production as possible.

"So, Mary Anne," I started. "Tell me about your class."

"It was a *wonderful* class. Even though I'm now thinking of writing a romance, I thought the class was great. And I'm so glad it was over before poor Nina's tragedy. I mean, it would have been awful to have it happen halfway through and have to go back and find her—well, not *there*." Mary Anne's teeth dazzled with whiteness. "Honestly, I don't think I could have gone *on*."

"So, how many were in the class?"

"There were five of us." Mary Anne looked stricken. "You don't think one of us, do you—"

"No, no, no." I waved my hand. "We're just looking for something Nina herself might have said or done. We're at a loss, you know . . ." I trailed off deliberately.

"I understand."

"So, tell me more about Nina's play."

Mary Anne offered the same synopsis as I'd read, repeating her earlier claim that it was heartfelt and emotional. "The teacher found it fascinating. Said it was compelling, a great start. Wonderful dialog as well. In fact, we all thought the dialog was very natural."

It didn't sound like anyone in the class had authored the notes on Nina's printed copy. "Who was the teacher?"

"Sylvia—" She snapped the fingers of her right hand, tastefully tipped with pale pink polish. "Sylvia Davies."

"Did anyone in the class have playwriting experience?"

"No, we were all true novices." Without waiting for my prompt Mary Anne said, "I'm trying to picture the rest of the class. I think I mentioned the sweet blonde woman who wrote an amazing play. And there was a young Indian—or was she Pakistani?—woman. She was *so* beautiful. But she never completed her assignments. Said she'd been too busy."

"Oh, and Beth. Actually, she works there, answers the phone." Mary Anne leaned forward and lowered her voice, making it hard to hear her over the whirring of the smoothies. "Beth is kind of snooty," she said. At least, that's what I think she said.

"Do you remember any names? Besides Beth's?"

"Oh, no. I shouldn't have even said Beth's name. I know I said I wasn't going to be a ninny anymore, but I have to protect everyone's identity."

"I understand." I knew that everyone in her class had been questioned. If it turned out that I needed names, maybe I could get Vince to give them to me. But that was unlikely.

"Did Sylvia collect written copies of your plays and write comments in the margins?"

If Mary Anne found my question odd, she showed no sign of it. "Oh, no. We didn't hand in any papers. Sylvia only listened as we read from our copies or from our laptops."

"Did you ever see Nina talking a lot to anyone in particular?"

Mary Anne thought for a moment as she sipped her drink. "I'm not sure. We all talked to each other."

While I tried to come up with another question Mary Anne leaned forward again, eyes dancing. "I think I mentioned that I want to start writing romance fiction. I want to write like you."

"Well, thanks, that's very kind of you to say. But you'll develop your own voice."

"Do you have any advice for me?"

"Yes, and I can sum it up in one word: write." I expanded on my terse advice, suggesting Virginia Romance Writers and James River Writers as good resources. "And take classes. The River City Writing Center should have some good ones."

"Can I send you my first draft for critique?"

"Absolutely."

I couldn't think of another Nina-related question. I finished my drink, fully expecting to see plants sprouting from my body. As we left the store, Mary Anne grabbed a shopping cart and went back inside to shop. "Hazel, let's friend on Facebook."

"Oh, you're on Facebook now?"

"Yes," she laughed. "Latecomer. I've found some great writing groups."

"Okay, I'll send you a friend request." I continued on to my car, texting Vince as I walked. I narrowly missed colliding with a stray shopping cart.

"Don't text and walk" needed to be added to the "Don't text and drive" campaign.

TWENTY-SIX

AT HOME, I friended Mary Anne Branch on Facebook and she accepted almost instantly. Her profile picture showed her flashing a Colgate smile at the camera as she, appropriately enough, leaned on a tree branch. I reviewed my conversation with the peppy aspiring writer and decided that Nina must have had a critiquing partner. Maybe she'd belonged to a writing group. But who was her partner? And what group could it be? There were countless such groups, many of them private. Since some of the criticism pertained specifically to plays, I assumed that the person who wrote the comments knew something about that particular format.

When I e-mailed the book group a summary of my conversation with Mary Anne, Eileen replied, "I know Sylvia Davies. Her father lives at the same facility as my mom. I see her a lot. I'll try to track her down over the next couple of days and see if I can find out anything about who might have written those notes."

We all thanked Eileen, and probably shared the hope that she would follow through without her unpredictable and volatile mother derailing her plans.

"So, do you think your chat with Mary Anne gave you anything useful?" Vince asked as we fixed dinner.

I shrugged. "Maybe. Only time will tell."

. . .

"According to Sylvia, Nina did show her play to someone, a man apparently, who was very disparaging. Sylvia couldn't believe it, because she thought so highly of Nina's writing. In fact, Sylvia encouraged Nina to keep developing her craft and to take advanced courses in playwriting."

"Did Sylvia have a name for the man?" I asked when Eileen paused.

"No, I asked but she didn't think Nina mentioned his name."

Another Wednesday had rolled around, finding us tethered to our computers or devices for a Skype session.

Trudy piped up. "It's a good thing that Nina didn't take the man's comments to heart and get discouraged."

"I remember this one instructor who deemed my writing crap. Thankfully I'd written enough by that point that I didn't believe him. But if I was just starting out . . ." I trailed off, thinking of the damage often inflicted on the fragile egos of writers.

I heard the sound of pages flipping. Sarah said, "These notes from the critiquer are interesting. Like this one—'Why did she get out of her car if she saw someone suspicious?' Now that's a good question, one I myself would have asked. Why *did* she get out of the car?"

"I think Nina was already out of the car before she saw the guy," I said. "In the actual situation, anyway."

"I would have gotten back in the car, and pronto."

"Anyway, the whole thing is creepy." I pictured Eileen tossing her long curls. "To think that she'd write this and recite it to her class."

"It's interesting that Nina set this at a country club," Lucy said. "I wonder what Hazel's undercover outfit would have been at a country club."

"What *is* country club garb on a Friday night?" I asked. "Certainly not low-cut tank tops and jeans slashed to ribbons."

"And no blue eye shadow, either," Eileen put in. "Probably business casual."

"Too bad. Not nearly as much fun," Trudy chuckled.

"Let's see, what else do we need to discuss?" I asked.

"Mary Anne," Trudy prompted. "Tell us more about your discussion with her."

When I expanded on my brief e-mail account of the meeting with Mary Anne at Ellwood Thompson, Lucy said, "Maybe Nina had reason to think the killer was someone in the class."

"So what was she doing—flushing them out?" Eileen sounded incredulous. "Who have we got? There's Mary Anne and a sweet blonde woman, a busy Pakistani woman, and Beth the snooty receptionist?"

"Sounds like a board game," Sarah quipped.

"Mary Anne?" Trudy sounded doubtful. "I can't see her killing anyone."

"Hey, perky, healthy folks can kill," Eileen said. "Anyone with a motive could have done it."

"What would be Mary Anne's motive?"

"Why, I don't know."

"Let's not forget Phyllis."

"For Nina's murder, perhaps. But what about Rox? Why would Phyllis have killed her?"

I broke into Trudy and Eileen's back-and-forth. "Phyllis and Rox were in the same line of work—development. Phyllis works for Infinity Center, and Rox worked for the Hamlin Group."

Sarah groaned. "We're doing it again, adding suspects before we eliminate other ones. Brad, for instance. I saw him yesterday at the ARS."

"How did he seem?" I asked.

"Subdued."

"I still think it was Brad," Eileen asserted. "We're just spinning our wheels. The killer is usually someone obvious. And Brad's obvious."

"Still, we need to find proof," Sarah pointed out.

"We'd need to find proof no matter who did it."

"True."

We heaved a collective sigh.

Sarah said, "I ran into Maria Muller the other day at the market and told her about all of this."

Maria Muller had attended our group for a while until

deciding that she didn't like reading mysteries. Maria liked to pose questions like "why did God allow killing and war?" She didn't like the usual answer that was our consensus: God gave us free will.

"So how is Maria?" I asked.

"Oh, she's fine. The same. She asked the usual 'why does God allow such things?' I didn't go into the free will bit, just said 'beats me'. I wasn't up for a long discussion. Besides, my ice cream was melting."

At one time, Sarah got involved with long discussions with Maria on the free will question as well as other weighty issues. Sometimes the two women lingered outside by their cars after the group meeting, but most often they huddled together in someone's living room. Sometimes others joined in, but we soon tired of the intensity.

"There are no free wills," Eileen quipped. "I just paid five hundred dollars for mine." Lucy and Trudy contributed their will stories complete with fees.

I thought of Rox, and presumably Marcie, attending to their wills. How much had they paid? Money should have been no object to either of them.

Except that from all accounts, it *was* an object.

TWENTY-SEVEN

MY BEST THOUGHTS always came to me when I wasn't thinking. That night, as I brushed my teeth, a memory came to me seemingly out of nowhere.

Nice to see you again. Wasn't that what Todd, the manager at Panera, said to me and Nina when we left Panera the day Phyllis christened Nina in coffee? It was such an innocuous expression that I was surprised I even remembered it. Did Todd say that to all his customers, with no real meaning?

Or had he meant it literally, meaning that he'd seen us before and was happy to see us again? If so, he was mistaken about me, as I'd never been in the Stony Point Panera before that dramatic day. But perhaps Nina had frequented the location.

That particular realization didn't amount to much—until I coupled it with another thought. Critiquing. I considered the people I'd critiqued with over the years, either in groups or on a one-on-one basis. My guess was that Nina met someone at Panera who critiqued her play. Maybe the same person helped her with editing as well. The person who wrote those notes.

Okay, great thought—perhaps. But only if I could verify it. The only person who might be able to help me with that one was

Todd. And that required another morning visit to Panera.

The next day was July fourth. Would Panera even be open?

No! I told myself as I completed my dental hygiene. Take a work holiday like everyone else did. Panera would still be there on Friday.

And Rox and Nina would still be dead.

• • •

The next day I was true to my word. I put aside anything to do with the investigation. As I did every year I watched the *Twilight Zone* marathon until late afternoon when we went over to Lucy and Dave's. Lucy's daughter, son-in-law, and granddaughter drove down from Northern Virginia to celebrate Independence Day. Dave's family lived in the area so didn't have as far to travel to join us. We grilled steak and chicken with all the fixings, and never once mentioned the name Rox or Nina. Until it came time to say goodbye.

When I had told Vince my idea about Nina meeting a critiquing partner at Panera, he'd suggested that I ask Lucy to accompany me. I hardly thought a bodyguard necessary for a field trip to a bakery café, but I agreed and approached Lucy.

"Sure. I'm game. When do you want to go?"

"Tomorrow. About eight."

"Okay. I need to be in the office by ten, but this shouldn't take that long."

"I really don't need a bodyguard."

"But I *want* to go with you. And I like their croissants."

"Okay, fine. I'll meet you at eight. The Stony Point Panera."

Lucy and I showed up at Panera bright and early the next morning and found Todd with no trouble.

"Hi, Todd. My name is Hazel Rose and this is my cousin, Lucy Hooper. I was here a few weeks ago."

"Yes, ma'am, I remember you."

"Do you remember the woman I was with? The one who got into a scuffle with another woman?"

"Yes, ma'am."

I told him of Nina's death, breezing past his awkward condolences. "When we left that day, you said 'Nice to see you again.' Did she often come in here?"

"Yes, I saw her a couple of times before that time I saw her with you. She was with this guy, an older guy." If Todd wondered why I asked these questions, he didn't show it. Panera likely offered their management full-day seminars on how to respond to inexplicable inquiries from the public.

"What did the guy look like?"

Todd shrugged. "White hair, glasses, nothing unusual. They had papers. A lot of writers come in here, so they might have been writers. And people meet to discuss business over coffee. Or whatever. To be truthful, I wasn't paying a lot of attention. I only noticed them because they had a heated discussion and she got up and left. She yelled, 'You don't know what you're talking about!'"

I looked at Lucy. She asked Todd, "Would you recognize the man if you saw him again?"

Todd shrugged again. "Probably. I'm pretty good with faces."

Now all I had to do was bring Todd a picture of this man. Someone with white hair and glasses. My sigh carried. I covered my rudeness with a smile and a warm "thank you" for his help.

"My pleasure. Can I do anything else for you ladies?"

"No, we'll just get some breakfast."

Over coffee and croissants, I said, "White hair and glasses, indeed."

"Standard older guy looks," Lucy laughed. "But who *is* this guy?"

I groaned. "He's another one of these strays we're collecting like cats. We haven't identified the women in the car from Florida and now we have this guy."

"The question is, was he Nina's critique partner?"

"It makes sense that he was. But sense doesn't give us answers."

"If he was, apparently Nina didn't take kindly to criticism."

"So—we find this guy, take a picture of him, and get a sample of his handwriting."

We threw up our hands in surrender and fell into fits of giggling.

• • •

"Vince, do you know any playwrights with white hair?"

"I don't know any playwrights, period."

"The James River Writers group had a panel of playwrights at the Writing Show a few years back. I didn't go to that one. I'll check with them and see if they can give me a list."

Vince and I sat in the family room eating lunch. Morris sat nearby, hyper alert for tidbits. "This is starting to seem futile. I just *know* that Brad killed both those women."

Vince held up his hand in a stop position. "Then leave it to the police and stay out of Brad's way."

Ignoring my husband's suggestion, I went on. "I've talked to everyone and his brother and her sister. In TV shows the detectives go from person to person, and each person leads them to the next person, until at last they hit upon the culprit. And it's all done in sixty minutes. We've been at this for weeks."

Vince gave me a wry look. "Welcome to my world. My former world, rather. Investigations take a long time and often go unsolved."

I thought of *Cold Case*, the TV show that dealt with unsolved cases. I pictured the Rox-Nina murders being solved by a team of TV detectives, all to the accompaniment of period music. What was music for this period anyway? Katy Perry? Taylor Swift? Hiphop? As I preferred popular music from earlier decades, I wasn't up on contemporary artists. I laughed as I realized I was stamping myself an old fogey.

Vince repeated, "Leave it to the police. Why don't you concentrate on your writing?"

Not a bad idea but I didn't admit it to my husband. I finished my sandwich and headed to my computer where I sent an e-mail to the address on the James River Writers contact page. Then I closed my e-mail program and took Vince's advice—I got back to my real job of writing a romance. Murder was not romantic.

The next time I checked my e-mail, I saw that I'd received a list of local playwrights from the executive director of James River Writers. Sylvia Davies was one of the names. The names I recognized belonged to either women or younger men. I looked up the websites for the two names I couldn't identify but the photos showed young, dark-haired men. No older white-haired men in this bunch. Of course, the roster included only members of the organization, so it didn't necessarily account for every last local playwright.

I e-mailed the book group an account of my and Lucy's conversation with the Panera manager. When I asked if anyone knew of any older male playwrights in the area, "no" was the unanimous response.

I groaned. I needed a "yes."

TWENTY-EIGHT

INVESTIGATING TWO MURDERS made me forget my upcoming biopsy—until the call from the imaging center confirming my appointment pushed out all other thoughts. Up 'til then I'd only confided in Lucy and Trudy, but during a Skype session I told the rest of the book group. I exchanged cyber hugs with my four friends, who wished me luck and promised to include me in their prayers.

Vince escorted me to my appointment. This time I had the waiting room to myself and only had to cope with my own anxiety.

The staff was pleasant and accommodating, binding my breasts with tape before I left. I could have reprised Julie Andrews's role in the film *Victor, Victoria* where she impersonated a male who in turn impersonated a female. The only thing I needed to pull off that elaborate stunt was Ms. Andrews' clear, soprano voice. Fat chance of that happening.

The only good part of the whole ordeal was the result that I summed up in one word and texted to the book group and to my sister: *benign!*

Vince and I spent several minutes laughing and hugging over my joyful news. Texts of "congratulations" and "great news" dinged from my phone.

And then I had a call of a different nature.

"Hi, Hazel. Uh, Brad Jones here."

• • •

I wouldn't have recognized Brad's voice. My sole experience with his voice had been at Nina's funeral and it had been delivered full blast. This voice was low key, almost tentative.

"Hello, Brad." My own voice sounded cool to my ears. Vince hovered nearby.

"Look, Hazel—I'd like us to get together and, er, talk."

What had precipitated this turnabout? Curious, I agreed to meet him the following morning at his office and wrote down the address he gave me. "Oh, and Brad—I'll be with Vince." I looked at Vince, hoping he'd be available, now that I'd committed him. Thankfully, he nodded agreement.

"Vince?"

"My husband."

"Oh, yeah, Vince. Okay. Fine. "

It would have to be fine.

"Well, I'm just stunned," I said to Vince once I ended the surprising call from my cousin. "I'm glad you can make it."

"You can hardly go off meeting that oaf on your own."

I grinned. "I'd never meet that 'oaf'—great word, by the way—on my own. I could always enlist someone from the book group. Or Kat."

"In this case, I'd rather be there. He's a major suspect, even if the proof is hard to come up with. It'll be interesting to see what he has on his mind."

"Yes, won't it? My guess is that his patients, and maybe even staff, are going elsewhere and he wants to rev up the investigation. See what we know."

I e-mailed the book group with this breaking news. All four of my partners in investigation considered this a possible turning point in our search.

• • •

The next morning Vince and I drove down Forest Hill Avenue to the Westover Hills section of Richmond to meet with Brad at his dental practice. His receptionist made no attempt to hide her lack of interest in us as she reluctantly looked up from her magazine and slid back her glass partition when we approached her desk.

"Hello. I'm Hazel Rose and this is Vince Castelli. We're here to see Dr. Jones."

"Do you have an appointment?" Her froth of purple hair matched her lipstick.

"He's expecting us at ten."

"Well, he's with a patient now. Have a seat." She closed the glass barrier and returned to her magazine.

As instructed, we sat in the waiting area. Vince took out his phone and I surveyed my surroundings. Brad, or whoever had decorated the space, favored a tan-and-burgundy palette. A couple of the oil paintings that covered the walls looked like they might have been the result of the paint-by-number kits I recalled from my childhood. An expandable, and empty, coat rack hung from one wall section. Elevator-type music filled the air. I picked up a magazine and started reading an article on aromatherapy.

After ten minutes, a man with a lopsided mouth appeared. Brad followed close on his heels. "Hazel. Vince. Thanks for coming in." We shook hands. Brad's white smock covered a gray shirt and matching tie. "Let's go on back to my office." The receptionist remained absorbed in her magazine.

"Sorry to keep you waiting," Brad said as we stepped into his office. "My last patient was late. Can I get you some coffee?"

"Sure," I said. Vince nodded his agreement. Brad stepped out, presumably to the coffee setup I'd spotted in the hall.

"Courtney, can I trouble you to make some coffee?" I didn't miss Brad's edgy tone.

"Sorry, Boss," Courtney said placidly. I recognized the voice of the purple-haired receptionist. "I don't do coffee."

We took seats facing a desk that filled most of the office and waited while Brad attended to the coffee. Vince and I looked at each other and smiled. When Brad finally reappeared in his office he said, "Coffee'll be just a few minutes," and sat behind his desk. He clearly had the power position—with us, if not with his office help.

Brad started. "First I'd like to, um, apologize for my behavior at Nina's funeral." He put up a hand as if to fend off our objections, even though we offered none. "I was very, very upset and it must have affected my judgment."

I made a dismissive gesture with my hand, but it didn't mean I was softening. There was also the matter of Brad's not acknowledging me as his cousin in the first place. Would he address that little oversight? "So, Brad, what can we do for you?"

"These murders have just devastated me. I think it's time I got involved in finding out who's responsible. I know you've been looking into it. The police are useless. They're pinning their hopes on me and they can't see the forest for the trees."

Did Brad know that Vince was a former detective, one of those useless police? If so, did he care?

"So I'm here to help." He managed a ghost of a smile.

"Do you have any information?" Vince asked. "If you do, you need to let the police know. Much as you think they're incompetent, they know their job." Vince's look was hard, but not hard enough to tip off Brad as to his true feelings. But I knew.

"I know, I know. But isn't there always information that only regular folks can find out? Things picked up in casual conversation with friends, acquaintances." Gee, did Brad read cozy mysteries?

"So what have you picked up in casual conversation?" I asked.

"Nothing. Well, Evangeline Goudreau threatened Rox."

"Evangeline?"

"She was Rox's accountant at the Hamlin Group. Rox had to fire her due to incompetence. And, like I said, Evangeline threatened her."

"That doesn't sound like a casual conversation," I noted.

"Yes, well . . . " Brad trailed off.

"So what was the threat?"

"Oh, she was vague. Said she had something on Rox that Rox wouldn't want made public. We both thought it was all hot air."

If you thought it was all hot air, why did you go to Evangeline's house?

"So do you think Evangeline killed Rox?" Vince asked.

"Could be. Although I don't think she could manage it

herself. The woman's enormous." Brad spread his hands to an improbable width to represent Evangeline's girth. "Her mother probably could, though." Brad's wry expression suggested a memory that he wasn't sharing, a ninety-one-year-old woman coming after him with her cane. I bit back a smile. Apparently he wasn't fessing up to that incident.

"Coffee's ready, Boss."

Brad closed his eyes and shook his head. I imagined he was counting to ten, perhaps to delay an angry outburst. "How do you like your coffee?"

We kept things simple and settled for black. Brad left the office and returned with overly full foam cups.

"Did Evangeline approach Rox again?" I asked. "Any more threats?"

"Uh, no. Not from her."

"From whom, then?"

He thought. "No one." I resisted the urge to roll my eyes. Threats shouldn't take much thought.

"Brad, why are you interested in joining forces with us at this point?"

"Truth?"

"Yes." I didn't add that the truth would be refreshing.

What he said next wasn't surprising. "My patients are leaving, going elsewhere. And now my staff. My best hygienist resigned yesterday. I'm down to one hygienist and a temp." He snorted and hooked a thumb in the direction of the receptionist. "Miss Congeniality out there."

So my guess about his patients and staff deserting him had been right.

Brad went on with his tale of woe. "When Rox was killed they felt sorry for me. But since Nina—" He shook his head. He failed to include Veronica, his first wife and the mother of his child, in the roster of women associated with him who'd met tragic ends. "And even Patty and Paul wouldn't come in the house the other night."

"Patty and Paul? I thought they went back to Pennsylvania."

"I never heard that. If they did, they're back."

"Where are they living?"

"I assume in the same place, near Stony Point. Like I said, I didn't know they'd gone anywhere."

"But anyway, you said they wouldn't come in. So why were they there?"

Brad looked like he might be regretting bringing up Patty and Paul. Because now he had to offer an explanation. "Promise not to repeat this?"

"Girl Scout's honor." I held up three fingers, with the tips of my thumb and pinky touching. I marveled that I remembered the sign. Had I made that many Girl Scout promises?

"I've, um, been helping them out. I give them money."

"Oh?" I hoped I sounded encouraging.

"Yes, well, Paul has a gambling problem. And IRS problems." That accorded with what Andy had told us. "They go through their monthly pension benefits pretty quickly. Patty and I have known each other our whole lives so I feel like I should help them out."

No wonder Brad hadn't wanted to meet me. He had Patty and Paul mooching of off him and apparently Andy had his hand out as well. But Brad had a lot of money. Although maybe three parasites were three too many and he feared I might make it a foursome.

"Well, this is quite a surprise," I said.

"So what have you guys turned up?" Brad asked.

I shrugged. "Nothing really. But tell me, Brad, who do you suspect? Besides this Evangeline. And her mother."

He thought. "There's Foster Hayden."

"Wasn't he in Atlanta?"

"Yeah, so I heard." His tone conveyed that he doubted Foster's alibi. I noticed that Brad didn't mention Andy. I supposed it was understandable that he not regard his son as a suspect, even though Andy had no qualms about pointing fingers at his father.

"Do you suppose the same person killed both sisters?"

"How would I know?" The scowling Brad was rising to the surface. He checked himself.

"Anyone else you suspect?" I asked.

"No. I was hoping you'd come across someone."

"No one I could tell the police about." As I said this, I looked Brad in the eye and held my gaze. He looked away.

After a moment's pause, Vince stood. "Well, Brad, if you

come up with anything else, let us know. Better yet, let the police know."

We agreed to stay in touch. Brad handed us cards. Vince and I didn't reciprocate. He'd called the day before, so I knew he had my number. For the first time I wondered how he came to have it. But I had called him months earlier when I was trying to arrange a meeting with my newly-discovered cousins. Had he kept my number for all this time?

We left our half-full cups of not-very-good coffee on his desk. As we walked away, I had a sudden thought. I called out, "Brad, were Rox or Nina on Facebook?"

"Rox was, said she needed to network for the Hamlin Group. I don't know about Nina. I don't have time for that crap."

On the way home I asked Vince, "So what do you think?"

"Brad's still a suspect in my book."

"So I was right about his staff and patients leaving in droves. And now he has to put up with a lazy receptionist who doesn't 'do' coffee." Our laughter felt good. We hadn't laughed much in recent days.

"I'm stunned about Patty and Paul being in the area," I said. "Do you suppose they never even left?"

I called their old number. Out of service. Vince and I detoured to drive by their apartment, looking for signs of the blue van that Paul drove.

As we approached the apartment, the next-door neighbor, who I'd seen before, was outside, yelling at her toddler and carrying an infant on her hip. It looked like another child was due at any moment.

She looked surprised to see me. "Haven't seen you for a while, honey."

"No, I've been busy. I just came over to see Patty and Paul."

The woman looked mystified. "But they moved. Didn't they tell you?"

"They said they were moving, but didn't say when."

"Oh, honey, they left a good long while ago. At least a month." Now she looked pitying.

So where were Patty and Paul? Did they go away and come back? Had they ever left? In any event, were they staying in the area? If so, where? Brad claimed not to know. Had their financial situation rendered them homeless? Paul had a van—maybe they were living in that. Or at some low-rent motel.

"Maybe they regretted meeting me and faked a relocation," I said to Vince when I got back in the car.

"That seems rather elaborate. And, as I recall, you felt ambivalent about them."

"True," I allowed. Was I hurt? Kind of, kind of not. Perhaps Patty, and maybe even Paul, didn't care for my company. Possibly they intuited my growing unease with them, or maybe they felt the same way. I think it's unusual for one person to like the other if the feeling isn't reciprocated. Another possibility was that they were embarrassed by their reduced circumstances. "Anyway, it's their business."

"But that won't stop you from poking your nose into theirs," Vince chuckled.

"I'll try Andy. He might know something." But when I e-mailed him he said he was clueless.

"If I hear from them I'll let you know," he said. "But it's unlikely."

I resolved to drop the whole thing. If Patty and Paul wanted to contact me, they had my number.

TWENTY-NINE

IT SEEMED STRANGE to see a dead person on Facebook, but Roxanne Howard looked very much alive as she smiled big for her Facebook friends from the helm of a boat. Rox posted up until the day she died, mostly about various goings-on at the Hamlin Group, but she shared postings from her colleagues in the non-profit world as well. She appeared in photos with local notables. I looked through her friends, thinking I might spot someone and nab the killer right then and there. And we had a mutual friend—Phyllis Ross.

I shouldn't have been so surprised. Rox and Phyllis were in the same line of work: development. I checked the pages that Phyllis liked. Since she worked as development director at the Infinity Center, I expected that she would like her organization's page; the page I didn't expect to find was Synanon. I clicked the link and found an abbreviated description from Wikipedia. I clicked further for the complete entry.

I had a sketchy memory of hearing about some questionable doings of the drug rehabilitation program based in Santa Monica, California—something about a snake. According to Wikipedia, in 1978 two Synanon members left a "derattled" rattlesnake in the mailbox of attorney Paul Morantz of Pacific Palisades, California after Morantz successfully sued Synanon on behalf of a woman who had been abducted by that organization. The snake bit—and almost killed—the attorney.

The online encyclopedia described a Synanon practice called "The Game," where members endured violent and humiliating criticism from their peers under the guise of group therapy. Wikipedia provided additional information that did nothing to dispel my belief that the organization had done more harm than good during its reign of more than thirty years: men forced to have vasectomies, women forced to have abortions, women shaving their heads—the list of indignities went on. Yikes!

Phyllis had lived in Southern California for a time. In San Francisco as well. The book group women nicknamed Phyllis, Sarah, and me "the California Trio." Sarah had gone to Berkeley and I'd lived in Los Angeles for twenty years. Had Phyllis been in Synanon? If not, why like the Facebook page? I wondered if Phyllis had honed her sharp tongue and hot-headedness during sessions of "The Game." All this was interesting, but I doubted that Synanon had anything to do with Rox.

Still, the fact that Rox and Phyllis were Facebook friends might mean *something*. And at this point, something beat nothing.

I checked my computer clock. Noon. If I waited until two, Phyllis should be back from lunch. While I waited, I went back to Rox's page and checked her likes. She had few—the inevitable Hamlin Group, other local non-profits, and a nail salon. Did the Moonshine Inn have a page? Nothing by that name came up when I searched, at least not in Virginia.

I told Vince of my plans. I thought I'd be okay on my own but, just as when I'd met Mary Anne at Ellwood Thompson, I vowed to text him on my arrival and departure from the center.

"You know, Vince, shouldn't the police have found this Facebook connection between Rox and Phyllis?"

"I didn't hear anything about that. Maybe they did check it out and it didn't amount to anything."

"Maybe." I wasn't convinced.

• • •

The Infinity Center was an adult daycare program, highly

regarded in the community, offering an impressive array of services for the elderly and their families. Good place, but I hoped I never needed it. On the drive over, I tried to think of what I'd say once I saw Phyllis. How would she receive me? I stopped at the reception desk. A harried-looking young woman with masses of auburn hair fielded calls. While I waited, I texted Vince the news of my arrival.

"Is Phyllis Ross available? I'm Hazel Rose."

"Phyllis?" The woman spoke into the phone. "There's a Hazel Rose waiting to see you."

Phyllis appeared wearing a beige pantsuit that revealed more of her figure than I'd ever seen. I never realized she was so slim as she usually favored loose-fitting, flowing garments. "Hazel. How . . . *nice* to see you."

"Do you have a minute? We can wait until you're off work."

"No, no. Come on down to my office."

Phyllis led me down a wide, sterile-looking hall, all teal and peach, those Southwest colors that prevailed in the late '80s. But the building that housed the Infinity Center was much more recent than that. We went through a door marked "Administrative Staff" into a hall lined with offices. Phyllis's lighting choice of a desk lamp, rather than the standard overhead fluorescents, made her office inviting.

I took the guest chair and Phyllis sat behind her desk.

I had to keep in mind that Phyllis was a suspect, so I needed to walk on eggshells. Still, I got right to the point with my opening line: "Phyllis, on that day at Panera, Nina told me about her sister Roxanne and how she was murdered."

"Yes?" Phyllis' dark eyes regarded me through black-framed glasses. "But you knew about that anyway. We discussed it at book group. What's your point?"

"How well did you know Rox?"

"Not well at all." Her eyes narrowed. "Did Nina ask you to investigate Rox's murder? I know you looked into Carlene's murder years ago. That probably means you're looking into Nina's as well. Probably the same person killed both of them, don't you think?"

"Oh, no, she didn't ask me anything like that," I lied. "But Vince is researching Rox's murder and I'm helping him by asking people who knew her. Like you." I figured it didn't hurt to bring Vince's name into the conversation.

Phyllis gave a short laugh. "Like I said, I barely knew Rox."

"I saw that you and she were Facebook friends."

"Ah yes, good old Facebook."

"But when you and I talked that day, after Panera, you sounded, um, negative about Rox."

Phyllis gave me a long look, perhaps weighing whether she wanted to reveal something or if it was best to string me along. I noticed that she didn't question why I was looking at her Facebook page. Hopefully the thought wouldn't occur to her.

The spill-all urge won out. She sighed and began. "Rox and I went to the same high school, but I was several years older so we didn't know each other from there. But we met at VAFRE." So Sarah was right when she suggested that the Virginia Association of Fund Raising Executives was how Phyllis and Rox knew each other.

"How long ago was this?"

"Oh, last fall sometime. I'd just moved into this position and was new at VAFRE. Remember, I was in marketing and promotion before. Anyway, Rox friended me on Facebook and asked me to have lunch with her. I accepted. She seemed so friendly."

"Did you know that she and Nina were sisters?"

"Not then. Later, at the lunch, she mentioned her sister Nina, and it turned out that it was the same Nina. But I figured that I shouldn't hold her responsible for her sister's actions. And like I said, she seemed so *nice*. At lunch she drank quite a few glasses of wine and was very interested in my life—what I did, had done. I told her I planned to run for public office someday."

"Really?" I broke in to Phyllis's account. "I didn't realize that."

"Just an idea I toy with," she said, waving a hand. "Anyway, Rox said, 'I see you like the Synanon page on Facebook. Were you there?'

"I told her about a drug problem I had back in the '70s. I told the woman *everything*." Phyllis stopped. "How much do you know about Synanon?"

"Very little," I allowed. "Wasn't there something about a

snake in someone's mailbox?"

Phyllis told a tale of Synanon, much of what I'd read about earlier. The Game, the snake, women forced to shave their heads, etcetera. I thought, *Phyllis with a shaved head?* How long did it take her to grow back her voluminous mane? I didn't ask Phyllis if she'd personally undergone any of those mandated indignities. Don't ask, don't tell—the policy had its merits.

Phyllis continued, "But back to Rox. She said to me, 'You probably don't want people to know about your past in Synanon. Or your drug problem. It wouldn't go over well with your voters.' That was when I saw the gleam in her eye. Then she said, 'But your secret is safe with me—for a fee.'"

"So she tried to blackmail you?"

"Yes."

I didn't want to play the "blame the victim" game, but I had to ask: "Phyllis, why did you like the Synanon page?"

"Oh, I don't *know*! I just did. You see, I hardly ever use Facebook. I check it about once a month. I'd forgotten all about the Synanon page."

"But what would be the problem anyway?" I asked. "Bill Clinton and Barack Obama both admitted to using drugs. Remember Clinton's famous 'I didn't inhale' line?"

"But they weren't addicted. And they weren't in Synanon."

"Yes, but how well known is Synanon, really? Nowadays, if people ever knew anything about it, they've forgotten the details." Like me, they might have a vague memory of the snake story.

"The point is that she tried to blackmail me. I said, 'Go ahead, do your worst.' Then I got up and upended a plate of Caesar salad in her lap. And walked out." Much as she'd done with Nina's coffee. Phyllis could benefit from an anger management course. Had she gone through a deprogramming process to release herself from the Synanon-style brainwashing?

"They're not going to care here," Phyllis waved a hand to encompass the whole of Infinity Center. "But in a political campaign? Hard to tell these days what will get voters up in arms. But thanks for the heads-up about that Synanon page. I'm going to unlike it right now." As she did so, I asked myself why someone would like a page if her association with the organization was so unpleasant. She'd claimed it was a nightmare.

Once Phyllis completed that task and pronounced it "Done!" she took a deep breath. "So that makes me a suspect. I know I'm already one in Nina's murder, thanks to your wonderful book group." Phyllis gave me a dark look.

I ignored the look. "Well, do you have an alibi for Rox's murder?"

"Not really. But I do have one for Miss Nina's murder." I didn't comment on that dubious alibi. As I recalled, Phyllis had left the museum fundraiser at ten o'clock and Brad made his call to the police at eleven. Phyllis had plenty of time to kill Nina. All we needed was the ever-absent proof that she did.

"Those two women—I didn't kill them but I haven't shed any tears over their deaths. *Not . . . one . . . tear*. That Nina character ruined my brother. *Ruined* him." I didn't roll my eyes, but I wanted to.

We parted on a sour note. As I walked down the long wide hall I found my phone in my purse.

"Leaving," I texted Vince. "Mission accomplished. Sort of." I only misspelled two of the five words.

At home I found Vince at his computer. He removed the headphones that circled his head and listened to my tale.

"What was Rox doing?" I asked, once I unwound. "Mining her professional network for extortion prospects?"

"Apparently not successfully, at least judging from her bank accounts," Vince said. "Remember when I checked with Dennis—"

"Right," I broke in. "Just the money from Marcie's estate."

"And her own salary. Nothing unaccounted for."

"Perhaps she stashed her blackmail gains under her mattress. If she did, I'm sure Brad confiscated it."

Had Rox blackmailed others? How would we find out? Was there a support group devoted to her victims? Rounding up that group sounded like a fun venture. I pictured the ad I could place on Richmond.com and *Style Weekly*.

And laughed.

• • •

I found e-mails in my inbox from the book group wanting a report on the meeting with Brad. I wasn't up to composing a lengthy e-mail, especially since it was Wednesday and we were meeting that night by Skype. I did offer a few tidbits on my visit to the Infinity Center, promising a complete account when we met. And I sent them a link to the Wikipedia entry about Synanon.

Once our Skype session was launched, I ran through my conversations with Brad and Phyllis.

"My word!" Eileen exclaimed. "Blackmail? Synanon? Where do we even start? I sure don't blame Brad's patients and staff for bailing on him. Who wants to be sitting in a chair with a murder suspect probing your mouth with sharp instruments?"

"I love the part about Brad and the purple-haired receptionist," Sarah laughed.

"Serves him right," Trudy said with asperity.

"What about Patty and Paul? What's the deal with them?" Lucy asked.

"Yes, if those two are so hard up, why doesn't she go back to teaching?" Sarah asked, sounding annoyed. "And did you ever find out what Paul did for a living?"

"According to Andy he taught Speech," I said. "Maybe Philosophy as well."

"And she taught English?"

"Yes."

"Well, she could tutor. As for him, I don't know if they offer tutoring for Speech and Drama. Or Philosophy for that matter. They both could get involved in something that could bring them at least some income. Instead of mooching off their relatives."

"Sarah, you mentioned Speech and Drama," I said. "Paul taught Speech. Why did you add Drama?"

"Did I? Habit, I guess. When I was teaching, the Speech teachers often taught Drama as well."

"This Synanon stuff is really bizarre." Trudy read from the Wikipedia entry. We tried, and failed, to visualize Phyllis bald.

Lucy said, "With all Rox's money she had to resort to blackmail?"

"Do you think it's even true?" Eileen challenged.

"Who knows what's true and what isn't? And we don't even

know that Rox didn't succeed in blackmailing." I felt a mounting frustration with this whole business.

"Just suppose Rox was bleeding Phyllis dry," Trudy said, "And Phyllis kills her. It's plausible."

"Sure it's plausible," I agreed. "Now let's come up with some proof."

"What about Patty and Paul?" Lucy asked. "Are you going to try to find out where they are?"

"No. I figure they either don't want to see me or they're too embarrassed to see me. At any rate, they know where *I* am."

I considered my newfound relatives: a murder suspect, an alcoholic deadbeat, and a possibly homeless former academic. I wished I'd met Marcie. She sounded like the best of this bunch.

Looking on the bright side, I suspected they'd supplied me with story ideas for years to come.

• • •

I thought back to Sarah's assuming that Paul had taught Drama. I looked him up online. And in no time, Paul Ratzenberger appeared on a WordPress site. As he'd looked two or three decades before. How long had he had this site? And did Patty know about it? I had taken her at her word that she and her husband hadn't yet ventured into cyberspace.

I clicked through the site, learning that my cousin's husband produced, directed, wrote, and acted in plays. His experience included set design, makeup, costume, and lighting. You name it, Paul did it. Halfway down the list of plays to his credit, I noticed *Greater Tuna*.

Why hadn't I ever heard about Paul's stellar theatre career? Had his gambling problem derailed it?

But, most important: as a playwright, was he Nina's critique partner?

I clicked on the photos link and found several pictures of theatre productions. Two showed Paul and Patty posing by a blue car that looked to be parked by a scenic overlook. I guessed the car to be a Camry dating from the '80s, judging by the boxy style that Toyota used in the original models. I only knew that because my brother purchased a Camry in 1985 and drove it for years. I recognized Paul's blue van in other pictures.

When I told Vince of my findings, he said, "Interesting. Now all you have to do is find them and then you can ask Paul about his stage career."

"And about whether he critiqued Nina's play. You know, I remember Patty saying Paul had run into Nina one day at Walgreen's. Maybe that's when she asked him to take a look at her play."

Vince smiled as he repeated, "Now all you have to do—"

"Is find them," I groaned.

THIRTY

Weeks passed, allowing us all to get back to living our lives. Rox and Nina's deaths appeared destined for the cold case files. I had no trouble filling my time: I completed my rewrites and sent them back to my editor. I felt the additional scene she suggested between the two lovers who decided to go their separate ways worked well. In what seemed like the blink of an eye, the second round of edits appeared in my inbox. I read it carefully, revised as necessary, added my own suggestions, and sent it back.

Mary Anne Branch e-mailed me the first three chapters of the draft of her romance. On that day at Ellwood Thompson when she'd ask me to critique it, I hadn't expected her to come through so soon. The story was quite good and I sent back some encouraging words as well as suggestions for improvement.

Along with writing one manuscript, editing a second, and critiquing a third, I filled my schedule with walking, book group, gym, laundry, cleaning litter boxes—you name it.

Brad called at least once a week, wanting to know if I'd learned anything new. Each week I said "No" and urged him to hire a PI. He whined about his dwindling patient base and having to pay his staff top dollar. I could tell that the man desperately wanted to scream and swear at me. The stress of holding his emotions in check was no doubt taking a toll on his health.

"All the more reason to hire a PI," I said to him each time.

"Why's he bugging me, anyway?" I complained to Vince. "With all his money he could hire a posse of PIs. He could retire his practice."

"Did you send him that list of PIs I gave you?"

"Yes. And Lucy managed to get the name of the one that Foster's mother hired to get the goods on her husband. I sent him that one too. Still, he calls me."

"Next time, hang up."

The book group "traveled" from the Dark Middle Ages to the High Middle Ages. We enjoyed Alys Clare's and Maureen Ash's tales of knights battling evil, as well as the renowned Ellis Peters's popular series featuring twelfth-century monk and herbalist, Brother Cadfael.

We continued to meet by Skype, but our visits got shorter and shorter. Beyond Brad's weekly calls there was little to discuss as far as the investigation went, so we became a normal group of women discussing normal topics—whatever "normal" entailed.

And then things started happening. Who knew that the Free Will Baptist Church would jumpstart this investigation?

• • •

The Friends of the Chesterfield County Public Library were partnering with several local authors for a fall fundraiser. One Thursday afternoon in late August I drove home from a planning meeting. Many churches dotted my route and I didn't pay them much notice—except for one.

It wasn't the unadorned white wooden structure with a simple cross above its front door that drew my attention. It was the sign on the lawn that jolted me: Chesterfield Free Will Baptist Church. *Free will . . . hmm.* I thought of Sarah and former book group member Maria Muller debating free will. And at a recent meeting we'd joked about wills in the legal context, where the costs involved in drawing up a will made "free" a laughable notion.

But now *free will* gave me an idea—one that probably had little to do with the theology of the Free Will Baptists.

Probated wills were public documents and it was high time I saw the actual terms of Marcie's will. The next morning, with that in mind, I found my way to the City of Richmond Circuit Court. I wound up paying a tidy sum in a corner parking lot for a spot two blocks from my destination. As I had the day Eileen and I visited the Hamlin Group, I vowed to start using public transportation for downtown jaunts.

As I approached the brick building that housed the Circuit Court, I noticed a woman with a cloud of yellow hair and volumes of smoke circling her. I asked her if I was at the correct entrance. She said I was, and cautioned me that I couldn't take electronic devices, including my phone, into the building.

"Oh, that's right," I sighed. Too late, I remembered the electronics ban from when I served on jury duty. So I trekked back to my car and locked my phone in the trunk. Back at the building I passed through security with no trouble and received directions to the Records Research suite.

Fluorescent lights blazed throughout the space where the color gray prevailed. My cursory glance took in no pictures, plants, or anything of even minimal beauty. Despite the dismal décor, or perhaps to counter its depressing effects, the Records Research employees were bursting with cheer, ready and willing to serve the public with a smile. One such employee found Marcie's will, made me copies, and gave me a receipt for the copying fees.

I retrieved my car and crossed the river over the Manchester Bridge and made my way to Crossroads, an independent neighborhood coffee hangout that operated from a converted gas station. The décor was funky and comfortable, with big purple couches and mosaic-topped bistro tables.

Once settled on a sofa with my latte, I read the Last Will and Testament of Marcia R. Jones.

There was no question about it, Marcie bequeathed her entire estate—by all accounts a considerable one, worth millions—to one Roxanne B. Howard.

When I went back over the document the first paragraph struck me with significance:

"I, MARCIA R. JONES, a resident of Richmond, Virginia, do hereby make, publish, and declare this to be my Last Will *and Testament, hereby revoking any and all former wills and codicils made by me at any time."*

Revoking. Had Marcie made a former will? If so, how did it differ from this one? To the point, to whom had she previously bequeathed her "property, real and personal, tangible and intangible?"

Where would I find another will? Would the lawyer who had drawn up this one have its predecessor? Foster had seen Rox and an elderly woman in the parking lot of his office building—were they en route to an estate lawyer? Foster couldn't identify the elderly woman as Marcie when Lucy sent him my picture, but I now felt certain that she was indeed my deceased cousin.

I checked the last page of the document and saw two names, Wendy Adamson and Fiona Darling, as witnesses. The date was October 14, 2011, just a month before Marcie's death.

I called Lucy and outlined what I needed from her.

Late that afternoon Lucy called me back: "Foster does know those two witnesses, they work down the hall from him. He asked them if they kept copies of former wills. The answer is no."

"Hmmm. But there might be a copy somewhere. Who could have one? And did they know they had it?" I flashed to Patty's remark about an uncashed check for a thousand dollars that Marcie had stuck in a book. Could Marcie have used her will as a bookmark?

"She may have had a safe deposit box. If so, probably Rox claimed the contents and Brad has them at this point."

"No, Lucy, if that's the case, we'll never find the will even if it does exist. Let's not even consider that option."

"If Marcie was as disorganized as everyone says she was, the will might have been buried in those piles of assorted items that Evangeline sorted through when she cleaned out Marcie's place. Hopefully it wasn't tossed or given to Goodwill. No pun intended."

How was I going to find answers to these questions? And what would the answers tell me? I might be wasting my time, but this investigation was dragging on too long, and doing something felt better than doing nothing.

I thought of Evangeline finding her blackmail material. Had she seen a will? The only way to find out was to ask.

"I'm going to call Evangeline. Talk to you later."

When I got home I looked up her number in the phone book. Thankfully, I found it and didn't need to get in touch with Nichole.

"Why, Hazel, how *are* you? You still need to sign my books."

"Sure, any time. Evangeline, when you were over at Marcie's helping Rox clear out her stuff, did you come across a copy of a will?"

"A will, huh? Let me think. Why do you need to know?"

I kept my response vague. "There's a family dispute going on."

"Hmmph. No, I put any papers aside without looking at them. Stupid of me, right? I might've found something really good."

Maybe Evangeline regretted losing an opportunity for blackmail. I didn't commiserate with her. "So you didn't find anything like a will?"

"No, I put the papers in a pile. Of course, I got over there late in the process. There were two other rooms and someone had cleared them out already."

"Who was there with you?"

"No one except for Rox."

"Evangeline, I need a favor. Will you look through those books you took and see if there's a will stuck in the pages? And call me back either way? Or text me? It's important."

"*Will* do." Evangeline giggled at her pun.

I ended the call after giving Evangeline my cell number and promising her that I'd come to Italian Delight the following Monday to sign her books. "But I can't stay. I have another appointment that evening." I didn't know if Evangeline knew of Nichole's unfavorable feelings towards me, or if Nichole still had such feelings. In any event, I didn't care to suffer a replay of my dinner with them. But I had to cater to my enthusiastic fans, and I counted Evangeline as one of them.

I should have asked Evangeline if she'd had an abortion or if she harbored some other secret. But how I'd have worded such a question was beyond me. Perhaps I could take her out for drinks. But using alcohol to trick people was sleazy and best left to the likes of Rox Howard.

I continued to mull over the will-stuck-in-a-book idea.

Patty had all those books from Marcie. Where were they now? Did she sell them to a book dealer? I dismissed that futile thought. If she still had the books, where would they be? In Pittsburgh? Still in Virginia?

I called Brad. Without preamble, I asked, "Have you seen Patty and Paul lately?"

"Yeah, a week ago. Maybe two. They came by. For their handout."

"Did they say where they were staying?"

"With friends. I don't know who."

Well, at least I now knew they were probably still in the area. Not wanting to answer questions, I ended the call as abruptly as I'd started it.

And then the answer, or at least a possible one, came to me out of nowhere: the storage space.

I had forgotten all about the storage unit. Did they still have it? Where was it? Had Patty ever said where it was located? When I checked my computer I found no dearth of storage facilities, including some that were close to the Ratzenbergers' former apartment.

I could see that I needed to visit these places. Didn't real investigators do that, pound the pavement? And would the facility managers tell me if Patty and Paul numbered amongst their customers? I really had to find the two of them and come up with a way to look through their books. I could say I'd heard they were packing up and I could offer my help. Why did I need to do this? Even if I found an old will, then what?

Frustrated, I headed for the gym.

• • •

Kat had lately been steering away from her signature leopard print, but that day she went all out. Her tank top, leggings and shoes all sported the distinctive design of the spotted cat.

"Hazel, I'm so glad to see you. You haven't been here for a while."

"I know." I felt sheepish. "I've been lax lately. I still walk a lot, though."

"Look, I have a class now. Why don't you work out and we can go next door to Starbucks? I want to know what's going on with the investigation."

I laughed ruefully. "It won't take long to tell you."

At Starbucks we took our lattes to a seat by the window. "So, what's been happening?" Kat asked. "Hear anything from Andy?"

"No, but Brad's still calling and bugging me." Kat knew about my now sort-of relationship with Brad, and the connection between Rox and Phyllis. Now I told her about finding Marcie's will.

"Sounds like you've unearthed a lot of information."

"True. But none of it amounts to a hill of beans. My latest quest is to find Patty and Paul's storage space. Actually I'd like to find *them*. I'm thinking that Marcie's former will, assuming there is one, might be in one of the books Patty got after Marcie died. And the books might be in the storage space. Provided they haven't been sold to pay Paul's debts."

"Why do you need to see her former will?"

I laughed. "I asked myself that same question. Answer is that I don't know. I guess because this investigation is stalled, and—"

"You're desperate, right?" Kat's blue eyes twinkled.

"Yeah. Curious, too."

"And you want to see justice done."

"That, too. And Brad, unpleasant as he is, is family. I have to know one way or another if he's the killer." I paused to sip my latte. "Problem is, I don't think Patty and Paul want to see me. Either because they don't like me or they're embarrassed by their reduced circumstances."

"But they're family, too."

I nodded. "I haven't a clue as to where the space is. I just remember Patty saying it wasn't far from where they were living before."

"And where was that?"

When I said it was on Forest Hill Avenue near the Powhite Parkway, Kat said, "Jake runs a storage facility in that area."

"Who's Jake?"

Kat waved a hand tipped with long red nails. "Jake Madden. We had a thing once. He looks like Alice Cooper. At least, the way Alice Cooper *used to* look. I haven't seen him in a long time, but he has to have a Medicare card by now."

"Who has a Medicare card? Jake?"

"No, Alice Cooper."

I tried to remember what the musician looked like back in the

'70s. I conjured up an image of unkempt long hair and copious amounts of makeup. "He still looks kind of 'out there.' Vince and I saw Alice Cooper a couple of years ago on a car auction show. He collects classic cars."

"Really?" Kat looked unimpressed. "I'll go by and talk to Jake in the morning. Of course, he'll bug me to go out with him again. But . . . whatever. He's kind of hard to resist. But there's Demetrios and I don't want to screw up things with him." Kat looked beleaguered at her romantic challenges.

"Are things serious with Demetrios?"

"Maybe." Kat looked coy for a moment before returning to the matter at hand. "Anyway, I'll call or text you afterwards. Oh, and Jake knows the owners and managers of other storage places, so he can check with them. Patty and Paul's last name is Ratzenberger, right?"

"Right."

Kat checked the time on her phone. "I gotta go. I'll get back to you as soon as I find out something."

"Thanks a bunch, Kat. I'll wait to hear from you."

• • •

The next morning Vince and I enjoyed our coffee on the porch. All was quiet with no lawn mowing, leaf blowing, or other noise-making activities disturbing the peace of the day. But when I booted up my computer to work on my writing, I glanced at my phone. A text from Kat.

It's Forest Hill Mini Storage. Unit number is J29. Jake says they're moving out by the end of the month and he's seen them there a lot lately. Packing, probably. Here's the address . . .

In the middle of telling Vince my plan to visit the facility in the hope of finding Patty and Paul, I stopped, struck by a sudden thought. "Vince, you don't suppose they've been living in that storage place, do you?"

A smile and a shrug answered my rhetorical question. He launched his Word program.

"Are those places air-conditioned? Are there toilet facilities? Maybe they've been sleeping in the van. Homeless, during the dog days of summer in Richmond." Did I really want answers to my questions? I shook my head as if to erase the unwelcome mental pictures.

"You're certainly running with this. You might find out if you go over there. But how are you going to explain how you knew where to find them?"

"That's an excellent question. I could say I saw their van turning off of Forest Hill. And figuring they were there to pack up, I came to offer to help."

"So you really think you'll find an obsolete will in a book?"

"We've been over this already. I think it's worth a try. Don't leave any stone unturned, as they say."

"Well, remember to text me when you get there and when you leave," Vince said, adding, "You know, they might be upset, angry even, by your showing up. Are you prepared for that?"

"I guess I'll have to be. But they're so polite they won't show their feelings."

THIRTY-ONE

I PULLED INTO the driveway of Forest Hill Mini Storage and parked under a stand of evergreen trees. I'd driven by countless times but it was the kind of place one sees but doesn't see—like auto parts shops or pawnshops.

After sending Vince the promised text, I sent one to the book group as well. I'd been remiss at not updating them about the past twenty-four hours—not that there was much to tell. Evangeline texted two words: "No will." After the flurry of texts, I locked my car and set off on foot, checking the numbers on the storage units as I went. Judging by the pattern, Number J29 was a good way down the long line of rental units. The roll-up corrugated metal doors were all closed and secured with padlocks, indicating little activity at this time of day.

A frisson of something like unease came over me and a loud internal voice boomed, "Go back. Go back *now*." I ignored the voice.

I came upon a parking area. Cars, trucks, boats, and a couple of RVs numbered among the dozen or so vehicles, most looking old and battered. A tan cover protected one of the cars but didn't hide the boxy lines of the model. Cars weren't my forte, but something made me think of the picture from Paul's website: the blue Camry that I guessed dated from the '80s. Was this the same car? If it was, why did they still have it? Patty didn't drive and they could probably get some cash for it. Not a lot, but some.

I walked around the car, looking for a hint of the blue color. Not seeing it, I lifted the cover over the back bumper.

I gasped.

The frame around the plate advertised Bremer Motors of Tampa, Florida. But it was the Commonwealth of Virginia that had issued the plate itself, with "IT" in the number.

I called the car color dark teal. But teal was a combination of green and blue, and so could appear to be either color, depending on the play of light, individual interpretation, and digital resolutions. On Paul's website, the color had looked blue. Carl Ellbee called it green when he saw the car in front of Nina's house the night she was killed. And the Florida dealer frame led him to believe the plates were issued by that state.

So . . . was this Patty and Paul's car? Much as I wanted to think no, I had to face it—the answer was yes. What was the likelihood that someone else stashed the car in the very parking lot where my cousins stored all their worldly possessions?

I thought of the two women Mrs. Ellbee had seen in the car in front of Nina's house. Who were they? A tall woman . . . hmm. Patty was tall. So was Paul. As for the white-haired driver . . . Paul or Patty in disguise?

I flashed to the conversation I'd had with Patty after Nina's murder. She'd heard on the news about a car with Florida plates and an "IT" in the number.

Had I stumbled upon Nina's killers and maybe Rox's as well? Was this why that voice inside my head urged me to turn tail and run?

Puzzle pieces bombarded my brain, but I had no time to assemble them. My hands shaking, I took my phone from my purse. To my dismay the camera feature displayed my mug. I felt sure I did not look this decrepit. Vanity aside, I needed pictures of the car, not a selfie. How did I switch the mode? I looked around frantically, hoping to get a few pictures before someone—like Patty or Paul—caught me in the act. But the place was a virtual ghost town and I turned back to my perplexing phone, vowing to replace it with the old flip phone I'd had, and enjoyed, for years. I touched an icon and *voila*, the car appeared in the camera window. Despite my trembling I got images of the plate and of the car itself. Before I could text the pictures to Vince, a voice behind me stopped me cold.

"Hazel! What are you doing here?"

Startled, I spun around to see Patty walking toward me, a red visor pushing her hair off her face. We hugged, but tentatively. Besides my recent realization that she could be either a killer, a killer's moll or, at the very least, a person of interest, I didn't want her to know how fast my heart hammered. Had she seen me taking pictures?

"I saw your van turning in here earlier. I figured you were here to pack up so I thought I'd offer to help." I hoped against hope that they *had* driven in there. If they were indeed homeless and camped out in their space or van, my cover story didn't serve me well. I didn't know how to explain my interest in the Camry, so I didn't even try.

Patty smiled and took my arm. "How sweet of you. Come on back and see the unit. Paul will be thrilled to see you. And you can look through Marcie's books and take any that you want."

I felt a strange combination of elation and fear—elation that I'd get my mitts on those books, fear of being in the unit with the two of them, who'd just leaped to the top of the suspect list. My mouth dry, I managed, "Uh, okay. I just have to finish this text to Vince. I need to remind him to get milk at the store." My hands trembled more than before and I'm not sure what I finally texted.

"I was just out for my morning walk," Patty said brightly.

"Nice weather," I managed, not up for small talk.

As we walked, I didn't spot a soul or even an open unit. At the far end of the property, the doors of Paul's blue van stood open, revealing a number of packing boxes. Paul added one more. He did a double-take when he saw me. "Hazel!" he greeted me with a false note of bonhomie as we drew near. "So good to see you." He planted a kiss on my cheek.

"Uh, hi Paul. Good to see you, too."

"Hazel saw us driving in here this morning and she offered to help us clear out the space," Patty said, her voice unnaturally loud. "I thought she could look through Marcie's books and take what she wants."

"Good idea. Come on in and we'll show you the boxes."

Not wanting to go in, I hovered at the entrance to the unit that measured roughly the size of a one-car garage. About a dozen cartons as well as a bare mattress and box spring filled the space. A packing-tape dispenser and thick black marker topped two of the cartons that served as a table. Had Patty and Paul been sleeping on that mattress? The van would be more comfortable, but perhaps they had air conditioning in here. What about toilet facilities?

I felt my mouth going even drier. "So, are you going back to Pittsburgh today?"

The next thing I knew, I was face-down on the mattress with a hand pressed over my mouth and my neck held in a vise-like grip. "Get some of that packing tape and put it over her mouth," Patty ordered. A section of packing tape replaced the hand. In no time the two of them bound my wrists and ankles. Patty's harsh tone and physical strength astonished me.

"Sorry, Hazel," Patty said. To my surprise, she sounded genuinely contrite. "After all, you *are* family. But we're not sure how much you know, what Nina told you."

"Come on Patty, let's get the hell out of here."

"Okay, *okay*. But where's her bag? She's got that frigging phone and I saw her taking pictures of the Camry."

Thankfully, the phone wasn't in my bag. After texting Vince I'd shoved it into the pocket of my jeans. In my present position on my stomach, the phone dug into a bone, the name of which escaped me, adding to my discomfort. Hopefully Vince wouldn't text or call just then. I held a dim hope that I'd muted the phone and then forgotten to turn the sound back on.

I turned to see Patty slinging my bag over her shoulder. "Just so you know, Hazel, this whole sorry situation is Paul's doing. I could have started a new life, gotten away from him and his gambling sucking up our pensions."

Then she stepped outside and said with great cheer, "Sit tight, Hazel. We'll be back." Then I heard the door roll shut, leaving me in pitch darkness.

What? They were coming back? With a knife? Maybe the knives were packed up in the van and they needed time to dig them out. Had Rox and Nina's murder weapons come from Patty's well-stocked kitchen?

Where was Vince? Did he get my text? At any rate, he knew where I was—as did Kat and the book group members. But none of us, including Vince, had suspected Patty and Paul so they wouldn't be worrying. I didn't know how long I could endure this Turkish bath-like atmosphere. Patty said they'd be back, but she hadn't said when. If they were en route to Pittsburgh it could be hours or even days before they reappeared. No telling what they had in store for me.

Every family had a black sheep. Mine had a whole flock of them. I cursed my sister for being such a thorough genealogist.

I once worked with an English woman who dubbed difficult situations "sticky wickets." I felt it safe to call being bound, gagged, and abandoned in a mini storage unit—emphasis on "mini"—a sticky wicket. Sweat leaked from every pore, making me doubt the units offered air-conditioning. I tried pulling my wrists apart but they wouldn't budge. My hands and feet were fast losing feeling.

What would Nancy Drew do? The famous girl detective had found herself trussed up countless times and always found a clever way to escape in the nick of time. In one adventure she located a box with a sharp edge and severed the cords that bound her ankles and wrists. Was there something like that here? There *was*, I realized with elation. The packing tape dispenser had a serrated edge. The same edge that had torn off the tape trapping me could extricate me. If I had my bearings right, the coveted dispenser sat on the cartons that should be inches from my right foot. To verify my estimate, I slid the lower part of my body to the right until my taped-together feet made contact with the boxes.

So far so good. Now all I had to do was hoist myself to a standing position and get my bound hands on the dispenser. If such a strategy could work for Nancy Drew—and any strategy worked for the beloved sleuth—it could work for me. The fact that she was a fictitious heroine and a flexible teenager to boot didn't matter. I couldn't let limiting thoughts discourage me.

I managed to roll over on the mattress—not an easy feat. After shedding rivers of sweat I at last stood. My victory was short-lived, however: the tape and my now-totally numb limbs made my position unsteady. When I fell against the boxes, the top one tumbled over and I followed. My heart sank when I heard the clunk of the dispenser on the concrete floor.

Tears streamed down my face, mingling with the sweat. I admonished myself to press on and not give in to self-pity. Where had that dispenser ended up? One advantage was the smallness of the space—but in my present handicapped situation it might as well had been a ballroom. Guessing that I'd find the dispenser to my right, I lowered myself to the floor and started inching my way along.

I hadn't made much progress before light flooded the space amid the sound of rolling metal.

Patty and Paul back so soon? Or a knight in shining armor arriving to rescue me?

"Holy shit!" The voice didn't belong to either of my captors. Neither did the face that appeared above me.

Alice Cooper? Alice Cooper rescuing a damsel in distress?

• • •

No, Alice Cooper was not my knight in shining armor. But Kat was right—Jake Madden bore an uncanny resemblance to the shock-rock musician. Jake produced a Swiss Army knife and freed me from my bonds. I ripped the tape off my mouth. Whew! I wouldn't need a lip wax for a while—assuming I still had lips. It felt like they'd been removed along with the tape, leaving a burning hole in their wake.

"Who did this to you? The Ratzenbergers?"

I tried to speak but only managed a nod.

"Incredible," Jake said, shaking his head. He took a phone out of his pocket and dialed 911. After giving a terse explanation of the problem along with our location, he called Kat.

"Soon this place'll be hopping with cops," he said as he shoved the phone back in his pocket. "And Kat's on her way."

I finally found my voice, even if it came out raspy. "How did you know I was here?" I croaked.

"You texted Kat a help message. She called me." He grinned and spread his arms wide. "Here I am."

"Well, I'm eternally grateful that you *are* here. But I meant to text Vince. My husband," I explained when Jake looked puzzled. "I never know what this phone will decide to do."

If my mischievous phone had to act up, at least it had chosen a good person to contact. Better Kat than someone in South Africa—or a telemarketer.

"You want me to call him now?"

"No, I will." I took my phone out of my pocket. To my surprise only forty-five minutes had passed since I'd sent my one-word text, meant for Vince, to Kat. I'd spelled Help *Heeeellp*. Thankfully, I wasn't too far off for Kat to decipher.

When Vince answered, I managed an abbreviated account of my situation before my voice broke.

"Are you all right?" he asked.

"Yeah, just a bit shaken."

"I'll be right there."

"Hazel!" Kat, redolent of soap and shampoo, descended on me, enveloping me in a hug. "I'm so sorry I didn't get your text right away. I was in the shower and then Tammy called and bent my ear. I never saw 'help' spelled that way but I imagine you were quite stressed."

"I'll say. And you're going to need another shower after hugging me." We laughed. "I could sure use a towel."

"Well, I don't have a towel, but—" Kat rummaged through her purse and pulled out a tissue packet.

The police arrived next. In no time, the small storage space swarmed with bodies and the police hustled me and Jake out into the blazing sun. Just what I needed—more heat. I hoped no one would snap pictures of me in my soiled, sweaty, and rumpled state. The tissues only helped so much.

I told the police that Patty and Paul had left not long before, probably no more than thirty minutes. "And they said they'd be back. Didn't say when, though. They're in a blue van. Ratzenberger's the name." I spelled Ratzenberger carefully. "I don't know if they took their Camry." I used my chin to point to the parking area. "It has a tan cover." I rattled off the license plate number that was seared on my brain. At that point it wouldn't surprise me if Patty's inability to drive was a sham.

Jake started off. "I'll see if it's still there."

One of the police said, "We'll get the license number of the van from DMV."

˙ Vince and Jake appeared at the same time. Jake said, "Camry's still there."

Despite the heat, Vince and I fell into each other's arms and didn't move for a long moment.

• • •

At home I treated myself to a long, hot shower, cringing at the many bruises that decorated my body. Then Vince and I drove to police headquarters where I gave my statement to Detective Fischella. Jake Madden was on his way out after giving his own statement. "You clean up well," he grinned.

Paul and Patty were stopped near downtown Richmond. I guessed they were headed for northbound Interstate 95. The reason for their slow progress in leaving the city owed to a stop at a state inspection station. Their inspection sticker was due to expire at the end of August, and it was then August 30th, and they didn't want to chance being stopped for expired tags. Who knew the DMV would be so helpful?

Later that day, Vince and I sat on the porch as he filled me in on Patty's confession. In an interview with detectives, she readily described her involvement in the stabbing murders of Roxanne Howard and Nina Brown. She named Paul as Rox's killer and herself as the driver. When they conspired to kill Nina, they reversed roles. Fortunately for them, the Florida dealer frame on their getaway car led Carl Ellbee to believe that the plate was issued in Florida as well.

Patty never expected to benefit financially from Marcie's death. After all, people didn't leave money to their cousins. She wasn't happy about Rox getting everything, but only because she didn't like the woman.

Everything changed the day Brad arrived on Patty's doorstep with Marcie's books. Remembering her cousin's disorganized ways, Patty riffled the pages of each book, hoping that money would flutter out. As I'd guessed, what fluttered out was a copy of Marcie's old will.

"So I was right about the will," I crowed.

"Yes, you were," Vince smiled. "And in the earlier will, Marcie left the bulk of her estate to Patty."

"Aha! Revenge motive. Understandable in a way. I mean, I'd be angry if I missed out on inheriting a fortune. Although I wouldn't resort to killing."

"Good to know that my wife has good anger management skills."

"So, go on."

"Patty was dead certain that Rox had a hand in the will being revised. She figured that Rox poisoned Marcie's mind against her and Paul—after all, they'd questioned Rox about Marcie's care and then they'd balked at taking their cousin into their apartment. Rox didn't like being challenged and that, in Patty and Paul's view, led her to convince Marcie that her cousin didn't love her, and only wanted her money to support her gambling husband."

"So I'm guessing that's when Rox and Marcie took themselves down to the estate attorney's office and revised Marcie's will. The date on the will was about a month before Marcie died. That's probably the very day that Foster saw them in the parking lot."

"That's the idea."

"So Patty finds the old will and realizes she missed out on a fortune . . . is that when she and Paul started planning Rox's demise?"

"Yes, but just in theory. After Marcie died, a year went by with no abating of their anger and resentment. That's when they launched their plan to kill Rox. They followed her around. They knew she had a drinking problem and discovered that she favored the Moonshine Inn. Paul disguised himself to look like Andy—only thing was, he hadn't seen Andy in some time and didn't know he'd shaved his head."

"I remember Susie at the bar saying that Rox looked like she knew him at first, then realized that he just reminded her of someone she knew. She probably thought Paul was Andy. And we now know that Paul was good at disguises. From his theatre background."

Vince continued. "In Moonshine's parking lot, Paul recognized Nina and caught her sign of recognition. He wasn't sure if she saw through his disguise, but didn't want to take chances. And he thought she gave him and Patty funny looks at Rox's funeral. Then Nina disappeared for a while. Until the day Paul ran into her at Walgreen's and she told him she was taking a playwriting class. She was surprised to learn of his theatre background and immediately asked him to critique her play."

"And that's when he knew that she knew he was the one she'd recognized in the parking lot."

"Exactly. When Paul read the play, he was shaken. He over-criticized it, even though he found it quite good. But he wanted to discourage her from presenting it to her class."

Vince paused for a moment before continuing. "They didn't want to kill Nina because they'd always liked her. But they agreed that they had no choice."

I rolled my eyes. "Of course they had a choice. So they knew where Nina lived? Of course, it might be in the phone book."

"When Nina gave Paul her business card, it had her address on it."

"Yeah, I remember thinking when she gave me her card that it was a bad idea to include her address."

"I have another question," I said. "When I talked to Patty after Nina's funeral, she asked me if I was an investigator. Apparently Brad told her that I'd looked into another murder. She sounded surprised. Do you think she knew all about Carlene, and her surprise was all for show?"

"Probably. But I didn't hear anything about that."

"So, what else did you find out?"

"When they killed Nina, they took the same car they'd used at the Moonshine Inn, an old Camry of Patty's that she doesn't like to drive anymore. This time Patty did the honors and wore a wig to make herself look like you. She's a bit taller but she figured Nina wouldn't notice. And the facial resemblance to you worked in her favor. Nina wouldn't have hesitated to open the door and let you in her house."

"So, again, Paul got to make use of his costume and makeup skills. He was in *Greater Tuna* so he has to be a good mimicker and quick-change artist." I described the play that featured two actors playing the entire cast of many characters. "It explains his performance at the redneck bar. And I suppose he was the 'older woman' driving the car."

When Vince nodded, I went on. "I rue the day I found out I was related to this bunch. Well, one good thing—it wasn't Brad. He could benefit from anger management sessions but at least he isn't a killer. Not of Rox and Nina, anyway. We still don't know about his first wife."

We sat in silence for a moment.

"What about my purse? Do the police have it?"

"I'll check," Vince said.

"Just before Patty left me in the storage unit today, she said 'I could have started a new life, away from Paul and his gambling sucking up our pensions.' I'd say that was yet another reason for her to be angry about getting cut out of Marcie's will."

"Yes, well . . . now she'll get that new life—"

"In prison," I finished.

THIRTY-TWO

ON LABOR DAY Vince and I threw a potluck party. Kat, Tammy, Jake Madden, and Mary Anne Branch joined the book group members and their spouses in celebrating the capture of two murderers. I felt sorry for Jake—he looked smitten with Kat, she not so much with him. We'd invited Brad and he said he'd be there, but might be late.

Vince and Dave carried platters of burgers and chicken in from the patio. Everyone crowded into the dining room and piled grilled meat, deviled eggs, lunch meats, tomatoes, bread, salad and fruit on their plates. With Olive out rounding up the neighborhood rodents and Morris giving this many people a wide berth, we didn't have to worry about felines stealing our food.

By now my guests knew of my harrowing but thankfully brief time as a prisoner in Patty and Paul's stifling storage unit. But they still clamored for details. With the help of the book group members and others, I covered every detail from meeting Nina at Panera to my shocking ordeal at the hands of my cousins.

Patty and Paul were safely locked up at the Richmond jail, due to be arraigned the next day. Their combined charges included first-degree murder, aiding and abetting, assault, and kidnapping.

The police found boxes of kitchen items in the van, including a knife with traces of blood in the hilt. The DNA results would take a while but Patty and Paul's confessions would suffice in the meantime. Had Patty used that knife to prepare those delicious lunches she'd served me? It didn't bear further thought. In the storage unit they turned up wigs, women's clothing, stage makeup, and cartons of books.

"It's surprising that Rox hadn't found the old will herself," Lucy said.

"Yeah, with her passion for money you'd think she'd have gone through those books hoping to find money, and lots of it," Eileen said.

"Do you think even if Patty had gotten all those millions from Marcie that she would have left Paul?" Trudy asked.

I shrugged. "Maybe. Maybe not."

Tammy had been remarkably quiet until now, but now she piped up. "Hazel, why did you go to the storage unit by yourself?"

"I thought Patty and Paul were okay. We all did. I thought they might have a copy of the will, but also thought they probably didn't know they had it. After all, Patty once told me she'd read all those classics. It didn't occur to me that she'd go through them on a treasure hunt."

"But being as they were so hard up for cash that's exactly what she did," Lucy said.

"Patty once told me she found an uncashed check for a thousand dollars in the pages of one of Marcie's books. Now I'm pretty sure she was referring to the books she got from Marcie, and that she had found the former will as well as the check."

"When did it all come together?" Mary Anne asked.

"It was all so gradual. So many of you helped in such big ways." I looked around the dining room and named the book group members as well as Kat, Tammy, Mary Anne, and Vince, crediting them for their contributions to the unraveling of this mystery.

"And of course, Jake, who rescued me from sure heat prostration." Jake took a bow.

"But things started coming together when I got a copy of

Marcie's will. And that's my biggest regret, not looking at her will earlier. And then the other day when I saw the car, the Camry, more pieces fell into place."

"Hazel, what made you look at the license plate?" Den Rubottom asked. Sarah had brought her paraplegic husband with her and I could tell she regretted the decision. The flirtatious Den was given to sitting in his wheelchair and openly ogling women. He cast an appreciative look at my chest as he added, "You said the car was covered."

"I don't know. Something about the shape of the car. I thought of the car I saw on Paul's website. As to what made me look at the license plate, I can't say."

"Women's intuition?" Jake offered with an arch tone as he tossed back his straggly mane. Sarah, standing behind him, executed a quick two-step back and dropped a chicken leg on the floor.

I laughed. "Some family, huh?"

"Well, Brad is family and at least he's off the hook," Lucy said. "As is Andy."

"And Foster, Phyllis, and Evangeline are off the hook—"

"Evangeline!" I broke off Trudy's rundown of ex-suspects. "What time is it?"

Vince checked his watch. "Six twenty-eight."

"I'm supposed to be at Italian Delight right now. I promised to meet Evangeline and sign some books for her."

"It's not that far," Tammy said. "Call and tell her you'll be late."

"I'll text her. See you later, I won't be long."

I grabbed my purse (retrieved with all its contents from the police) and reached for the doorknob.

"Brad!"

Brad Jones stood on my doorstep, a bouquet of colorful flowers in hand. He wore shorts and a polo shirt. Lucy took the flowers and went to look for a vase while Vince introduced Brad to the assembled.

"Brad, I'll be back in about forty-five minutes. Help yourself to some food." I swept my arm to indicate the table.

"Thanks," Brad said. He walked to the door with me. "And thanks for solving these murders. I still can't believe that Patty and Paul were behind them."

"Yes, well . . ." I trailed off. What could I say?

I looked at Brad. That day at his office I'd doubted the sincerity of his apology. But now I felt that he genuinely wanted to change. Maybe this whole experience had taught him something. I still didn't have an answer about Veronica and how she'd drowned. I probably never would. I resolved to give my cousin the benefit of the doubt.

"I'd like to meet your sister," he said. "Ruth is her name?"

"Yes, Ruth. I'm sure she'd love to meet you. After all, we're family."

ACKNOWLEDGMENTS

I am immensely grateful to the following:

John Koehler, Joe Coccaro, and their team at Koehler Books. Thank you for your suggestions which made this a better book.

Mel Berger, for your wise counsel.

The City of Richmond Citizens Police Academy. The program introduced me to many wonderful people and I learned much that helped me in my writing. And my life.

City of Richmond Circuit Court, for your assistance with my research.

Rhonda Keyes Pleasants, mortician at the Joseph Jenkins Jr. Funeral Home, for helping me depict an emotional funeral scene.

Marie Molnar, my "redneck consultant." Your advice was invaluable.

Author Pat McDonald. We shared cyberspace laughs over my questions about British slang. Thanks for assuring me that I was up-to-date on the lingo.

Glen King, Evette Lamka, and Marcia Phillips. I'm a better writer thanks to your sharp eyes and suggestions.

Justin Lineberry and Maria Scott, for brainstorming with me on a title. You came up with a great one.

Heather Weidner and Rosemary Shomaker for Skyping with me.

Sisters in Crime, James River Writers, and American Association of University Women. Your support and camaraderie inspires me.

The *Virginia is for Mysteries* authors. Thanks for the friendship, road trips, and all your hard work.

Glen King (again!), my "research assistant" in various redneck bars. It was quite an adventure.

Olive, Morris, Daisy, and Shammy. You're great cats on and off the page.

Book groups everywhere, especially the AAUW mystery group of Santa Clarita, California, the model for Hazel Rose's book group.

My readers, for your encouragement and enthusiasm.

CPSIA information can be obtained
at www.ICGtesting.com
Printed in the USA
LVOW12s1521071016

507863LV00002B/312/P